A Dangerous Inheritance

SUSAN YAWN TANNER

Also by Susan Yawn Tanner
The Bellamys of Texas historical series:
Winds Across Texas
Fire Across Texas
Storm Out of Texas

The Bellamy Legacy contemporary series:
A Dangerous Inheritance

New editions from Secret Staircase Books
The Scottish Highlands Romances
Highland Captive
Captive to a Dream
Exiled Heart

A Warm Southern Christmas
(a historical romance novella)

Scan the QR code to sign up for Susan's newsletter
where she announces new books and exciting giveaways.
https://susanytanner.com/

A Dangerous Inheritance

The Bellamy Legacy
Book 1

SUSAN YAWN TANNER

Secret Staircase Books

A Dangerous Inheritance
Published by Secret Staircase Books, an imprint of
Columbine Publishing Group LLC
PO Box 416, Angel Fire, NM 87710

Book layout and design by Secret Staircase Books
First trade paperback edition: June, 2023
First e-book edition: June, 2023

Publisher's Cataloging-in-Publication Data

Tanner, Susan Yawn
A Dangerous Inheritance / by Susan Yawn Tanner.
p. cm.
ISBN 978-1649141361 (paperback)
ISBN 978-1649141378 (e-book)

1. Colter Bellamy (Fictitious character)—Fiction. 2. New
Mexico—Fiction. 3. Private Investigators—Fiction. 4. Western
Contemporary Romantic Suspense—Fiction. I. Title

The Bellamy Legacy Series : Book 1.
Tanner, Susan Yawn, Bellamy Legacy romantic suspense.

BISAC : FICTION / Romantic Suspense.

813/.54

For Ainslee, my sixth-born grandchild. She is our sunshine, bright and beautiful, and loved so very much!

Acknowledgements

I'm grateful to my editor, Stephanie Dewey, and her team of beta readers who are crucial in helping to make a book *shine*. They are: Amy Connelley, Georgia Ryle, Eve Osborne, Dawn Hasiotis, Liz Dawson, Sharon Hurley, and Tammy McCabe. And special thanks to the eight who trusted me enough to make the leap to a new genre. You are appreciated.

Prologue

Colter Bellamy glanced up as the phone rang, but Jonah was already reaching for the handset even as he continued searching through the scattered papers and folders that littered his desk. The rising sun outlined the Albuquerque skyline in the wall of windows behind his cousin and work partner.

Jonah tugged a notebook closer. "Slade Agency."

Colter waited in silence. Because it was an outside line, the call meant potential business. Personal calls and existing cases went straight to the internal line or cell phone of the working lead.

When Jonah shifted his feet from his desk to the floor and hit the speaker button, Colter tossed aside the case file he'd just opened. He flipped open his laptop, listening to the conversation as he accessed the company database. He recognized the caller's voice. Another cousin and one of the office agents who monitored for family names—Welles or Slade or Bellamy—to pop on news reports, adverse news in particular. The scattered descendants of six generations from those three families made it happen with enough regularity to keep them busy.

"Deceased? Say the name again," Jonah said. "Pederson?"

"J.D. Pederson."

With a few keystrokes, Colter began creating a new case file.

"Pederson Ranch?" Jonah's brow furrowed as he glanced Colter's way but Colter shook his head. He recognized the name but wasn't aware of a connection to any of the family. If there was one, he'd know soon enough. "An apparent blowout?" Jonah's frown deepened. "Is there anything to the contrary?"

"Four new tires."

Still possible, Colter thought, mentally reading between the lines. A defect. A sharp object in the road.

"Net worth?"

Jonah gave a low whistle at the amount and met Colter's eyes. People were murdered time and again for a hell of a lot less. They saw the proof in the bombardment of daily news, and, all too often, within their own sphere.

After a moment more, Colter accessed a separate database and pulled up the name, as well as a series of photographs. The most recent photos were of the man, a young woman, and two boys. If the woman was Pederson's wife, he was a cradle snatcher and she might just be a grave maker.

When Jonah ended the call, he gave Colter a nod. "This one's yours. May as well start digging."

Colter grunted. If he remembered right, the last one had been his, too. On the one hand, he didn't mind anything that would take him out of the office and into the field.

On the other hand, he couldn't help but realize that the whole damned family was trying to keep him busy. Too busy to think, too busy to regret, too busy to wonder if he should have stayed longer, tried harder.

Chapter One

Miranda took a deep breath, then another. A soft wind sifted through her hair in the same sweep that rustled the leaves on the branch above her. The carved box felt heavy in her arms, heavier than it had been when filled with ashes. Her eyes stung as she gazed across the low, rolling hills at the sizeable herd of beef cattle but she had no tears left to cry.

She didn't know how she was going to do it. This place had been J.D.'s dream. She loved it as much as he did, every inch of dirt, every blade of grass, every stretch of fence row, but the dream had been her father's … as was most of the knowledge it took to run it. She knew her part, of course, and she was good at it. But she didn't know all of it. Not even half of what she'd need.

"Randa?" The quaver in Dillon's voice tugged at her.

She glanced toward Riley and the foreman took the wooden urn from her, leaving her free to put her arm around the nine-year-old at her side. "We've got this," she said quietly. She lied, but by the time Dillon and his twin figured out she didn't know what the hell she was doing, she'd learn what she needed to know. Dane, who was not as tall nor as bold as Dillon, pressed a little closer on her other side and she placed her free hand palm down on his head.

At her nod, Riley walked toward the stone carved only with J.D.'s name and the dates of his birth and death. J.D.'s foreman and best friend sank to one knee to position the urn at its base. Silence floated around the mourners as Riley bowed his head in silent pain. Miranda took a ragged breath and shifted her gaze to the stone just to the right of J.D.'s. Her mother's. There was nothing for the twins' mother. Jerica had left the ranch not long after their birth. Miranda had no idea where the stupid woman was or if she was still alive. To be honest, Miranda hoped she was dead and buried. J.D. had long ago ceased to hunt for her and Dane and Dillon had long since ceased to ask. "Let's go home, guys," Miranda said huskily.

The ranch hands and what looked to be half, if not most, of the town parted as the trio passed through their midst. There had been no service, no pastor, no words spoken in some futile effort to invoke comfort for their grief. J.D. hadn't held with organized religion. Miranda was vaguely aware of Riley moving toward the horse ground-tied at the tree line. Most of the ranch hands had chosen to ride as well.

With the twins settled in the back seat of the pickup, she climbed behind the wheel. Someone had washed it and wiped every surface on the interior. Within a day or two, though, it would again be coated with late summer dust. Like everything else on the property, it had a job to do. J.D. had little use for slackers or luxuries. Miranda was a lot like him in that regard. A lot different in others.

She kept a foot lightly on the brake for most of the way back down the steep hill to the ranch house but kept her ears tuned to the backseat. The boys usually had plenty to say about nothing, as J.D. had always liked to put it. They'd been quiet since the accident. Too quiet. Every now and again, she heard one whisper to the other, nothing of consequence, until one comment took her breath.

"What did you say, Dane?" Miranda kept her voice calm and quiet, but her heart thudded.

Silence.

"Dane?"

It was Dillon who answered. "He—he wondered when we'd have to leave the ranch."

Very carefully, she put the truck in park and twisted in her seat to look at them. Two grief-stricken little boys trying to be men stared back at her. "Get up here, guys."

"Up front?" Dillon sounded uncertain. They always rode in the back. It was one of the safety rules Miranda had latched onto when she was trying to figure out how to step into their missing mama's shoes.

"Up front." Her voice was firm.

They scrambled over the seat and she didn't bother to remind them that both front and back doors worked perfectly fine. Dane tucked himself close to her and Dillon sat forward so that he could see her around his brother.

She studied their faces. They actually looked more like their mama than they did J.D., but they were as stubborn and good-hearted as their daddy. They had his grin as well, but it was not in evidence on either freckle-dusted face at the moment. Two sets of tear-drenched, copper-colored eyes looked back at her.

"Why would you want to leave me and the ranch when I'll need you more than ever with J.D. gone?" Just saying his name was hard. He was the twins' natural father and the only father she'd ever known but all he'd ever wanted to be called was J.D.

Dane's upper lip trembled, but it was still Dillon who answered. "Mr. Wes said he'd probably be job-huntin' as soon as you got rid of us."

She caught her breath at the words, at the look of trepidation on their faces. "He told you that?"

Dillon squirmed. "Not 'zactly. He was talking on his phone."

Miranda let that pass. The twins knew how she felt about listening to conversations that didn't belong to you. Now wasn't the time for a scold. Later, maybe, but not now.

"He might just be job hunting after I talk with him but it won't be because you're going anywhere, not before college at any rate."

"J.D. said I didn't have to go to college."

She stifled an unexpected chuckle. Dane had spoken at last.

"Nor will you have to, but I hope you'll want to. J.D. hoped that as well." She put the truck in gear. "Now, let's go home. We've all got work to do."

She knew some, probably most, of the mourners would follow her truck across the hills to the house. They'd bring casseroles and cakes and tales of J.D., some humorous, some not so much, but that wasn't what his sons needed now. They had memories of their own that were best dealt within the reassuring familiarity of tasks that couldn't wait until they all felt in a better frame of mind.

She'd already done as much grieving as she could stand, huddled for hours alone against a scrub tree and letting the sobs rip through her chest as surely as the pain of loss ripped through her heart. Terror at what faced her had taken second place to the heartache for the first day or two. Now it nipped like anxiety at the edges of her mind because failure wasn't an option. She had two boys to raise and the ranch that was their birthright to run.

She sent the boys to change and to find Riley at the barn. Then she sent him a text to watch for them. She'd talk with their tutor later. She couldn't begin to fathom taking on the task of homeschooling along with running the ranch, but she would if she had to. For the next few hours, her place was at the front entry to greet the people who were J.D.'s friends and mourners. Riley had already asked to be relieved of any responsibility there. She didn't blame him nor did she begrudge him that freedom. For as long as she could recall, he'd been J.D.'s right hand. J.D. didn't need him now, but J.D.'s sons surely did. He'd keep their hands busy and their minds occupied.

Feeling far older than her twenty-eight years, she squared her shoulders and opened the door to the first knock. She and Lila, who was much more than a housekeeper, moved unobtrusively through the ever-shifting crowd of friends and neighbors and business associates, accepting condolences, offering coffee or a 'nip of something more' as J.D. would have put it. Not until the last person had left with assurances that they would answer any call and be there for her and the boys in any need, did she give in to the exhaustion cascading over her. Lila gave her a hug, murmuring about the need to cook a meal Miranda knew none of them would be hungry enough to eat.

Miranda wanted nothing more than to change out of the dress she never wanted to see again. She was across the room and at the base of the stairs when the doorbell rang again. As tempting as it was to just sink to the bottom step and ignore the sound, she turned back and opened the door. Her heart dropped at the sight of Sheriff McEnny, back and in uniform. He'd been at the funeral but hadn't come to the house after. Now she understood why. But she hadn't expected it, not this soon. She had an appointment with J.D.'s attorney first thing Monday morning.

"You're not taking the boys."

McEnny studied her face without speaking for a moment. "No, Miranda. I'm not. And I'll help you fight anyone who tries."

Miranda felt color flood her face even as the relief shuddered through her. "Of course, Sheriff. I'm sorry. I've just been so anxious, worrying about Dane and Dillon, trying to think what might happen next, and head it off."

The look on his face didn't reassure. "We need to talk. May I come in?"

She stepped back and nodded. "Of course. You're always welcome, but I take it this is business, so we'll go in J.D.'s office." She suspected a decade from now she would still think of it as J.D.'s office.

The sheriff closed the door behind him and followed her to the back, through the great room to the library J.D. had used as his office.

After asking, "May I," McEnny closed the double doors and turned to look at her. His expression had been sad and solemn earlier. Now it was grim.

Miranda sank onto the sofa. She'd sit at J.D.'s desk soon

enough. Today was not that day. McEnny turned one of the armchairs that faced the desk so that he was seated directly in front of her.

He removed his hat and twisted it slowly in his hands while Miranda waited in patient silence, a skill she'd learned from J.D. "I've had a phone call," he said at last.

She leaned against the smooth leather at her back. Was this about the boys, after all?

"A private firm … suggesting I take a closer look at your dad's accident."

Miranda's heart thudded. Her mouth suddenly dry. "A closer look?"

The sheriff nodded but didn't elaborate.

"I thought Flynn's garage looked the truck over … after. They didn't find anything that could have been the cause of his truck flipping over that outcropping."

"Ronnie and Nathan," McEnny named the mechanics with a nod. "And after the call, I asked Flynn to have them take another look. A closer look."

"And?"

"Flynn called me back yesterday after lunch. He looked at every possible thing that could have failed mechanically or electrically. Looked for hours. He didn't find any reason for that wreck. Just two of the tires flat and pretty much shredded."

"One of which could have been a blow-out, causing the wreck, and the other could have happened at any point during the roll-overs." The words, part of the report she'd been sent, had haunted her dreams. Multiple roll-overs. A familiar wave of nausea swept through her. She couldn't bear the thought of J.D. afraid or hurting. He had to have been both.

McEnny nodded.

Miranda took a deep breath. "So, who—or what—is this private firm and what did they say when you let them know?" She paused. "You *did* let them know, right?"

"I talked with Mr. Bellamy and a Ms. Welles this morning ... a conference call, I guess."

She stilled. "Bellamy? Welles?"

McEnny frowned. "Those names mean something to you? Beyond the obvious," he added dryly. Those names—along with Slade—were either revered, feared, or hated throughout the state.

Her nod was reluctant. "The twins ... their middle names. J.D. gave them their first names but their mama insisted they be named after her side, too. Dane Bellamy and Dillon Welles."

"Huh," McEnny grunted, looking thoughtful and more than a little discomfited. "Reckon I never heard their middle names, at least not that I recall."

"No reason you would have unless you were around when J.D. was experiencing some frustration." She smiled faintly. "It happened from time to time."

"I imagine." McEnny smiled. "With three boys and a girl it happens a lot at our house." The smile, which never quite reached his eyes, faded. "Anyway, Mr. Bellamy wasn't satisfied. Asked if he could arrange to have the truck delivered to Albuquerque."

Miranda shook her head more in bewilderment than refusal. "They think someone—or something—caused J.D. to wreck? Did they give a reason? And how did they even hear about it? And why would they care? The twins' mama left this ranch, and them, nine years ago. If these people are family, they haven't cared to visit or check on them before now."

"I can't answer any of those questions but they asked

me to place a guard on the property here, someone to watch over the twins until they could send someone out here."

A mix of emotions, too many, hit Miranda at once and she got to her feet. "Send them the damn truck if you want or have it towed to a salvage yard. I could care less. If you think there's a danger to the boys, put someone patrolling from time to time. Just let Riley know what to expect so none of your men get shot for trespassing." She stopped her pacing and turned to look at him. "Beyond that, I've got no use for any relatives that woman might have anywhere. You can tell them that."

McEnny stood as well. "I don't know what to think," he admitted. "I can't imagine anyone anywhere wanting to hurt J.D. He could be hard-headed but he was also good-hearted. Folks liked him in spite of himself. But..." He scratched his forehead, hesitating.

"But...?"

"I don't know. This Mr. Bellamy seemed certain something was wrong. He didn't share his reasons, but his concern was Dane and Dillon and keeping them safe."

"Or maybe he just wants an 'in' to getting his hands on their inheritance," Miranda said slowly. The ranch and all it entailed was worth a fortune.

"It crossed my mind," McEnny answered, "so I looked and I dug deep. Welles Enterprises is still rock solid, has been from the beginning, and the partners all have more land, free and clear of debt, than J.D. ever dreamed of owning. Land and money and all that comes with it."

"Greed knows no boundaries," Miranda said dryly. She opened the doors of the library and walked the sheriff to the front door where he stopped and turned to face her.

"I don't know that I put any credence in Mr. Bellamy's

concern but I wouldn't mind sending a patrol through now and again for a few weeks. I'll walk out to the barn and let Riley know."

"Not today," Miranda shook her head. "Please. The boys are with him now. I'll give him a heads up and you can call him later and let him know specifics."

She watched from the door as he walked to his car. There would be some questions floating around the ranch at his return in uniform. Sooner or later those questions would be aimed at her and rightfully so. For now, though, she had far too much crowding her mind. She walked to the barn to saddle one of the young horses that needed riding. She could think on a horse's back. And no one could talk to her.

When she returned, she found Riley on a low bench in front of the barn. He held a bridle in one hand and an oil rag in the other. She stepped down from the stocky appaloosa and loosened the girth. The last rays of the lowering sun filtered through the leaves that lined the drive to the barn and glinted on the silver of the foreman's brows and moustache. She wondered how old he really was, if he ever thought about retirement. All she could pray was 'not yet'. Beyond the grief, he'd be disheartened by J.D.'s death, maybe wondering if she would make changes, maybe worrying some.

They hadn't had that talk. It was time. But first there was the business of the sheriff's visit.

"You got a minute?"

"Always."

"I'll turn this guy out to stretch and roll and be right back."

She focused on unsaddling and brushing the gelding, fought the heaviness of grief that threatened to roll her under. They'd get through. She knew they would, but it wasn't going to be easy.

Once she had the appaloosa through the gate, she leaned against the fence, watching as he sprinted across the small paddock and wheeled about to race to the other side. As if they hadn't just ridden for over an hour.

Riley seemed not to have moved while she was gone but the first bridle hung on a peg and he was buffing oil into a second.

"You've got plenty of hands to do that," she reminded him, "and you're about to run out of daylight."

"Yep."

He'd answered her just as he'd always answered J.D. Riley didn't argue. He just agreed with their logic, then did things his way. She hoped he always would.

"The sheriff came back to the ranch, after everyone else had left."

He glanced up, meeting her eyes. "In uniform." It wasn't a question.

"In uniform," she acknowledged.

"He's not fool enough to make problems for you with the boys." His voice held solid assurance which she knew came from years of familiarity with the lawman.

She sat on the bench beside him. "It wasn't about the twins. It was about the wreck."

Riley's hands stilled. "He find something?"

"No. He had a phone call from a private company. They asked to look over the truck."

He shook his head. "Damned muckrakers. You don't have to let them. You don't have to do anything you don't want to."

"I told him he could send it. There's no reason to refuse. They also asked the sheriff to have deputies watching the place until they send someone to guard the ranch."

Riley set the bridle aside. His brows lowered but he looked more bewildered than angered. "What the devil? Who are these people?"

"Welles Enterprises." She kept her voice steady but it was an effort.

"Ah, hell." Riley spat on the ground between his boots. "Jerica's kin. We don't need them here." But he looked anxious.

Miranda felt less stressed than when she'd talked with McEnny but she hadn't changed her mind. "No, we don't. The sheriff can have his men come out from time to time but he's to give you a heads-up about when and where they'll be. They've got sense enough not to spook the cattle but I'd as soon the boys not catch sight of them. You can let Wes know when to keep them close to the house."

He nodded but asked, "You think there's something to worry about?"

"I don't know what to think," she admitted, "but I won't take any chances where Dane and Dillon are concerned."

She sighed. "Speaking of which, I've got to go in before long. Wes let the boys overhear a conversation he shouldn't have been having and they shouldn't have been hearing. They heard him tell someone he'd be job hunting as soon as I got rid of them."

"Damn." He gave her a look. "Is he fired?"

"That was my first thought," she admitted. "But he's good at his job and hasn't caused any problems before now. What do you think?"

"You mean what do I think J.D. would do?"

"There's some of that," she admitted, then took a deep

breath. "He seemed to always know the best approach to take, the best words to use."

But the look he gave reminded her of J.D. "Plain talk works best. Let him know his mistake and your expectations. He's maybe a little anxious about his future. Made a stupid mistake. Doubt he'll make another, once you call him on it."

Riley would never have made that mistake, she thought, but Riley had a couple decades, at least that, on the tutor. She nodded, rethinking her gut reaction of wanting to blast the man. "It upset me because it upset Dane and Dillon. I felt like I'd been slapped and I'm pretty sure they felt gut-punched. Those boys are mine and nobody messes with them," she said fiercely.

Riley got to his feet and put a hand out to help her up. A hand she didn't need, but accepted, because he needed her to. "And it's best you go in to them. It's dinner time and bed won't be far behind. They need you more than ever."

She studied him a moment, grateful for the wisdom she saw in him, the strength of his shoulders and the straight back. As long as Riley lived, the boys would have more than just her to watch out for them. "I know they do. They need both of us more than ever. And because of that and because I've got to catch up on the other side of the ranch, I won't be out with you as much. It's going to take some studying and learning and making mistakes and fixing them." Her world felt upside down. It had for days. She turned to go then turned back again. "You may want to step someone up to foreman to replace you. You can't be here for the boys, manage the ranch, and be your own foreman, too." Even if ranch manager wasn't his aspiration as she suspected it had never been, he wouldn't refuse. He never refused her or J.D. anything. And it would reaffirm that he was needed. And he always would be.

She didn't wait to see his reaction to a promotion he'd never have wanted, just turned to hide the sting of tears, promising they'd be the last she shed. J.D. was gone but he was still counting on her. As long as she had Riley to take control over the physical aspects of the ranch, she could handle the business end. Grief had to take a back seat to that.

In the end, Miranda left her conversation with Wesley Harper until the following morning, giving herself time to think things through, to consider every angle. She wasn't looking forward to their talk but felt at least settled enough to deal with it. She looked up as the tutor rapped at the open door to J.D.'s office—hers, now, she corrected the thought with a sharp pang.

"You wanted to see me?"

"Yes. Coffee?" She gestured toward the carafe on the side table.

"No, but thank you. I've just come from the dining room and Miss Lila made sure I had my fill."

It was with their housekeeper that Miranda had left her request for Wesley to see her before lessons.

"Sit down. Please." Miranda had chosen to sit in one of the two arm chairs in front of the desk rather than being formal.

He took the other and stretched his long legs before him, managing to look attentive yet comfortable. "How are the twins? Did you wish them to have a few more days off from their lessons?"

"They're … coping. I did think about time off but it might be best for them to be busy rather than not."

He nodded, pushing his glasses more firmly against the bridge of his nose. It was a habitual gesture she'd noticed before. The eyes behind the glasses were a warm brown. She'd always thought them wise and kind and sighed at the possibility she'd misjudged him as someone she could trust to keep the twins' best interests in front of him.

"I think busy is better for those two," he agreed with her comment. "They're thinkers, which can be both a good and a bad thing."

"They are, yes," she said, taking that opening, "which is why I'm concerned."

At her words, he pulled his legs in and leaned the slightest bit toward her. "How can I help?"

"By explaining why you think I'd 'get rid of' my brothers." She kept her tone level and her face expressionless through sheer determination.

For a moment, Wesley wore a look of confusion which faded to dismay. "Ah, damn, I'm so sorry. I was overheard, wasn't I?"

"Yes, by the twins."

And the look of dismay slowly darkened to a kind of horror. "Jesus." He met her gaze without flinching. "If you'd like my letter of resignation, I'll have it to you within the hour."

She hadn't expected that. His self-revulsion eased her more than abject apologies could have. "At the moment, all I want is what I requested … an explanation."

Wesley released a deep breath. "Fair enough. More than, actually. I was on the phone with my dad who's been fired. Again." He rubbed the back of his neck. "And it won't be easy for him to find another job because he has another DUI and swears he can't afford the recovery program the state requires to have his license re-instated.

I've sent as much as I can this past year, but…"

"But you're enabling him."

His shoulders slumped. "Yes, and, even knowing that, it's still hard to say no. So hard. Fortunately, I've been wise enough not to let on where I am. Unfortunately, my stepmom figured out early on that my salary was stable. I don't fault her, mind you, a son should help his father."

"Again … but." Her tone was softer.

He nodded. "His call caught me at a bad time so soon after J.D.'s wreck. J.D. was a good man, a decent man, and he'd become a friend and a bit of a mentor perhaps. His death … well, I guess it angered me some. Without anyone to be angry *at*."

"Then your dad called and you had an outlet. You could be angry at him." It was a guess but an easy one.

"That, and I didn't want another blasted phone call asking for money. It was an unplanned, hare-brained thought that I could make him think I'd lost my job and was wandering with pockets as empty as his." He shook his head. "It was stupid and thoughtless and careless beyond belief not to be sure that no one was about to hear. And for it to be my guys." His breath came out on a long sigh. "I don't know how to make this right."

"Take them fishing."

"Excuse me?" He stared at her, clearly baffled.

"Do what J.D. would do. Take them fishing this morning. Talk to them. Tell them you made a mistake. Apologize."

He gave a grunt of laughter. "You make it sound so simple."

"Isn't it? That was the foundation of J.D.'s success. Honesty. Decency. Doing the right thing. Saying the right thing."

He smiled. "And the fishing?"

"A breather, of sorts. A distraction. Then lessons, this afternoon. Something fun but challenging."

She stood and he did the same.

"Thank you."

The words were simply said but she heard his sincerity, saw him take a deep breath and straighten his shoulders as he walked from the room. Without a doubt, the twins were academically ahead of their peers in the public system, although she'd had the thought lately that they needed more time with kids their age. Would that have made a difference? Would it have helped them through their loss? She didn't know. Besides, J.D. had liked Wes. A lot. They'd both counted on him to keep the twins' well-being first and foremost. She'd continue counting on him for the time being but considered it a silent probation.

Chapter Two

The county was more rural than not but prosperous enough that the sheriff's office was well maintained. Not fancy, by any means, but solid and it appeared to be scrupulously clean. Dayshift had just ended and the receiving counter at the front entrance sat vacant. A deputy hunched over a desk in the back got to his feet as Colter pushed open the glass door at the front and stepped inside. "Mr. Bellamy?"

Colter nodded.

"This way, sir. Sheriff McEnny is waiting for you." Not with pleasant anticipation, judging by the deputy's tone.

Colter followed him down a short hall and stepped past the door held back for him to enter.

The sheriff rose as they entered. He nodded at the deputy who closed the door behind him. "Mr. Bellamy."

He held out a hand to shake, then gestured to a corner where two leather chairs had been pulled close to a small table.

Colter took stock of the other man. Their photo of McEnny was ten years or so old, a shot from a local magazine article when he'd won his election yet again. Except for a few strands of silver at his temple his hair was still as black. The slight bump on the bridge of his nose suggested it had been broken or hinted at Native American or Spanish bloodlines. Colter could have gone either way. He didn't look like a man who'd back down from a fight. But it was the blue eyes that tipped his ancestry away from Native American toward Spanish descent despite the Gaelic surname. None of which mattered as much to Colter as McEnny's reputation for doing the right thing the right way.

Once Colter declined a polite offer of coffee or a soft drink, McEnny didn't waste any time, something Colter could appreciate, even brusque as it was.

"I've heard about you Bellamys … that you don't mind crossing the line where you can."

Colter considered the comment a moment and decided not to take offense. "Then you've heard wrong," he said. "We flirt with it, skirt the edges at times, but we don't cross over."

McEnny's shoulders relaxed but his stare didn't. "See that you don't. Not in my town." When Colter matched his stare without blinking, McEnny leaned back into his chair, looking satisfied he'd made his point. "So, your team found something suspicious with J.D.'s truck? You wouldn't be here if it wasn't solid."

Colter acknowledged the comment with a nod as he pulled an envelope from his front pocket. He handed it across the table.

McEnny withdrew the small stack of photographs and looked through them one at a time in the order Colter had arranged. Colter watched his face. He'd already studied the pictures. Damn near had them memorized. A broad shot of the mangled truck, then close ups of a tire sidewall from the outside. The hubcap was destroyed and the rubber shredded, typical of a hard crash. The remaining shots shifted to the interior of the tire at the bead, the steel and rubber belted cable that sealed rubber to metal rim. A progression of shots, the first of which showed nothing definitive but each succeeding photograph zoomed closer and closer. The change in expression was barely perceptible but Colter knew the moment the sheriff spotted what he wanted him to see. The final shot showed the precision cut made and the cause of the crash exposed.

"You can keep the photographs. I have several sets," Colter said when McEnny looked up.

"A hunter, maybe. Scared to come forward, afraid of the consequences. Hell, maybe he didn't even know he'd hit anything."

Colter didn't comment.

"Damn it to hell." McEnny laid the photographs to one side. "What caliber?"

"Seventeen."

The sheriff took a deep breath. "Fast. If what you're thinking is right, and that's still a big if for me, he went for speed not distance or power."

"Or she," Colter said, then nodded. "But, yeah, fast. Had to be, to bury it that deep in the bead."

McEnny's eyes narrowed. "She? You know something?"

Colter shrugged. "I know it happens. Wouldn't be the first daughter who wanted things now rather than later."

McEnny scowled at him. "Don't go barking up that tree, Bellamy."

"Barking isn't my nature, but there's no trail I won't follow."

The scowl faded to a look of disgust. "It'll be a waste of time, but it's yours to waste." With a shake of his head, he glanced back down at the photographs. "The bullet? Where is it?"

"With me."

McEnny's voice took on an edge. "This is my jurisdiction."

Despite the fact he had every intention of leaving the bullet with McEnny, Colter was determined to take his measure and push just a little in the process. "It is but the Pederson boys—the twins—they're family. Their grandfather was a Bellamy. And here's my problem. That team of yours? They had two opportunities to find what mine found. Two. They failed both."

"Yeah, and if my team had the resources of the private sector, you wouldn't be sitting here."

"Oh, I'd be here," Colter disagreed, keeping his tone even. "We take care of our own."

"You Bellamy's aren't above the law." Given the right tone, the sheriff's words could have held antagonism, even a hint of threat. The tone wasn't there. Colter judged it more resignation, maybe even a trace of acceptance.

"No, we aren't. We've never tried to be. Never will." Colter reached into his pocket and placed a bullet in a plastic pouch upon the table between them.

McEnny grunted in irritation and leaned against the leather-backed seat of his chair. He knew he was being played. "You've made your point and my team will take a closer look at J.D.'s death. So just what is it you want?"

"Everything you know as soon as you know it." Small town lawmen could be touchy and Colter knew McEnny could go either way. He also knew the sheriff was sharp enough to know that the case itself could go either way. A failure by the sheriff's team could be career-ending. A failure on Colter's part would be a place to point a finger and save face.

They exchanged stares for a moment before the sheriff stood and crossed to his desk. Leaning down, he turned a key in the lock of a bottom drawer. When he returned, he placed a deputy's badge on the tabletop and slid it toward Colter. "I did a little digging after I got your call. I know you were on the force in Albuquerque a while back. Even so, there ain't but one way you'll get that information."

Colter got to his feet. He'd been down this road once or twice in the past. Without hesitating, he repeated the oath of office after the sheriff then picked up the badge and slipped it into his pocket.

"Don't get attached to that," McEnny warned, opening the door of his office.

Colter paused in the opening long enough to say, "I'll be in touch."

"I never doubted it." If the sheriff's tone still held a hint of animosity, Colter couldn't blame him. There wasn't a man alive who appreciated being pushed into a concession. But, as Colter told himself, sooner or later it happened to all of them.

Colter called Jonah on his way out of town. He'd promised to brief the other man on his meeting with the sheriff. No better time than now.

"How'd he take it?" Jonah's tone indicated he already

knew the answer.

"With an attitude. Willing to accept help, but not happy about it."

"No decent lawman would be," Jonah pointed out, "not under these circumstances."

"Yeah, well, they should've been showing those photographs to us … not the other way around."

"I don't disagree," Jonah admitted, "but you know that would never have happened. Still, with that, having the upper hand here gave us the edge to get you on the inside."

"I would've gotten there either way."

"I'll take the easier. Where you headed now?"

"To the ranch. To see the girl." The girl in the photograph, who'd turned out to be Pederson's daughter by a first marriage and a grown woman who, in all likelihood, stood to inherit a lot. He couldn't confirm that information until the will was submitted for probate but the prospect was enough to go on for now.

"McEnny didn't object to that?"

"I didn't ask."

Jonah grunted. "Likely, he guessed, now that he knows what a pushy son-of-a-gun you are."

"Likely." But Jonah knew as well as he that their work didn't allow for reticence.

"And the girl? She know you're coming?" Jonah could do a fair amount of pushing himself.

"No."

He could almost hear the disapproval in Jonah's silence. He didn't bother to explain himself. Jonah understood the value in catching people off guard but it still wasn't something he approved. Particularly not in a case like this. Miranda Pederson had just buried her father. But all Colter wanted to know was if she was responsible for his death. If she'd killed him or hired someone to kill him. It happened every day in this great country of theirs.

Colter stepped out of his truck at the far end of the drive and studied the house. Behind it, a sunset flamed the sky with gold and rose which gradually deepened to orange and purple. The two-storied structure wasn't new but, even from this distance, he could tell that it was well-kept and solid, sprawling in multiple directions from add-ons over the decades. He'd seen pictures of what the place had looked like in the beginning as well as what it looked like now. The change was substantial but not in the impressive way that said old money. J.D. Pederson, like his father before him, had been nobody's fool. Anything the ranch had made above what was needed to sustain a growing household had gone back into the ranch, making it a prosperous and still-thriving business even in uncertain times.

The metal arch over the double gate framed the name 'Pederson' in simple block letters. Colter wished he'd known this branch of the family before now. He liked the style he saw reflected here. Plain and unpretentious.

Climbing back behind the wheel, he continued down the drive. As tempting as it was to follow the wide paved curve around to the back, he settled for stopping at the front. An older woman answered the tinkling chimes of the doorbell. Not the daughter.

"I'm here to see Ms. Pederson."

She gave him a long, slow, less than welcoming look. "May I ask who's calling on her?"

"Bellamy. Colter Bellamy." Her eyes flickered in recognition of the name.

She opened the door and stepped back, giving him space to enter a wide hallway. "Wait here a moment," she gestured toward a carved bench. "You may take a seat if you'd like."

Colter didn't like. He propped one shoulder against the wall on his left while she disappeared through an opening to the right.

The wait that followed didn't surprise him. He doubted anyone here would be expecting company. This soon after a funeral the family was usually left in peace. Then there was the added element of his last name which might or might not be concerning to those left behind. Either way, his presence would hardly be welcomed.

The woman returned and nodded to him. "Miranda has agreed to see you, Mr. Bellamy. Please follow me." He almost smiled but didn't. Miranda Pederson would get every courtesy from him, as women always did, but— welcome or not—refusing to meet with him had never been an option. But that was something they couldn't have known and there was no need to express it now.

His boots were not as quiet as the woman's shoes on the slate floor. Almost but not quite. He followed her through an oversized room with three different groupings of comfortable furniture. Pricey but not new. He didn't make notes. He didn't need to. He simply observed and stored it away. At this point in an investigation, any and every thing mattered until he knew it didn't.

The double doors of the room beyond stood open. A large window framed the wall behind a massive, mahogany desk and book cases lined the walls on either side. The hardcover spines of the books, which ranged from ranching to political discourse to histories of the area, showed years of use.

Colter took his hat from his head and stepped into the room and the woman seated at the desk lifted her eyes. He'd thought of her as a girl until that moment. She wasn't. She was young but she was a woman. The look in her eyes was both haunted and haunting. And those eyes were like none he'd seen before. Photographs hadn't come close to capturing the color. Neither green nor brown nor gold but somehow swirls and flecks of all three. A pale scattering of freckles across even paler cheeks should have been a detraction from her looks. They weren't. The uneven streaks the sun had left in her brown hair should have looked washed out. They didn't. Her features were even and regular and completely unspectacular, but they caught and held his attention for one unguarded moment before he pushed that distraction aside.

He hesitated a moment longer, taking in the scene. An open ledger lay on the desk in front of her. She held a pencil, the ends gripped loosely between the fingers of each hand.

He stepped forward. "Ms. Pederson."

She nodded, watching him. "And you're Mr. Bellamy."

"One of them." One of several as a matter of fact. He kept his tone agreeable. She didn't offer him a chair, and he didn't think she planned on it. He took one anyway.

He didn't fault her for being wary or unwelcoming. And he didn't look forward to rocking her world with the knowledge that the father she'd just lost had been murdered. Unless she was guilty. Then he wanted to rock the hell out of it.

"How can I help you?"

"I'm sorry about the loss of your father."

Her fingers tightened on the pencil. "Thank you."

"I'm sorrier still to inform you it's doubtful that his death was an accident."

The pencil snapped between her fingers. "Where is Sheriff McEnny? Why are you here telling me this?"

Those first two questions surprised him, if only because neither was who or how. "McEnny deputized me earlier."

"I don't believe you."

He pulled the badge from his shirt pocket and held it for her to see before placing it back in his pocket.

"J.D. would never have intentionally harmed anyone. I don't believe anyone intentionally harmed him." She placed the broken ends of the pencil carefully upon the ledger and put her hands in her lap. Those startling eyes pinned him in place with their intensity. "I don't believe *you*," she said, emphasizing the last word.

"Fair enough." He got to his feet. "I've said what I thought you should know. If you don't have any questions for me, I have an investigation to conduct."

He got no more than a step or two before she said, "Wait." Her voice was low and tense and as unwilling as he expected it to be. He stopped and turned.

"What proof do you have?"

He waited a heartbeat or two, as if deciding whether or not he would share, although that was never really in question, then withdrew a second set of photos from his shirt pocket. An abbreviated set this time.

Her hand was steady as she reached for them. The picture on top was the mangled truck. Her knuckles and her face whitened in equal measure. The next was of the exterior of the tire. The third revealed the exposed bullet on the interior.

She sucked in her breath, giving herself a moment to

absorb what she saw, but then her reaction was the same as McEnny's had been. "An accident."

He met her look and shook his head.

"It must have been. There are hunters all over these hills."

"This time of year?" Late summer wasn't exactly prime hunting anywhere. "But let's say you're right. A hunter. With that caliber, the prey would be a rabbit or squirrel. Forensics has already established the distance the bullet traveled from gun to target somewhere between fifty and a hundred yards. An inept hunter could have missed what he or she was aiming for but he would've been close enough to see the crash." At which point, he'd be guilty of walking away from a dead or dying man but Colter wasn't crass enough to put that thought in her head. Bad enough that her father was dead. Worse if he could have been saved and someone had refused to help him. Unless that someone was her. In that case, he was being considerate for nothing. He shrugged and acknowledged, "Anything's possible."

"But you don't think so."

"I don't think so." He waited a heartbeat and added, "I wouldn't be here if I did."

"So, what now?"

"Now I find J.D.'s killer and make sure his sons are safe."

She got to her feet and the impact on his senses was immediate. She was slender but sturdy-boned, full-hipped, and full-breasted. He felt a flash of male appreciation that was as unexpected as it was unwelcome and pushed it aside.

"My brothers are *my* concern," she all but spat the words at him, "not yours or anyone else's."

"Unless you're the killer."

"You can go to hell!"

"I might, at that. Or maybe I've already been there." He matched her glare for glare but caught himself before he matched her curse for curse. He'd known from an early age, the Bellamys lived in a rough world. But Reginald Bellamy had taught his sons to treat a female with respect until they proved they were no lady.

When she stayed silent, he settled his hat on his head and met her angry gaze. "How long have you been calling your father J.D.?" It wasn't an idle question. He'd seen some sick relationships over the years.

She lifted her chin. "Since I turned seventeen and he started handing over pieces of the ranch for me to manage. He said a woman didn't need to call her business partner daddy."

"Were you a woman at seventeen?" He didn't filter the question or soften it and he could tell by her expression that she understood it.

She leaned forward, palms flat on the desk. "By sixteen, I could ride better, rope better, and brand a cow as well as any of his ranch hands. By seventeen, I'd homeschooled myself through high school and was in my first year of college, focused on business management. Woman enough, Mr. Bellamy. Now, if we're finished, I still have work to do."

That makes two of us, Colter thought as he walked back the way he'd come and opened the entrance door to let himself out.

Always watchful, his gaze went instantly to the man in faded jeans and a chambray shirt—a ranch hand, maybe—who leaned against a support post near the door. As Colter stepped out onto the porch, the man straightened and moved forward to position himself not quite in Colter's way. But close enough.

Colter met his gaze head on. "Problem?"

"Not with me … unless there's one with Miss Miranda."

"That remains to be seen. But I'll figure it out and you likely won't be the first one to know."

The ranch hand narrowed his eyes. "Who are you and what are you figuring out?"

"Bellamy. Colter Bellamy. And you?"

"Riley. I'm the foreman here."

"Well, good to meet you, Riley. I'm sure you'll be seeing me." With that Colter walked on toward his truck. He heard the door reopen behind him and suspected Mr. Riley would get his answer as to what Colter was 'figuring out' soon enough.

From their earliest days, when New Mexico was a territory rather than a state, the three couples who had banded together near Taos to become ranching partners had taken care of their own and given back to the county and to the state in gratitude for a new start. They still gave back to the land that sustained them and took care of their own with equal fervor. Anyone who wanted could turn their back on the family but no one could be taken from them by force. Not without a fight and not without retribution.

Chapter Three

Miranda woke early, as she always did, and stepped out of her room to the balcony beyond. The mug she cradled between her hands would be the first of the two cups of coffee she typically allowed herself each morning. She'd learned long ago that caffeine killed her appetite and she'd lived on coffee since the phone call telling her about the crash. Time to back off.

The first cup was here, in solitude. The second cup had always been with J.D. as they planned their day over breakfast.

Sinking into a chair, she watched as daylight slid over the hills. She let herself think of J.D. for a moment, let herself miss him, but she didn't let herself think of murder, then she pushed her thoughts forward to the day ahead. Her appointment with J.D.'s attorney was at ten. She had things to do before then.

Lila met her at the base of the stairs and Miranda suspected the housekeeper had been waiting for her.

Her suspicion was confirmed when Lila folded her arms in front of her and said, "You need to eat before that office swallows you up."

Miranda smiled through the stab of pain. How often had she heard Lila say those same words to J.D.? She wasn't hungry, but she obediently followed the housekeeper into the dining room. J.D. had always been there before her and the empty chairs mocked her.

"Have the boys eaten?"

"They'll be down to the kitchen before long."

Miranda looked thoughtfully at the full sideboard and single setting on the long table. "Send them in here, please. I want them to eat with me each morning. Wes, too, if he chooses."

"They'll talk your ears off," Lila reminded her but she looked pleased.

"I'd rather my ears fall off from their chatter than from the quiet."

"I'll get their places set. Shall I pour your coffee first?"

Miranda shook her head. "We'll serve ourselves. And, Lila? If you haven't eaten, you're welcome to join us this morning and any other."

"J.D. enjoyed his quiet time with you," Lila acknowledged, "talking out what each of you would do that day but I think this is a good change for you."

Miranda suspected there would be other changes but she was taking one day at a time. Today was the first of the many tough ones that lay ahead, and she didn't want to start her morning in solitude. She was genuinely pleased when the housekeeper took her up on that offer and joined them at the dining table.

With her ears still filled with chatter and a heart not quite so heavy, Miranda stepped into the sports car J.D. had bought for her twenty-first birthday. It was no longer new and shiny but it was well cared for and she loved it as much as ever. She intended to drive it until the wheels fell off and, if possible, she'd put them back on and drive it some more. Especially now.

The distance to town gave her too much time to think, but when she turned on the radio the sound jarred and she turned it off again. Forced to drive past the site of J.D.'s wreck, she clenched her jaw and felt a corresponding stab in her chest. To occupy her mind, she pushed it to run through the list of things she would need to accomplish that week and realized there would be things that J.D. had planned and she didn't yet know about. Things she'd have to figure out before an unexpected problem caught up with her. She'd let the days since the accident and the days after the funeral pass in a blur. It was time to buckle down.

She turned onto a tree-lined street on the outskirts of town, then turned again onto a wide paved drive beside a stately home. Next to a brick walk leading toward a side entrance, a discreet sign bore the words Langley & Langley, Attorneys-At-Law. Elizabeth and her daughter, Katherine, shared a partnership on the lower floor of their home with private apartments on the floors above. Miranda had been in Liz's for a holiday open house. She'd thought it as original and classy as the woman herself.

Liz opened the door before Miranda could lift the old-fashioned knocker. "Come in." And when she did, Liz pulled her into a light hug. "I'm sorrier than I can say to be doing this today."

Miranda swallowed against the lump that tightened her throat before stepping back. "Thank you. It's … hard."

"Impossibly so," Liz agreed on a sigh. "Sit down." She gestured toward a sofa with a low table in front of it. A file folder centered the table and an envelope with Miranda's name on it lay atop it.

Miranda sat and studied Liz's face. The attorney wasn't flashy though she had the money and means to be. Her pixie-cut hair, more chestnut than brown, was matched to the color of her eyes. She'd added a touch of color around those eyes and on her lips but that was about the extent of her make-up.

"I have coffee or tea, iced or hot," she offered. "Or anything else."

"Water, maybe."

Liz stepped out then returned carrying a small tray with a pitcher of iced water and two glasses. She set it beside the folder and poured them both a glass before taking the envelope and handing it to Miranda.

Miranda stared at it a moment and blinked back a sting of tears. Her name was in J.D.'s hand-writing. Opening it, she extracted and unfolded the single sheet and read in silence.

Miranda, my dearest daughter, if you're reading this, it's too soon, and I didn't mean for that to happen. I know it's too soon because Liz makes me review my will once a year, every year and I rewrite this note to you although it hasn't changed much since the first one I left for you. I'm not ready to go, not ready to leave you and Dane and Dillon. But, then, I'm sure I never would be. I'm also sure

I don't want to spend my last years in bad health, physical or mental, or bedridden but … well, I'm hopeful for another year or a dozen running the ranch with you and watching the boys grow to men. But they aren't nearly old enough yet so I'm counting on you now to finish their upbringing. They'll make fine men in time.

I've set aside enough … well, more than enough, I reckon, but hell, they're mine and I can … for each of them to make their way in the world. They're to have one-fourth of that account balance when they reach the age of twenty-three. Not one minute before and don't you let them sweet talk you into sooner. Another fourth when they reach age twenty-five and the balance when they turn thirty. I'd like to see them in college or the military but I'm not opposed to them making a start in a craft or a business they love. You can share that with them when the time is right. You'll know.

You are sole executor to my estate and there's some other paper Liz has which names you as their legal guardian at the moment of my death.

A sense of relief swept her. He'd named her guardian for Dane and Dillon. They were safe.

As for the ranch and the remainder of my money, it's yours.

Miranda's breath caught in her throat and looked up at Liz, shaking her head, but Liz gave her a small, sad smile.

From the first time you helped me pull a calf from its dying mama and kept it alive with a bottle and a warming light, I knew it was yours. I like to think that one day, a 'way in the future one day', you'll pass it on to my grandkids. So be sure you marry someone good enough to be their daddy.

Now, dry your tears, baby girl. You have work to do. I love you and I always will, J.D.

Staring down at the paper in her hands, Miranda drew breath after breath, trying to stop the pain. She'd thought she had no more tears to cry. She was wrong. They burned in her eyes and blurred her vision when she looked up at Liz.

"I've got to fix this."

Liz chuckled. "It's not broken, Miranda. And it's already done. The deed was refiled as a Transfer on Death to you several years ago."

"Transfer on Death?"

"Your father signed and had me record a deed for the ranch that states the property—the land as well as the house and any other structures, excluding Riley's home and the acreage promised him—was, and in fact did become, yours upon his death. Once recorded, that would've happened even if he'd left no will which, of course, he did. The will ensures the remainder of the ranch holdings, the cattle, horses, equipment, any subsidiary rights are now yours."

Miranda shook her head, trying to absorb the words and their meaning. "This isn't right. Couldn't you have talked him out of it?"

"You know better than that. When his mind was made, it was made. Nor did I think he *should* do any different."

"But—the ranch—it's their birthright." Miranda felt bewildered.

"Yours as much as theirs."

"Not really," Miranda said, reminding Liz without the words that she wasn't J.D.'s daughter by blood. She'd been a toddler when J.D. had married her mother.

"Yes, really. I was there when the adoption papers were drawn and signed. You belonged to J.D. every bit as much as the twins. You know that's true, don't you?"

Miranda took a deep breath and nodded. She did know J.D. loved her. He'd never made her feel less than his and she suspected he would have taken a horse whip to anyone who might have. No one ever had.

Liz studied her face for a moment and sighed. "Listen, Miranda, your father had strong feelings that a man should make his own mark on the world. That's what he wants for his sons. And he's leaving them more than enough to make their dreams—whatever they prove to be—a reality. The amount they'll have when they turn twenty-three is more than most people make in a lifetime and that's only a part of it. But the ranch ... it's yours. That's what he wanted for you."

The will itself wasn't lengthy. Liz had written it in the straightforward language J.D. preferred. The terms were exactly as he'd outlined in his letter. On a separate page was a list of bequests he'd made to Lila and each of the hands, all of whom had been with him for some years.

As Miranda read through that final page, Liz said, "I've taken the liberty of preparing the checks. All you'll need to do is verify the amounts against the list and sign the checks."

Miranda knew she wouldn't need to verify the amounts. Liz would have been scrupulous in her accuracy. "What about the money for Dane and Dillon? Where is that?"

"J.D. placed it in trust funds so neither the money nor the ranch is part of probate. Speaking of which, I'll file probate this week and push the will through as quickly as possible..."

Liz stopped mid-sentence as Miranda held up one hand. "So soon?" She felt as if she couldn't catch her breath. It was all too much, too fast.

"Delaying the process won't bring him back."

And, that, Miranda knew, was what she was trying to do. Stop time. Make this not be real. Her breath caught on a hiccup. Tears burned and she saw the hurt and the sympathy on Liz's face. The other woman hadn't only been J.D.'s attorney. She'd been his friend.

"I know," Miranda said on a sigh. "I know you're right."

"Finalizing probate means you'll have one less thing taking your time, but everything is straightforward and I don't foresee complications. You'll have access to working capital throughout the process. J.D.'s money is with Clark & Sons. Now that you have the will showing you're the sole executor, and I've sent him a copy as well, he'll go over that aspect of things."

Liz paused, read her expression. "Overwhelmed?"

"A little," she admitted. A lot, if she were honest.

"Take it one step at a time." Liz let out a sigh. "And I hate to add to those steps but you also need to be thinking about making your own will. To safeguard the twins' futures."

Not today, Miranda thought, feeling weary to the bone although it was barely noon. She had a lot to process.

Colter followed the GPS until he reached the coordinates for the wreck. He pulled to the shoulder of the winding, rural highway and sat in silence, scanning the rugged landscape on both sides of the pavement. Traffic was light, almost nonexistent for the moment. Even so, he switched on his flashers for safety before he stepped out.

On the same side of the road, he walked several yards in front of his truck then several yards behind. Not until he crossed over, did he find evidence of the roll-over. Most of the debris had been gathered and removed. He'd seen the greatest part of it, but a sideview mirror had been missing. He found it, now, amidst a scattering of glass. The fact that both front and back windshields had shattered so completely said volumes about the force behind the roll-over. The impact when the truck bounced against the ground, not once but at least twice from what Colter was seeing, had to have been significant. What looked to be a third roll could be, instead, where the tow truck had been stopped to lift the wreckage but even two flips spoke volumes. The last speed limit sign had been for sixty-five miles per hour. He suspected Pederson had been going every bit of that and perhaps a little more.

The distance from town to the ranch and the speed the well-maintained road allowed would have ensured the tires were hot. Anyone with a little gun knowledge who also knew the rancher's habits could easily guess the outcome of firing a bullet into a sidewall under those conditions.

Colter turned and walked back past his truck toward a cluster of small boulders, pausing long enough to lay the bits and pieces of scrap metal he'd found in the bed of his truck. He walked around the rock formation, close enough to form perceptions but far enough not to disturb the scene, although he supposed enough time had passed that it hardly mattered.

Lost in thought, Colter winced at the squeal of locked tires and glanced up to see a small sporty looking car leaving a layer of rubber on the road beside him. He wasn't the least surprised when Miranda Pederson stepped out. His first thought was that she had surprisingly long legs. His second was that she looked furious to see him there. And *that* was not a surprise. He knew for a fact that, on both sides of the road and as far as the eye could see, they were surrounded by Pederson land. The highway, however, belonged to the state.

"What the *hell* are you doing here?"

For half a heartbeat Colter wondered why an angry woman was so off-putting. In the second half of that heartbeat, he realized that what he was feeling was the opposite of repelled. He also realized she knew exactly why he was there and the question was rhetorical and designed to provoke an argument. Colter didn't like arguments.

But she was hell-bent on one, it seemed. When he didn't answer, she pushed harder. "This is Pederson land. You're trespassing."

"I was," he admitted. He didn't mention the few pieces of the demolished truck he'd retrieved and placed in the back of his. He supposed she'd consider that theft. And maybe it was. "At the moment, I'm on government property."

Her chin jutted further at the words. He stared into her eyes and recognized a mule-like stubbornness behind the anger. He knew a few Slades and Welles and Bellamys who could have equaled that look. Including himself.

By force of effort, he relaxed his stance. "Do you want J.D.'s killer brought to justice?"

For a moment, she didn't speak. "More than I want anything else, other than for the twins to be safe."

"Then our goals are the same."

She brushed strands of hair away from her face but the wind whipped them back just as fast. She gathered the length of it in one hand impatiently. "You make it sound so reasonable until I consider the fact you think it possible that I killed J.D."

"I've seen enough cases to know anything is possible, but I won't be looking at you any harder than I am anyone else."

After a moment, she turned and got back into the car,

leaving him with a silence that lasted less than a heartbeat before she put her foot to the gas and laid rubber once more.

He watched her car disappear over the next hill before calling McEnny.

The sheriff pulled in behind Colter's truck. He didn't look pleased as he walked up to where Colter had one hip propped against his tailgate. "What've you got?" His tone indicated he wasn't expecting much.

"When was the last rain?"

McEnny scowled. "To amount to anything? Two days before J.D. was killed. A couple more weeks of this heat and no rain and we'll be fighting wildfires. Dry as tinder with a wind to fan the flames." The scowl deepened. "Why?"

Instead of answering, Colter asked another question. "Where do you position the shooter?"

McEnny eyed him a moment then pointed back toward the same cluster of rocks that Colter had been studying. "There. Figure he was lying down on one side or the other. He'd be about sixty maybe seventy yards from the highway. Damn good marksmanship to make that shot at the speed the truck was moving."

Colter agreed. Much farther and the drop of a .17 caliber wouldn't have allowed the bullet to hit that tire straight on, not with the force that it had upon entry. Either someone got extremely lucky or they'd had more than average range hours with moving targets.

"Why? You come up with something different?"

"Not different, no."

McEnny's gaze sharpened. "But what...?

"Play it out like you see it in your mind."

He'd half expected the lawman to tell him to go to hell, but McEnny looked more intrigued than irritated.

The sheriff stared at the group of boulders. His tone was still acerbic when he started talking, but Colter expected that never changed by much. "I don't think it was spur-of-the moment. I think he knew J.D. and knew his plans for the day or knew his habits well enough to guess at them."

Again, Colter agreed. It didn't feel like a random act. He wasn't altogether convinced on the timing. An opportunity may have presented itself, but the thought was already in place. "If the killer knew Pederson's plans, he was either a part of those plans or someone close enough J.D. had mentioned them."

The sheriff nodded. "If we go with habit, it broadens the pool. J.D. was a creature of habit without a doubt. Tuesday was haircut and lunch at the café, usually with me. Every third Wednesday was the farmer's auction at the edge of town."

Colter was silent for a moment, thinking. J.D. had died on a Wednesday afternoon. His overturned truck had been spotted some distance from the road later that day by a passing motorist.

"Can you make me a timeline of those two—the farmers' auction and lunch with you—and anything else that comes to mind?" He'd also talk with J.D.'s daughter about his habits and then he'd verify every word she said.

"Sure. There's pool night and poker night." McEnny chuckled as if at a good memory, then cleared his throat. "Yeah." He took a deep breath. "Yeah, I'll get all that to you."

Colter relaxed a little. It seemed the sheriff wasn't going to fight him on every step of the investigation and that was a big plus. He appeared, even, to be willing to let Colter stay involved. Colter suspected the sheriff had done some research, enough to add facts to all the gossip about Welles Enterprises. "Anybody mention seeing him at the farmers' auction?"

"No, I didn't see a need to ask before I saw those photographs. I put a deputy on that first thing this morning. He's out tracking people down." The sheriff rubbed the back of his neck. "Even, then, it's a huge auction, pulls people from several counties. J.D. could've been there and not been noticed."

Colter didn't think so. J.D. seemed to have been a larger-than-life kind of person but he wouldn't argue the point. He gestured around him. "Keeping in mind that J.D. was a creature of habit, and his killer may have known him well, how do you think the killer made the approach?"

"Probably pulled his truck to the back of those boulders." They were substantial enough to have hidden a car or even a pickup if carefully positioned. "Got out, lay down in the brush alongside those rocks and waited for the right truck to come along. Not likely he'd be seen, not if his truck wasn't."

The lawman was still certain the killer was a man. Colter's internal jury remained out on that one.

Colter rubbed his jaw. "That's pretty much how I figured it. Until I got closer." He glanced at the sheriff and started walking toward the boulders. McEnny followed looking disgruntled, as if already suspecting he'd missed something. And he had.

They stopped where Colter wanted the lawman to focus. "So, the rain a day or two before the wreck was enough to amount to something, which means the land here at the base of these hills would've held moisture."

The sheriff took a moment to study the hardy wildflowers, a litter of purple against the otherwise dull landscape. "And there're no tire tracks." McEnny sounded more than disgusted with himself. "Which means the killer likely came on foot."

"And this is all Pederson land," Colter reminded.

"Well, yeah, right here along the road, but over that hill the land is leased to Robert Bentley."

Colter turned to look where McEnny pointed. That fact hadn't shown up anywhere in the information he had. And it put a definite spin on possible suspects. "Any hard feelings between Bentley and Pederson?"

McEnny gave a bark of laughter. "You could say … but that was once upon a time a long time ago. J.D.'s ex … Jerica … was Bentley's wife when she and J.D. decided they were in love."

But maybe, Colter thought, it wasn't long enough ago. Maybe something had fanned the fire on the ill will. It would be enough to poke at.

Chapter Four

Miranda went with Riley at daybreak the next morning, headed to sections not difficult to reach by pickup. Riley drove the old ranch truck, not breaking the silence until they reached the first gate which Miranda got out to open. When she climbed back up into the cab, he gave her a look. "Something not sitting right with you?"

Miranda stared through the dusty windshield. "J.D. left me the ranch. All of it."

"Yep. And?"

She turned her head and stared at him long enough that he glanced at her before returning his attention to the potholes in the rough dirt road. "You knew?"

"I don't reckon there was anything J.D. was of a mind to do that I didn't hear before he made it happen."

Closing her eyes, she took a deep breath. Riley knowing

made it real. And somehow right. "All of it except your house and the acres surrounding it." She looked at him.

"Me and J.D. walked that land down five, six years ago when he told me it was a done deal and to quit bitchin' like an old woman."

That made her smile.

"I don't rightly have much use or time for it now but maybe when you and them boys don't need me as much, I'll buy a few more head and watch them grow."

Miranda glanced out the side window and blinked back the tears that threatened to fill her eyes. "I'll always need you, Riley, but that doesn't mean you have to work for the rest of your life or mine. You're as much home to me as J.D. and this ranch have ever been."

"I ain't goin' anywhere."

She let the silence sit between them as they checked fence lines and water sources and watched cattle graze. Riley had lead hands for each section of land but he and J.D. had inspected every inch of the ranch at least once a week, by truck or by horseback.

After the last stop, Miranda settled into her seat and stared through the windshield. She surprised herself when she said, "Colter Bellamy thinks J.D. was murdered. That the wreck wasn't an accident."

When Riley didn't answer, she turned to look at him. His face was set in stone.

"Riley?"

"He got proof?" His voice sounded as if it were being sifted through gravel and he cleared his throat.

Fighting the ache in her throat, she told him about the photographs, about the bullet.

"Damn," he murmured, then put the truck in park and sat in silence a moment, as if absorbing and accepting her words. "McEnny fumbled the ball on this one."

"It could have been a hunter."

"Higher up in the hills, I'd agree to a maybe on that. Down here, right along the highway … I don't know. The whole county knows this is Pederson property, that we run cattle right up to the fence line." He shook his head. "Even if it was a hunter and he walked away from that wreck, it's still murder, intentional or not."

Colter Bellamy had made the same point but it hit home coming from Riley.

The sick feeling in her stomach deepened. "So, you think it *could* be intentional? That there's at least a chance? But … why? Everybody loved J.D."

Riley grunted. "We loved him. Maybe most folk who knew him did." He sighed. "But not everyone."

"You know someone who could have disliked him that much?"

"Nobody with enough courage," he answered, evasively. "Maybe it wasn't dislike. Maybe greed. Could be someone wanted some of what he had, what you and those boys have now." He shifted so that he faced her, holding her eyes with his. She could see the concern, maybe a touch of real worry, and that frightened her. "If anyone asks you about buying anything—even so much as an acre of land or a bull we ain't listed in a sale—you don't tell them *no*. You tell them *maybe*, that you'll give it some thought, you hear me? Then you come find me and we'll go to McEnny. I ain't so sure about this Bellamy fellow yet, but I'll check him out."

Riley's words were still in her mind when he stopped the truck at the back of the house, keeping a good distance from where Wes and the boys were tossing a basketball into the hoop attached to the garage. She watched a moment as the tutor sank one with neat precision, caught it, and tried again.

Dane darted between Wes and the goal, capturing the ball with a swift play that delighted her. He gave a crow of laughter which drew a quick grin from his tutor. Before Dane had a chance to get too cocky, his twin stole the ball from him mid-dribble. Dillon let out a whoop as he made the goal with a move almost as smooth as Wes' own had been.

"That's good," Riley said. "J.D. would want them to get back to normal as soon as possible." He looked at Miranda. "And you, too."

"Not as long as his killer is walking around a free man."

"Yeah," he agreed heavily, "there is that and it puts a different spin on everything. But J.D. wouldn't want any of you to grieve forever."

"A part of me will." There was no getting around that.

Riley gave her a look and acknowledged, "You'll miss him forever. We all will. But unrelenting grief…" he shook his head and rubbed his hand over his face. "A grief like that will turn everything around you to shadows and destroy your soul almost as surely as hatred. That would break J.D.'s heart."

Miranda didn't answer but she took Riley's words with her as she stepped out of the truck and closed the door softly but securely behind her. She watched a moment as he pulled around the house and took the drive toward the barn then reminded herself to smile as the boys rushed toward her.

"Miranda! Miranda!" Dillon appeared to vibrate with his excitement. "Did you see me steal the ball and make the goal?"

"I did." She tousled his hair as he wrapped his arms around her waist. "Who's winning?"

Dillon looked at Wes who shook his head and smiled. "Today is a free for all. No score kept. The focus is on speed and agility, in getting their hands on the ball, and skill in keeping the ball. So, why don't you boys get back to it for another fifteen minutes or so?"

As they took off to wrestle for control of the ball, Miranda said, "Sounds as if you're letting them work off energy."

"This morning wasn't as productive as some days," Wes admitted, "but I don't think it was excess energy as much as lack of concentration. After lunch we'll try to get back on track."

The shouts and laughter from the twins lightened her heart but didn't ease her mind. Not after what she'd learned about J.D.'s death. She wasn't sure how much to tell Wes. She'd told Riley but she'd known Riley all her life. He told people what they needed to know, no more and no less. Anything nonessential just never entered a conversation. But Colter Bellamy hadn't said the investigation was a secret or so much as suggested she keep quiet as to why he was hanging around. And Wes was with the boys more than any of them.

She took a deep breath. "Wes, there's a chance that J.D.'s death wasn't accidental. The sheriff is looking into that."

"I...," he rubbed his hand through his hair, "I don't know what to say to that. They think someone ran him off the road?"

"They still have the truck. I guess they're not through looking," she said, deciding not to mention the bullet, in case that wasn't supposed to be broadcast. She'd have to remember to ask McEnny. She'd told Riley, but he didn't talk about much of anything to anyone unless it had to do with ranch business which was why J.D. had never hesitated to confide in him and Miranda felt the same.

"Who would hurt J.D.? And why the hell would they?"

"I don't know why. And I can't think of a soul who would have hurt him, much less want him dead." Then, wondering if she'd said more than she should have, she added, "Of course there's always the possibility that it was the accident it seemed. I guess it's the sheriff's responsibility to question everything." She trusted Wes, but sometimes the less said, the better.

Wes shook his head, looking as much in disbelief as she still felt.

"But it does make me worry some about the twins. About their safety."

His stunned expression deepened. "Damn, Miranda." The worried creases in his forehead deepened as he shifted his gaze from hers back to the boys. "Look, I'm licensed to carry. A bit rusty as I haven't been to the range since I started here but I could take some time to practice if that would make you feel better."

It was hard to picture Wes with a handgun. He somehow didn't seem the type. "Let me think about it. I don't like the idea of a handgun around the boys, but I'd rather you had one than not, if someone else did. Do you? Have it here, I mean?"

"Not with me here, no, but that would be easily remedied. All you have to do is let me know."

"I will, and ... this puts me at odds with another thought I'd had, about Dane and Dillon having some outings which gets them in contact with others their age."

"I actually think that's a good idea, Miranda, although I see the concern and share it under the circumstances. Academics are critical, no argument, but so is social interaction. I'd checked into some things. There are several excellent science museums in Albuquerque, nuclear and natural, as well as a historical and cultural. And it's been some time since we visited the history museums in Taos. One or two public schools allow their outings to be joined by home-schooled students."

"I'm sure some of it in hopes that a parent or two will change their mind about home-school." Beneath her quick comeback she felt good that Wes was a step ahead of her on this. He was getting paid well to be, but she appreciated the evidence of it.

"Which I hope you don't."

She snorted. "Not likely at all." She and J.D. had never wavered on that. The boys were happier and safer not being on the road twice a day for the long trip into town. That time was better spent exposed to the work that ran the ranch, the day-to-day effort that put food on the table and clothes on their back. And now, more than ever, she wanted the boys close.

The alarm on Wes's phone drew his attention and he gave her an apologetic look. "Time for the boys to wash for lunch. Miss Lila is particular about scrubbed faces and combed hair at her table … as you well know."

She watched as he gathered and herded them toward the house. His mention of the housekeeper reminded her that she still had to speak with each employee, reassure them that nothing on the ranch would change, and hand out the checks that J.D. had left for them. The prospect tightened her already-tense muscles. This afternoon, she told herself. Or tomorrow. Soon, but not now. She'd never make it through, not yet.

Colter had driven back to the city to spend most of the day working with Jonah. He made notes on his laptop as he and Jonah talked through what the research team had unearthed and forwarded to them regarding Pederson's friends and neighbors and business associates, starting with the most obvious.

"Since leaving New Mexico, Jerica Pederson has resided in Wyoming, *living the life* with an oilman. According to this rag, they're currently enjoying yachting along the coast of Australia."

"The ex? She's still Pederson?" Jonah asked curiously.

Colter nodded. "They're married but she kept her ex-husband's last name."

"Odd."

"Not so much," Colter pointed out. "Not these days. Seems most anything goes as far as names."

"Guess I'm old-fashioned," Jonah admitted. "You saw the magazine? The photo?"

Colter nodded, studying the woman. Dark, designer sunglasses, tendrils of light hair slipping from under a trendy, broad-brimmed hat. She would appeal to most men. Behind her, white sand beaches curved around turquoise water.

"How high is Robert Bentley sitting on your list?" Jonah tapped his pen against a file folder.

Colter shrugged. "Not as high as I'd expected he'd be."

"Even though the local paper milked the story of J.D.'s entanglement with Jerica Bentley for all it was worth at the time?" Jonah asked dryly.

"Even though," Colter acknowledged.

It was true, there had been more than a few seemingly benign stories in the social section on the Bentleys. But from garden parties to art exhibits to charitable auctions, Pederson had been visible in the background in almost every photo of the couple. He didn't appear to be paying them much attention and if the angle of camera had been different, he wouldn't have been included at all. But he was … consistently. It occurred to Colter that someone at the paper had gotten wind of an affair or at least a flirtation between J.D. and Jerica and wanted the readership to see it as well. He wondered if McEnny had been deliberate in downplaying the publicity, and the animosity, that would have generated, not wanting an outsider to stir up trouble the sheriff, himself, didn't believe existed. Or, perhaps, the sheriff hadn't seen what he hadn't wanted to see in an old friend.

Then came the dramatic announcement of the very young wife divorcing Bentley, her older and very rich landowner of a husband. It hadn't been on the front page but it might as well have been. There had been photos from the now-unhappy couple's engagement party several years back, photos of their lavish wedding, then the stark notice of divorce.

The paper seemed to have dropped the subject of Jerica Bentley from the moment she became Mrs. Pederson. There had been little more than a brief mention of the private ceremony of J.D. and his bride in the social section and an even briefer one of her second divorce, this time from J.D., a few years later. Nothing after that.

Even with the scandal it must have been at the time, Colter couldn't help but think there had to be someone with more reason to murder J.D. Pederson. Something more than a decade-old romantic feud with nothing between now and then that amounted to friction of any kind.

"So, who else do you have on your list?"

Colter leaned back in his chair and propped his feet on his desk. He stared at the screen of his laptop, not reading, not even seeing. He knew everything that was there by heart.

"J.D.'s business partner when the ranch first started. A man named Newland. He committed suicide last year."

"Huh." Jonah looked thoughtful.

"Dead broke and with a small fortune in bills but he and J.D. hadn't been in contact in more than two decades."

"Doesn't sound like much to go on there."

"Not until you factor in how the partnership ended. The guy broke a point of the contract between them and J.D. came out with damn-near everything after a miniscule pay-off to the partner."

Jonah tapped his pen against the top of his desk. "The payoff amount, who decided that? Did it go to court?"

"It ended there, yeah, but the exit amount was already in their original agreement. J.D. didn't argue the pay-off, his objection was the amount that the partner was asking."

"Which was what … double?"

"Times ten."

Jonah sat up straight. Yeah, Colter thought, agreeing with his unspoken reaction. Some grudges could be carried a long time when enough money was involved.

"Was his share worth it?" Jonah asked. "Worth the times ten?"

"More like times twenty."

"That's a lot to feel is owed to you and not be allowed

to collect."

"Yeah. So, I'm thinking I'll take a look at his relatives. See who might be holding a grudge."

"Worth a look," Jonah agreed. "What else you got?"

"Not much. Still digging." Colter closed his laptop. "I'll do a little more tonight, then head back to the ranch in the morning. There're a few people I need to talk to."

"Have dinner with us tonight," Jonah suggested.

"You already asked. I already said no." Not that he was looking forward to spending the evening in the apartment. Even now, he still wasn't used to the silence.

"Colt—"

"I'm fine," he cut in. On some levels, he was. On others, he wasn't. Not quite yet. But he would be.

Before Jonah could argue, a knock at the half-open door drew both their gazes. Jonah's dark-haired, dark-eyed secretary-turned-fiancée smiled at them. "We have reservations in an hour," she reminded Jonah before turning toward Colter. "For three." Her eyes held the barest hint of sympathy, but she lightened the mood with a wink. "Time to get you out and about."

Colter opened his mouth to say he wasn't ready to be out and about in the way she meant then shrugged and nodded, giving in. He had to eat, might as well be in decent company. There wasn't any food in his apartment. He knew that for a fact.

Chapter Five

Jonah's call came late the next morning as Colter was leaving the city. "The will went into probate late yesterday."

"And?"

"And the adopted daughter gets pretty much everything tangible, the ranch including cattle, horses, equipment, the profit and the loss. So far, it's been pretty much profit. The twins get the bulk of the old man's money, but not for a few years yet."

"Their guardian?"

"The daughter."

"So, by the time they cross those few years, there could be nothing left."

Jonah snorted. "She'd be a fool."

"Some folks are," Colter countered, but he heard the

doubt in Jonah's voice and was inclined to agree with it …
but not fully … not just yet. There was too much at stake.
"I need to talk with her."

"The daughter?"

"The attorney."

"How soon?"

"This afternoon."

"I'll get back with you," Jonah said and broke the
connection.

Jonah came through as Colter knew he would. When
he neared Taos, he didn't turn toward the small hotel where
he'd booked a room, but toward the center of town.

Pederson's attorney was pretty much what Colter
expected and she looked like her photograph, proving it a
recent one which wasn't always the case with public records.
A woman of middle years with a subtle softening along the
jawline and faint age-lines around her eyes, but those eyes
were shrewd and, at the moment, sharply questioning.

He hadn't expected her to open the door herself.

"Thank you for seeing me," he said as he shook the
hand she extended.

"You can thank Joe McEnny." Her tone was dry but
not insulting.

Apparently, Jonah hadn't been able to get Colter on her
agenda without local help, he thought without rancor. "I'll
do that, Ms. Langley."

She stepped back from the doorway. "Please, come in,
but I give you fair warning. How long you'll be welcome
depends on what you have to say and how you say it. Until
that's decided you may call me Liz."

He might have chuckled if he wasn't so certain she was dead serious.

He followed her through a small sunroom to an open set of wide double doors. The opposite set were closed. He'd read she had a partner. Her daughter. "Would you like a glass of water?" she asked over her shoulder as she stepped into an office that was somehow both large and cozy.

"Thank you but no."

"Coffee, then?"

"Please." It had already been a long day and it was far from over.

She gestured him to a seat on the sofa while she took a wing chair. A long, low table in front of the sofa held a coffee service with mugs heavy enough to be comfortable in his hand as well as sugar and cream, which he ignored. The coffee, dark yet smooth, needed nothing more.

Colter knew the badge he wore counted for something. McEnny's word counted for something. Elizabeth Langley would need more than either of those things if he wanted her cooperation.

The silence stretched between them and Colter almost smiled. She was that rare person, one with the ability to put patience into play and outlast someone she considered an adversary. He opted to go with the question she wouldn't be expecting.

"Why does Robert Bentley hold a lease to Pederson land?"

Her gaze didn't so much as flicker. "That acreage was a recent acquisition and the lease was in place when the land was put up for sale. The previous owner tried to buy out the lease at J.D.'s request after J.D. offered his asking price, plus the amount that remained on the lease. Bentley refused. I petitioned the court to break the lease but was unsuccessful."

"Did Bentley know Pederson was the prospective purchaser?"

"Doubtful. The owner chanced losing the sale if Bentley refused and refusal would have been certain if he'd known it was J.D."

"But the sale went through," Colter stated the obvious.

The attorney shrugged. "It was a ten-year lease with eighteen months to go. J.D. wanted the land enough to wait it out."

"A patient man."

"He could be—when it suited him."

"And when it didn't suit?"

She leaned back in her chair and studied him a moment before answering. "When it didn't, he usually had money enough to make things happen sooner rather than later."

"I would imagine that fact irritated Robert Bentley almost as much as finding out it was Pederson who'd bought the property, ending any chance he could renew that lease."

"I would imagine."

"Do you know if there was any contact between Bentley and Pederson after the sale?"

"I don't."

"Pederson wouldn't have mentioned it to you?"

"After the purchase was complete?" She shook her head. "There would've been no reason for him to have done so. J.D. trusted me to handle his legal affairs, we were friends after a fashion, but I wasn't a confidante. And you aren't here to talk about the history of that piece of land." She lifted one brow. "And now that we've gotten the easy question out of the way…?"

"All of my questions are easy … it's the answers that are sometimes difficult, but I'm not on a witch hunt," he said. "I'm here to find out who killed J.D. Pederson."

"If someone did."

"I don't believe in coincidences."

"Nor do I."

"Who stood most to gain from J.D.'s death?"

"The will's been probated. It's all public information now."

"I'm aware."

She sighed. "The twins gained the most in purely monetary terms. I would hope you're not looking there."

"I'm not."

"His daughter, Miranda, would be next in terms of gain. If you look there, you're a fool."

"Maybe. Sometimes the obvious is obvious for a reason," Colter remarked. "The daughter is executor and in charge of the twins' inheritance."

The attorney lifted one brow but stayed silent.

"The ranch proper was recorded as a Transfer on Death," he pushed. "Tempting for some."

"Not for Miranda," she said firmly, "even if she'd known about it, which she didn't."

"To your knowledge."

She smiled faintly then nodded. "To my knowledge."

"And then there's all that money she controls for her stepbrothers."

This time his words drew a flash of anger but she was quick to hide it and he admired her restraint as she gave him a cool look. "If you're set on Miranda as your villain, you will waste your time and be disappointed in the end."

"Not set on her, no, but neither will I avoid considering

the possibility. And who would be after Ms. Pederson in terms of gain?"

"Riley or Lila, equally unlikely."

"The foreman became owner of what he must have already considered his home and property plus a chunk of money. The housekeeper an equal chunk of money."

The attorney leaned back and crossed her legs. "Accurate on both counts."

"Maybe one of them wanted that inheritance sooner rather than later."

She shook her head. "What probate doesn't show was the current salary of both—above comfortable and guaranteed because J.D. loved and trusted both of them. His death could have cut short both of those salaries. Miranda makes that decision now."

"Would you consider her life in danger?"

"No," she said flatly. "J.D. was an excellent judge of character. I don't think his judgement was misplaced in either his foreman or his housekeeper."

"Who, then?"

Liz gave him a sharp look. "I suggest you look beyond the obvious. If J.D. was murdered—and I don't know that Joe McEnny is any more convinced of that than I am—you'll need to cast your net farther than Riley or Lila or Miranda."

Colter knew her patience was at an end before she got to her feet. He stood as well. "Ms. Langley, I'd ask you to consider two things. First, the obvious suspect is often the murderer, and for the obvious reason. Second, J.D. Pederson trusted you." He walked toward the entrance and stopped. "You cared about him and you'll care when I'm proven right—that someone hurt him intentionally. If something occurs to you, I'll hear from you."

She nodded. "Yes, you can be certain of that," she said as she closed the door with a soft click behind him.

He hadn't planned to return to the Pederson ranch this soon but he had questions and didn't see a real need for a delay in asking them. It was early yet with plenty of daylight to make the drive and not be considered harassing the family with a late hour visit. He got lucky when Pederson's daughter stepped out of a side door as he pulled into the drive.

To her credit, she neither pretended not to see him nor not to care that he was back. Her jeans were well-worn and faded. The long-sleeved work shirt was just as worn with sleeves rolled up to the elbow and the top few buttons open to expose the tank top beneath. Her long-legged stride carried her across the short expanse of lawn to his truck. He tried not to think about those legs which proved easy enough to do by focusing on her scowl at the sight of him.

"Mr. Bellamy."

That was it. That was her greeting. No, 'how can I help you' or 'what are you doing here?' Not even a 'go to hell.'

"Ms. Pederson," He returned, nodding in acknowledgement of her own greeting. "If you have a few minutes, I need to ask some questions."

"And, if I don't have a few minutes?"

"I can wait in my truck."

The devious glint in her gaze gave fair warning of the comment that followed. "Not the most pleasant place to spend the night."

"Not the worst, either." He kept his tone bland and his expression affable but it wasn't easy.

She hesitated, then sighed. "Fine. Let's get it over with. There are some chairs in the back." With that, she spun on her heels and left him to follow.

Colter didn't want to like her, didn't want to be entertained by her attitude, didn't want to admire her strength.

The chairs faced a swimming pool, empty of all but an excess of floats and toys, more water pistols and plastic swords than anything else. The large expanse of water gleamed crystalline in the late afternoon sun.

Miranda Pederson sat and said, "Ask."

"I'd like you to walk through that last morning with J.D. You saw him before he left the ranch?"

She took a deep breath and glanced toward the distant peaks but not before he saw the bleak look in her eyes. "I did. We met over breakfast every morning to plan what we'd each be doing that day, compare notes, any concerns."

"And did he have any concerns that day? Anything he mentioned as a worry?"

He could appreciate that she took a moment to think before speaking. The crash was some days ago now with a lot of shock and grief and coping afterward. Or, if she were guilty of her father's death, days of tension and fear of discovery.

When she did answer, it was with a shake of her head. "We talked about which beef herds to rotate this month. Whether to try a new brand of feed for the working horses."

"Why would you do that? Change feeds?"

She shrugged. "Good reviews plus the fact that it contains some supplements we now add in to our current feeding program which doesn't have them."

"What did you decide?"

The question earned him an odd look but he didn't bother to explain that more lies were caught in unguarded conversational moments than otherwise. Somehow, he doubted she'd have any great appreciation for what tactics worked when questioning a suspect.

"I've put that decision on a backburner."

He didn't let the cool glance she gave bother him.

"What else did you talk about?"

"Not much. Just what we were going to do that day."

"Which was?"

"I had paperwork to finish, a few bills to pay. He was leaving right after breakfast for the farmers' auction."

Which matched what McEnny had mentioned as his habit. "You didn't normally go with him?"

She gave a faint smile that wasn't aimed his way so much as at her memory. "No, that was J.D.'s thing. He used to take me as a kid and I loved it then just because I loved the time with him. Now we each have our own work load. Had," she corrected herself, the smile absent now.

"Did he seem upset that morning? Edgy? Or even angry?"

"No. Not at all. It seemed a normal kind of start to the day. He said he'd see me after lunch."

She turned her face away from him but not fast enough for him to miss the sheen of unshed tears. He reminded himself that she wouldn't be the first person to have the ability to cry at will.

It also wasn't the first time he'd felt like dirt after questioning someone. He doubted it would be the last.

Miranda stayed silent, waiting for the next question to cut the silence between them. Instead, she heard him stand and walk away without another word. When the anger came, it swept through like a biting north wind and she reached for her phone.

The sheriff answered on the first ring. "Miranda? What's wrong?"

Although she heard the alarm in his voice, his fear for J.D.'s daughter and sons, she didn't let it soften her question. "Why the *hell* are you letting an outsider run this investigation?"

His sigh was heavy. "What'd he do, stomp in like some rogue elephant?"

Miranda let that sink in … his tone of frustration, even discouragement. It tempered her own question. "If you knew that was apt to happen, why did you let it? Why even open that door?"

"You're savvy enough to know the answer to that without asking. He's a Bellamy and this is New Mexico. But … it's more than that," he said with a firmness and authority that reminded her why he was voted in time after time. "Your daddy was a good man and I'd play poker with the devil himself to make whoever caused his death pay for the rest of his life, and may God make it a short one."

Miranda let some of the starch ease from her spine. "So, you think Colter Bellamy's a devil, too?"

"Devil? No. Ass? Yeah, maybe at times. Let him do his job, Miranda. I'll for sure be doing mine."

And how, Miranda thought, did you argue with that? She couldn't. When they'd said good-night, more amicably than not, she laid her phone aside and stared at the wall in front of her. She hadn't a clue how she was going to get through the days ahead but she didn't have a choice. She'd have to find a way, a moment at a time.

* * *

Colter walked into the room and looked around. The place had been listed as a hotel but the setup was a step beyond expectations. McEnny had given it a thumbs up and the hacienda a few miles away a thumbs down. Colter had wondered if he was being set up, but that seemed not the case.

The room was larger than typical, comfortable, with a sizeable sitting area in front of a double set of windows with drapes heavy enough to block the exterior security lighting. A quick check proved he faced a small square of lawn with trees and heavy shrubbery blocking the neighborhood beyond. It seemed the hotel had been established before any city zoning, if that existed here.

He called Jonah after a shower and a call down for room service.

Jonah answered the call after the first ring. "Anything?"

"Nothing new."

He could almost hear his cousin thinking before he asked, "And you're not looking at the foreman or the housekeeper very hard, are you?"

"It's hard to see that either would benefit. Not unless you've turned up some recently discovered dirt."

"No dirt," Jonah admitted. "Not even a little dust."

"So, both were as comfortable, or more than, before Pederson's death as after it. Riley's been living on the property left to him for a couple decades and the cattle promised to him already had his brand on them. The housekeeper … Lila … got a very generous check but doesn't lack for anything as far as I can tell."

"All true," Jonah agreed. "So where does that leave us?"

"My guess? We need to be looking at someone who has a grudge, either a recent one or something that's been burning long enough to leave a hole in their gut."

"You're taking the daughter off the list along with the foreman and housekeeper?"

"Off? No, not entirely. But they're all far from the top right now."

Chapter Six

Miranda waited in silence as the housekeeper opened the envelope with her name on it and read the note J.D. had written to be included with the check. They were in Lila's domain, taking a moment together before the hustle of the day. The kitchen was large and homey, a mix of old and new. Original but well-maintained cabinets and tile flooring with every modern appliance known to the cooking world lining the countertops.

After a long moment, Lila lifted her eyes to Miranda. "There was no need for this. I have all that I need. Your father paid me well in life. He didn't need to leave me anything in death."

"You took good care of him. Of all of us."

"As I plan to continue." The words were firm, but her gaze held a question and Miranda understood. They both knew death could bring changes, most of them unwelcome.

"As long as you're willing, this will be home for you," Miranda assured her. "Dane and Dillon need you and so do I. We always will. You're one of the first people I remember." The truth was she barely remembered her mother. Nothing more than eyes the color of her own and a soft, sad voice. In fact, she sometimes wondered if her recollections weren't memories of her mother at all but were, rather, things J.D. or Lila had told her about the woman whose child she was.

Her recollections of J.D., however, were planted deep. Sitting in front of him in the saddle as they rode over his kingdom. Doing schoolwork at his feet while he made notes in a ledger or read newspapers and ranching periodicals at his desk, a fire blazing in the hearth. She'd grown up the only child of J.D. Pederson, a good life of hard work and simple pleasures. J.D. had not lived rich, and the child she'd been never realized they were.

She hadn't wanted to leave that life, that home, for college and she recalled the words he'd used to convince her. "Things are changing, Miranda, everything around us is changing. The whole world is different now. I need you to learn that world and bring it back with you. The ranch will need that and more." And so, she'd gone with her entire focus on the day she would graduate and return.

The memory of that evening, of the argument he'd won which convinced her to write an acceptance letter to the college and pack her bags, could still make her smile but so many things changed—too many things—before graduation brought her home to take her place with J.D. at the head of the ranch.

"Tell me about Jerica." She'd never before asked, never wanted to know more than the superficial.

For a moment, Lila looked at her without speaking, then she shrugged. "She was your step-mother."

"Hardly that." Miranda knew that was blunt, but it was honest. "I was away at school through their courtship, if you can call it that, and what little time they were married. Maybe if I'd been here…" She stopped. Maybe if she'd been around, J.D. wouldn't have acted like a fool with another's man wife. But then they wouldn't have the boys.

Lila nodded in understanding; her expression wry. "Exactly. You can't wish his foolishness and her selfishness away without wishing the twins away." She hesitated and sighed. "They were both selfish."

Miranda caught Lila's expression, understood it. "So, you're saying I can't blame one without the other and I know that. I do. But I knew J.D.'s heart. He wasn't a bad person. I guess I'm asking if Jerica *was*."

"Bad? No. I wouldn't call her that. She wasn't any more sinful or wicked than any other human. She was, however, way less mature than she should have been at her age."

"Was it J.D.'s money?" She'd always felt that it had to be. Not that Jerica's parents or the man she'd married first didn't have plenty, but J.D. hadn't flinched at spending his on her. Maybe the others hadn't been so open-handed. "He was years older than her."

The older woman hesitated. "Miranda … no. She fell in love with J.D., or at least with the idea of being in love with him, lots of women did, you know."

"He wasn't tall, dark, and handsome." But he was her daddy and a prince in her eyes from the first moment he'd swung her up in his arms. She'd felt as if she could reach the sky.

"No. He wasn't classically handsome but he was smarter than most and his heart was kinder than most.

Half the town fell in love with his smile and the other half with his sense of humor." Lila's eyes reflected the smile in her voice.

Miranda stared at her and lifted one brow. "You, too?"

The housekeeper rocked back with a laugh. "Oh, my, no. We were too much alike, J.D. and me. Too much like best friends or maybe even cousins. We bickered together and we surely loved each other, but not in that sense of the word."

"If she loved him, why did she leave him?" Tears stung her eyes. "How could she leave her sons?"

The humor left Lila's face and a heavy sigh escaped her. "Because she did love him and she realized too late, he didn't love her and he wasn't ever going to be faithful to her. He put a ring on her finger when she told him she was pregnant, but he wouldn't have if she hadn't been."

"So…" she stopped, feeling gut-punched, wishing she hadn't started this conversation, wondering why she hadn't known or at least guessed some of this. She glanced around at the room. A place where she'd learned so much and, now, it seemed, also too little. She took a deep breath. "So, J.D. was the bad guy?"

"Ah, honey, no, not bad. Just that selfishness again. Jerica came after him, there's no doubt of that. She was young and bored with her marriage and J.D. looked like all she'd ever wanted. And she looked like all he'd ever wanted in his bed."

"Ugh. You make him sound like one of the studs picking out a mare for the day."

"Some men are like that." A faint grin crossed Lila's face then faded. "And some women make it easy. A few too many in J.D.'s case."

Miranda felt a heaviness in her chest. She didn't want

to ask another question, certainly not the one that was haunting her after Lila's revelations. But it was the only one that mattered now, after hearing more than she'd wanted to know. "Did my mother?" Her throat felt tight. "Did she make it easy?"

Lila's face softened. "Your mother was already sick, bad sick, when her car broke down a mile or two from the drive. And she was battered and bruised." Her expression saddened as she studied Miranda's face. "J.D. never wanted you to know what a bastard she'd been with before she ran."

"My dad," she said flatly, feeling a little sick at the realization that she might have come from a monster who preyed on the weaker around him.

Lila nodded. "But you got nothing of him left in you, I'm certain of that. You're all J.D.'s. He raised you and taught you and loved you more than anything on this earth. I almost wondered if he could make room in his heart for Jerica's sons but he did, for sure."

"Of course, he made room for them. They're his. His blood." And she wasn't but she'd never been jealous of her brothers. From the start, she'd loved them with the ferocity of a mama bear.

"Not more than you, honey." Lila touched her hand. "Not ever more than you. J.D. married your mama but it was a ragtag little girl who stole his heart. But he took good care of Elise, right along with you, the best doctors, the best home nurses, so y'all could be together and she could get the care she needed right up to the end. He may never have been *in love* with her but he *did* love her."

Miranda pushed to her feet, feeling far more shaky than she had since the day J.D. had died. Shaky and overwhelmed. There was so much of her own story she'd never been told. And she'd never asked. But she needed one last answer. "Where is he now? My dad? I thought he was dead, I thought I remembered my mother saying he was dead, but…"

Lila hesitated then took a deep breath and gave a little nod, more to herself, it seemed than to Miranda. Miranda braced herself at the look on the other woman's face. "He landed himself in jail robbing a liquor store. That's when Elise threw your belongings and hers in the back of her car and lit out while he wasn't there to stop her. He killed a man for raping him in the exercise yard with half dozen other men watching, maybe one or two of them deputies. Someone—J.D. or more likely Riley—kept you close to us day and night until he was sent to prison for life. J.D. said he expected he'd die there and, if he didn't, J.D. would find a way to send him back." Lila sighed. "And that look on your face is why J.D. never told you."

"I asked him. Who I was and where I came from." Miranda felt as bewildered as she did sickened by Lila's revelations. "All he said was that my mama was sweet and smart, but that he didn't know much about my dad."

"He didn't lie, honey. He didn't dig for anything more than what he needed to get your mama her divorce and make sure you were safe. And Elise was a sweet soul and smarter than most. Every inch of that old car she drove was filled with the books you have in your room now. She didn't pack many of her clothes, told me she knew she wouldn't have much use for them soon enough and the books were what she wanted you to remember her by."

"I don't even know what to think," Miranda admitted.

"Then put it aside for now. What lies your mama told you were to protect you. There'll always be some things you can't do anything about. Your daddy, whoever he was, whatever he did, is far in your past and nothing to do with your future. J.D. raised you so you have the best inside you that he had to give and it's more than good. And you have your mother's intelligence and her beautiful voice. Elise could sing like an angel."

At Miranda's stare, Lila's eyes softened. "You don't remember her singing to you, do you?"

Miranda shook her head.

"I wish you could hear the sound of it. You have that … her voice. There was a time or two, as you were turning to a woman, I heard you singing to the boys and it was like I was hearing her all over again." She chuckled. "Don't you remember how hard J.D. pushed you to consider that school of arts in New York? He always said you could have been a star, but all you wanted to do was chase cows."

The tightness inside of Miranda eased a little and she smiled at the housekeeper. "I remember you pushing back at him."

"You would've been miserable away from here." The housekeeper studied her face. "J.D. didn't like anyone talking about your past around you and I think he was right for the most part. You needed to focus on being a little girl and you never asked much as you got older, either. J.D. and the ranch seemed enough for you."

"More than enough," Miranda said softly.

"Even so, you've asked some now and I'll tell you. Your mama used to talk to me, not all the time and not a lot about your daddy but she did say that he wasn't a bad man, just a weak one. I think you need to know that because there's no bad in you, either. The difference is that J.D. gave you strength enough for ten men. He was proud of the woman you became. You should be, too. Now, go on. You've got work to do and so do I."

Miranda knew she was right. They'd talked long enough and she had more than enough to think about. But, before she turned to go, she gave Lila a hard hug. And her back was straight as she opened the door to the patio and walked out into the sunshine. It was a Friday and Wes had a long weekend home planned, so she and the twins were going to ride to a few of the hill pastures and check on cattle. The same way she used to do with J.D. all those years and memories ago.

Dane and Dillon were waiting for her in front of the barn. They stood motionless on either side of Riley, each holding the reins to a horse, but as she drew closer, she could almost feel them vibrating with excitement for the day ahead.

Their horses, handpicked for them by J.D. a few years back, were saddled and ready, as was the appaloosa she favored. She loved all of them but the appaloosa had been her first real cow horse. J.D. had sent him off for training as a three-year-old and gifted him to Miranda for her twelfth birthday. He was getting on in years, over twenty, but he was sound and solid as a rock and could outwork most of the youngsters around him. When he let her know that he was ready, he'd be retired to pasture for a life of ease. He wasn't ready.

Riley stepped away from the barn and handed her the reins. They exchanged rueful smiles as the twins began talking. And not in unison.

"Riley said we could take our rifles," Dane said.

In the same instant, Dillon asked, "Are we riding near the lake? Can we go swimming?"

Before answering, Miranda cast a quick glance at the rifles which were properly secured and then at the bulging saddle bags, no doubt stuffed with food and, if she had to guess, swim trunks.

She looked at Dane first. His cheeks held a few more freckles than Dillon's and his eyes were a darker shade than his brother's, not much darker but enough to notice. "Riley is right, rifles are allowed as long as they stay secured until I give permission for you to remove them." Her gaze shifted to Dillon. "How about we plan to eat lunch by the lake?"

Their grins couldn't have been more alike and tugged hard at her heart. She'd never encouraged, would never have allowed, them to call her mom or mama but no mother could have loved them more than she did.

She swung into the saddle and watched as they did the same. Riley stepped close and looked up at her. "You got your cell phone?" She touched the leather case at the back of her saddle and Riley gave a satisfied nod. "Stay in touch with me."

"I will, Riley." And didn't she just hate that necessity. She'd ridden every acre of this ranch alone, without a worry. Now, with the boys at her side with their trust in her, their safety *on* her, the worry was there. She didn't wholly believe—or maybe didn't want to believe—that anyone had murdered J.D. but … what if?

Putting that thought aside, she took a deep breath. She refused to live in a state of worry and she wouldn't put the boys in a state of fear.

The further they rode, the lighter her heart felt. The fresh morning air would soon give way to midday heat, but she turned them toward the foothills where a breeze always sang through rocks and scrub and trees hardy enough to find a toe-hold. They moved from section to section, counting head while checking the sky for carrion birds that would signal a downed animal. Every so often she sent a text to Riley, assuring him all was well and letting him know where they were headed next, sometimes mentioning an animal or pasture that might need attention of one kind or another.

In years past, she'd carried a small pad and pencil, making notes as J.D. pointed out the various needs. On their return to the ranch, they'd go through her notes together and J.D. would give those notes to Riley who would turn them into actions. Technology made the process more efficient, but she was determined not to let it become impersonal.

Dillon gave a whoop of sheer joy when the lake came into view and Miranda chuckled. "You can swim for an hour or so, then we'll eat and head back. Sound good?"

The twins gave her vigorous nods and scrambled from their horses. She stepped down and watched with pride as they unsaddled and led their horses to drink before doing anything else. She followed suit and kept one eye on the twins as they swam and one on the ground-tied horses and tried not to think of the many times she and J.D. had ridden these hills. Thoughts of the man who'd been her actual father crept in and she hated that. She hated what she knew now, but she couldn't hate Lila for telling her. Knowledge is power. She wasn't sure who'd said that first, but J.D. had said it often. With knowledge came the tools to change what needed changing and to defeat what needed defeating.

Before she could get too deep into thoughts best pushed aside, the twins came racing up the slight incline toward her. They were hungry as they always were and maybe a little more so. They unpacked their lunches, and Lila knew them each well enough to know what to send with them. Miranda lay back on the grass for a moment, letting the peace of the place and the sound of happy voices roll through her. Whatever whim of fate had allowed her mother's car to break down where it had all those years ago had been a blessing, and she was grateful for every hour she'd been given with J.D. She'd called him daddy for years, the term coming effortlessly to her, and she supposed her mother had done well at keeping her out of sight and sound of her real father even when they'd lived together. Miranda honestly didn't remember him at all. Nor did she want to.

She sat up with a twinge of regret. "Let's go, guys."

They were too well behaved to complain as they rerolled their lunch bags and saddled their horses while she did the same. As she swung her leg over her saddle, she realized she needed to check in with Riley or he'd be texting her on the trail when she needed to focus on the ground ahead and the horse beneath her. And she felt a little guilty that she hadn't done it when they'd first stopped. As she shifted in her saddle to retrieve her phone, she caught a flash of sun glint on metal or glass on the hill above. The sound that split the air a heartbeat later chilled her blood. "Guys, hit the ground, hurry!" Her brain knew that any bullet had passed before she could have heard the crack that followed but she couldn't trust another wouldn't follow.

Throwing her leg back over the cantle to dismount, she felt the appaloosa shift beneath her. Please, God, please, no. She wasn't sure if she spoke the words aloud but either God didn't hear them or it was already too late. She heard the second shot as the appaloosa staggered on his feet then swayed as his knees buckled. She swung her legs free in time but her head hit the ground hard and the breath was knocked from her lungs as the horse rolled, flinging her to one side.

"Randa?" Dane's voice was a soft wail.

She wanted to tell him she was fine but she couldn't speak. And she wasn't sure she *was* fine, she thought, as she lost consciousness.

The sheriff had agreed to a meeting over a late lunch. Colter knew there'd be eyes watching no matter where they went because he was an unknown, but at least any interested onlookers would be left guessing between casual conversation or sheriff's department business.

They took a table near the back of the small restaurant and the sheriff placed his hat in the seat of the chair next to him.

The waitress, quick to come to their table, gave the sheriff a warm smile and Colter a lingering glance. She was cute and curvy and not his type. Hell, he wasn't even sure he had a type anymore. Dana had been perfect. Until she wasn't. Or, rather, until she decided he wasn't.

McEnny didn't waste time once they'd placed their orders. "What do you have?"

"Not as much as I'd like," Colter admitted. "What do you know about Arthur Newland?"

The sheriff lowered the glass he had halfway to his mouth. "Haven't heard that name in a long while. He's still got kin here but he moved away years ago."

"We might need to talk to those kin. Newland put a bullet through his brain right after the first of the year."

"Did he now?" McEnny looked thoughtful. "There was bad blood, but that was a long time ago."

"A bad memory can last longer than a good one."

"There's that." The sheriff leaned back as the waitress

returned, her movements quick and deft as she slid one plate in front of him, the other in front of Colter. After a discreet glance at their intent expressions, she murmured, "I'll be back with more tea," and left them to their conversation.

Colter studied the sheriff's face in the moments that followed her departure. "You're still not convinced."

"That it was murder? No. Not convinced. But not ready to rule it out either."

"So, what are you doing on your end?" Colter kept his tone benign. He was more inclined to like McEnny than not, but he wasn't willing to let the investigation stall due to lack of enthusiasm on the sheriff's part.

McEnny chewed another bite of his chicken fried steak before he pointed his fork at Colter and answered. "Me? I'm appointing you lead."

That surprised Colter until he considered the resources of Welles Enterprises. He could bring far more to bear than the sheriff of a rural county. McEnny, it seemed, understood that as well as he did.

"Before you leave town," McEnny added, "stop and see Irving at the office. He's setting up a two-way for you." He fell silent as the waitress returned and topped off their tea glasses. As she walked away, he added. "Keep that badge on 'til this is done." He pointed his fork again. "And I don't mean in your pocket."

Colter nodded but circled back to his topic. "You were around when Pederson took Newland to court?"

"Been here all my life. Was a deputy back then, not much more than an errand-runner earning my place in the department, but I had a badge and I was proud of it."

"Do you remember the case?"

"Well enough. The two went in halves on some fancy

bull from overseas that cost more than either of them could afford at the time. Both signed an agreement that the bloodline would stay on the ranch or the offending partner would be bought out for the original amount that each contributed in either cash or land."

"Fancy, indeed, to require that kind of agreement." Colter murmured. "And the amounts were recorded."

It wasn't a question but McEnny nodded. "To the penny. But it didn't amount to much stacked against the value of the ranch after a few years under Pederson's management."

"He was the driving force?"

McEnny snorted. "J.D. never took a back seat to anyone on anything. Most folks were content to let him take the lead because he never failed to get good results."

"How much of the good results for the ranch came from that bull?"

"Hard to say without a look at the ledgers but I would imagine a significant amount. Restaurants in other countries praised the beef that came from the steers. It was mentioned in a number of cooking magazines and chefs called it by name in some of their recipe books."

Despite arms loaded for another table, the waitress managed to slide dessert menus in front on them on her way past. Colter pushed his aside but McEnny pulled his closer. Before either could comment, the sheriff's phone rang. He flipped it open and said his name, then his gaze went straight to Colter. "On my way," was all he said as he flipped it closed and stood.

Colter was already pushing his chair back as McEnny grabbed his hat and said, "Shots fired at the Pederson ranch. The call came in from Riley. An ambulance has been dispatched."

Colter was in his truck before the sheriff had the door open on his SUV.

Chapter Seven

As the patrol car peeled out, Colter fell in behind, satisfied at the pace the sheriff had set. They caught the ambulance moments before it turned under the rectangular sign perched high upon metal posts. Two of the Pederson hands waited on four-wheelers at the gate. One jumped out to speak with the ambulance driver, the other strode toward the sheriff's car.

The ambulance moved forward behind one of the four-wheelers. The other driver waited while the sheriff pulled his car to one side, then came toward Colter's truck on foot. McEnny stepped up into the passenger side, closing the door after him, and said, "No fatalities. Looks like we're headed out toward some rough terrain. Low profile squad cars might not be the best."

"Are the twins safe? Who needs medical?" Colter

managed not to growl the questions.

"Dane and Dillon are scared but unharmed. Miranda's horse was shot out from under her and went down hard. Rocky ground up here. Got some scrapes and cuts ... maybe a concussion."

The tension in Colter's gut eased somewhat with McEnny's first words but his anger edged up a notch. The twins hadn't been hurt. Colter intended to make certain they stayed unscathed. And it appeared he could lower Ms. Pederson a few notches down on his list of suspects. He wouldn't remove her altogether. Not just yet. It wouldn't be the first time a partner-in-crime had been double-crossed.

He chanced a glance toward the sheriff's profile before returning his gaze to the four-wheeler bouncing recklessly up the hillside in front of him. "Another hunting accident?"

McEnny held his tongue at the chide, just kept his stare in front of him. But Colter didn't miss his low grunt of frustration.

In the silence that followed, Colter kept his focus on navigating the terrain ahead of them. The ride wasn't smooth but neither was it the worst Colter's truck had made. Even though they'd been told the twins were unharmed, he felt a quick relief when they topped the next rise and he saw them standing with the EMTs a short distance from the felled horse and the woman who sat curled next to him. Riley squatted at her back.

"Ah, hell." McEnny breathed the words as Colter eased the truck to a stop beside the ambulance and cut the ignition.

"Who's the guy behind Riley?"

"Vet."

Colter studied him a moment. A big guy, standing motionless, his gaze fixed on the horizon. "He's not doing anything." It didn't take much effort to guess why.

"Reckon he's already done what he had to do. If I were to guess, I'd say he was called before we were but I'll be careful not to ask that question." McEnny shook his head and sighed. "She's had that horse forever. J.D. gave him to her when she was a kid. Used to rope steers off him at some of the local rodeos." He opened the door on his side and turned to meet Colter's look with a hard one of his own. "Somebody's going to pay for this. Damned if they won't. I'll make sure of it."

Colter stepped out of the truck. He didn't bother telling McEnny he didn't plan to wait on the sheriff to mete out justice. McEnny walked toward Riley and the woman but Colter headed for the twins. He turned to the EMT who stood closest, an older woman with cropped hair and an unhappy look on her face.

"Do either of the boys need to be seen by a doctor?"

She took a quick look at his badge and shook her head. "No, we checked both of them, no injuries, no sign of distress other than worrying about their sister. She needs to be seen and treated but, so far, we can't get her to leave the horse."

"She was unconscious," one of the twins interjected. "Dane called Riley and I put water on my bandana to wipe her head."

So, Colter thought, this one was Dillon. He was an inch or so taller and a pound or two stouter than his twin. Not enough to be noticeable unless you were inclined to pay attention to details. It was enough to tell them apart until he learned the nuances of their voices and facial expressions.

"Who're you?"

"You can call me Colter." He didn't think now was the time to spring a family name on them, if they were even aware it was one. Besides, he planned to be around enough that Mr. Bellamy would get cumbersome.

"Is Randa going to be okay?" Dane's voice quavered.

Eyes the color of old pennies stared up at him. Colter could read the anxiety in their depths. "She's conscious now so I suspect she'll be fine in a day or so." Colter's glance took in both the boys as he spoke. "She does need to see a doctor to be extra safe and she may need the two of you to stick close by when she gets home again." He planned to do the same but more for their sake than hers.

To his relief, the medic was quick to back up his reassurance. "That's right. It's a requirement to have a doctor give the all clear when someone has been unconscious, but she's talking fine and her vision is clear so don't you worry."

"Why don't we go see if we can help Riley convince her to go with the ambulance so we can take care of things here?" Colter suggested.

Dane nodded resolutely and Dillon lifted his chin in a show of steadfast courage. Their Bellamy legacy, Colter thought with an unexpected touch of pride.

Miranda shifted at their approach and Colter winced. The cut across her right brow still oozed blood. If it weren't stitched back with skill, it would leave a scar and might anyway.

"The ambulance person says you need to see a doctor."

Dane's voice had held firm as he spoke but Colter could see his hands clench when he got a close up look at his sister's face, and he recalled that Dillon had been the one to wipe her face while Dane had called the foreman for help. Along with the cut and the blood, the darkening skin warned of an ugly bruise to come along one cheekbone. It had to hurt like hell, he thought, but he suspected the tears that wet her face were for the horse rather than her own pain.

"She's going," Riley said heavily. "I already told her. She already agreed."

The foreman was more than rattled, Colter thought, noticing the clenching and unclenching of his hands.

"As long as you get Gabby back home where he belongs." She glanced at her horse and then at the boys. "He'll need your help."

"I'll get things settled and be into town later to bring you home," Riley said. His voice broke on the last word and he cleared his throat.

"You'll need to see to the boys' protection," Colter inserted. "I'll get Ms. Pederson back to the ranch safely after she's treated."

Miranda gave him a look but didn't argue. Colter wasn't sure if pain or a concern for the twins was the deciding factor but thought it more apt to be the latter. Riley gave him a look, as well, but his prior animosity seemed banked by the enormity of what had just happened. Colter didn't take his gray-faced silence as approval, though. Far from it.

He stood back, watching as she let Riley help her to her feet. She was quick to shake her head at a suggestion from the second EMT of putting her on a stretcher and took a step toward the veterinarian who placed his hands on her shoulders. "I'm sorry, Miranda. More sorry than I know how to say."

"Thank you for coming." She stopped and took a deep breath. "For easing his way." Her voice held steady but tears soaked her face.

Behind her, Riley cursed long and low as the EMTs stepped forward, one to either side of her. Even with their help, her progress over the uneven ground was slow and appeared painful. Colter suspected she might have a cracked rib or two from the fall. One technician climbed in the back of the ambulance behind her and the other stepped up behind the wheel to drive and Colter turned to look at Riley.

"Did you hear the shots fired?"

He didn't miss the hard look Riley gave his badge before deigning to answer. "No. I was on the other end of the ranch. Took me two lifetimes to get here."

"And Miranda said she couldn't be sure which direction they came from," McEnny added. "Sounds ricochet around these hills. Still, I've already made a call to put a couple of my men out here checking the area. We've got a few hours' daylight left. They may see something."

Or, just as probable, they wouldn't, Colter thought, and he wasn't counting on the slim chance that they might. When he returned with Miranda Pederson, he'd be checked out of his hotel and bringing his clothes with him. He'd deal with his lack of welcome when he returned to the ranch.

He caught McEnny's gaze, tilting his head toward the vet, still standing beside the horse. "He knows to retrieve the bullet?"

McEnny sighed. "He knows."

Miranda stared at the bright fluorescent light above her, waiting for the emergency room doctor to return. Her forehead had been numbed and stitched, but her head still ached. The doctor had been unhappy that the cut might scar, but that was the least of Miranda's worries. The fiercest being the twins' safety and the increasing likelihood that J.D. had been murdered. Her ribs were sore but not broken. The radiologist wouldn't confirm but had been willing to hint she didn't see anything of concern, only mentioning the likelihood of torn cartilage. All Miranda wanted was to go home. She needed to be near the twins, needed to see for herself that they were safe and to keep them safe.

She hadn't been frightened when Colter Bellamy had implied J.D.'s death had been no accident. She was frightened now. The twins had been inches away from her. Inches. She had no idea who had fired those shots or where they'd been aiming. Could no longer rule out that J.D.'s death had been murder.

The door eased open and she forced a smile at the familiar face. "Am I good to go?"

The doctor's expression didn't lighten. "You are. I'd rather keep you for observation." He'd known her forever, known J.D. since they were in high school.

"I need to be home. The twins…" she hesitated. "It's all been too much. They need me."

"I agree. They need you but they need you whole and sound and healthy. They need you to allow us to take care of you."

"I won't lift a finger for as long as you say."

He sighed but his lips twitched and she knew she'd won. "You're as bad as J.D."

"I am," she agreed, feeling unspeakably exhausted. She'd agree to anything as long he signed her out.

"Is that your ride back to the ranch, pacing the waiting room and glaring at the nursing staff?"

She would have rolled her eyes if she didn't suspect the movement would be painful. Even her eyeballs hurt. "I'm sure it is."

"Where's Riley?"

"He was at the scene of the—of the accident—with

Sheriff McEnny."

He eyed her steadily, and she could read the questions in his gaze, but he didn't voice them. Miranda had no doubt he had other patients waiting for his time, his skill, and his attention.

"I'm going to release you to go home but I need your promise to give yourself a minimum of forty-eight hours downtime before you're out and about. I'm serious about that, Miranda."

She took a deep breath. "You have my word." Little as she liked giving it, she'd keep her word.

He turned to go and stopped just before he left the room. "If you need help with anything, anything at all, you have only to call. J.D. was a good friend. I owe him that much." Then he stepped through the doorway and was gone.

Miranda slid from the bed as soon as the door clicked to a close behind him. She'd already replaced the emergency room gown with her own clothing when an aide stepped in, pushing a wheelchair. "I don't need that, but thank you."

"Oh, but ma'am, I'll need to wheel you to the sidewalk and see you safely into a vehicle."

"Not happening." Miranda wasn't unkind, just firm, and she wasn't up to persuasion.

"It's a policy."

Miranda did her best to hide a grimace of pain as she pulled on her boots. She eased past the young woman with the most reassuring smile she could muster. The aide trailed behind as Miranda followed the signs to the waiting area.

Halting beside the nurses' station, she glanced around at the scattering of persons seated on uncomfortable-looking chairs. Only one person was on his feet. Yeah, that was her ride home. He slowed his pacing at the sight of her then walked her way, stopping in front of her. "Ready?"

"I'm ready."

He cast a glance at the hapless aide who still looked hopeful, standing there, holding the handles of the wheelchair. Miranda noticed as his lips twitched but he didn't say a word as they walked toward the exit. She thanked him as he held the full glass door open for her to walk through.

She supposed it wasn't fair to wish him far away, but she did. She didn't want to feel or think or talk. Feeling, however, proved inevitable, fear for Dane and Dillon, grief for Gabby, renewed grief for J.D. rolled through her with every breath she took.

And she had little doubt that the man at her side was going to make her think *and* talk. But she'd delay as long as she could, she thought, as he placed a light hand on her arm to guide her toward the only truck pulled up to the curb. Even if it hadn't been, she would have known it to be his. The small parking lot was almost empty with an SUV, a worn-out work truck, and a couple of sedans. Theirs was a small town and the emergency room wasn't often busy. She didn't appreciate being their excitement for the night, she thought wearily.

When Colter stepped past her to open the truck door, she heard it unlock to the key fob in his palm. *Fancy*, she thought. Seemed most everything was these days, whether that was someone's preference or not. Yet one more reason to prefer her small roadster. Fast but simple, same as the ranch truck was powerful but plain.

Colter stood poised to help her climb in but she appreciated that he waited for her to ask. She didn't ask. When she was settled with her still-aching head against the back rest, he closed the door behind her and walked around to the driver's side. For a moment, his silhouette was backlit by the security lights scattered around the parking area. Straight nose, strong forehead, stronger jaw and square chin. He was a good-looking man.

"Were you given pain meds for later?"

"They called in a prescription," she said. "They gave me a shot of something so I won't need them tonight. I'll send someone to pick it up tomorrow." She wouldn't. She didn't like how any of them made her feel and, more than ever, she needed to be alert every minute now. The twins' lives might well depend upon it.

His truck was smooth, his driving even smoother, as Colter exited the parking lot and headed out of town. Fast but smooth. His silence didn't last long but then she hadn't expected it to. "Tell me everything you remember about this afternoon." She gave a sigh which he didn't entirely ignore. He cut her a look. "McEnny's going to ask you the same. I'm sure he's waiting for us now. Talking it through ahead could help you recall details and have them clear in your head later when you go through it with him."

She supposed that was true enough. "I decided to take the boys with me on a cattle check this morning."

"On a school day?"

She didn't bother opening her eyes to look at him. "I thought you'd ask me what a cattle check is."

He snorted. "Self-explanatory."

"So is home school, but," she kept on before he could comment, "the boys are ahead of the public-school curriculum at this point. They're smart and they love learning. Wes makes it fun. But right now, they need something more. They need … time. Time with family. Time on the land."

He didn't comment so she started again. "The cattle

are in different pastures. We started in the lower ones and headed up from there."

"Anyone know where you were going?"

"Riley. Most of the hands, I would imagine. I'm sure Riley's going to have a few things to say to me."

"About?"

"I was supposed to check in with him after every stop. I ride alone most of the time so he's rigid about me letting him know when I move from one place to the other. I failed to do that when we rode toward the lake. He was probably frantic when he didn't find us where he thought we'd be. Where I'd last told him."

Colter didn't comment on that. "How many shots did you hear?"

"Two. One went past us and I called for the boys to get down on the ground."

"Where were they?"

"They'd just saddled and were getting ready to mount." She shuddered hard at the memory of that moment. The terror that had struck her, knowing they were exposed against the hillside. And then the horror. "I felt Gabby sway an instant before I heard the second one fired." She paused, took an unsteady breath, then another. She heard again the moment when Gabby's breathing rattled into silence. And her heart shattered in her chest all over again. "I knew it was too late."

"Bullets travel faster than sound," he agreed. He gave her a look. "I'm sorry. Really sorry for Gabby and for you."

His words struck a chord and for a moment she couldn't identify why that was so. Then she did. He'd said his name, not *the* horse or even *your* horse. He'd called Gabby by his name.

"Thank you." A whisper was all that she could manage.

Another shudder, this one soft with grief, went through her.

His voice was even as he asked, "Did you get a sense of anything off before you heard the first shot? Any kind of awareness?"

"You mean like some supernatural sixth sense?" She shifted her head on the backrest to eye him. "Is that something you believe in? Something you think you have?"

She felt the faint ripple of amusement that went through him. Not a chuckle, not a sound at all, no more than a consciousness that this wasn't the first time he'd been asked that question although perhaps not in quite those same words.

"Not supernatural, no. More like an enhancement of the natural five senses. I think we all have the capability. Some develop and make use of it. Some don't."

She put herself back in that moment, made herself think beyond feeling Gabby topple beneath her, beyond the chill of knowing the boys could be in danger. "No. I didn't feel anything but I think I saw something," she hesitated. "On the hill above us. A flash, like a mirror or glass."

"Or a gun," he said.

"Or a gun."

They fell silent but she didn't relax against the backrest, didn't close her eyes. She watched as he made the last turn before reaching the long drive into the ranch house. And, again, he was the one to break the silence.

"You're not married," he said.

She heard nothing in his voice, not curiosity, not insult, not humor. It wasn't a question. She didn't have to answer. "I was engaged once. I was twenty. He was twenty-seven. He was killed in a car crash." She turned to face him.

"That's when I discovered he already had a wife."

He looked at her, then back at the road where his headlights cut through the dark surrounding them, and they finished the remainder of the trip in absolute silence.

Chapter Eight

The sheriff had parked his car front and center of the driveway. Colter maneuvered past to get Miranda closer to the door. When he was satisfied, he put his truck in park and looked at her. He'd thought she'd fallen asleep but she was watching him.

"My legs aren't broken, you know."

"I know." He also knew she had to be sore as hell.

She proved that point when she chose to sit motionless as he walked around the hood of the truck where he opened her door and helped her step down. He ignored the sharply drawn breath she took when she had both feet on the ground. She might accept his help but he doubted she'd want his sympathy, even though today's event had all but eliminated her from his list of suspects. She hadn't ranked high, at any point, but there had been that possibility.

He wasn't surprised when she stepped away from his assistance. He didn't argue, just stayed close and watched as she made her way to the door.

Doubtless alerted by the headlights, the woman who'd admitted him on his first visit—the housekeeper—opened it before they were halfway from the truck and watched as they walked toward her. She made a soft sound of distress at the sight of the bandage across Miranda's forehead. "You'll need to go straight up to bed," she urged.

"I'm fine, Lila. Sore here and there but nothing that won't heal soon. I want to hear what the sheriff has to say."

"They're in the great room." Colter thought Lila looked more resigned than irritated at having her concern dismissed.

"The boys?"

"Upstairs … well, never mind that," she finished as a commotion on the stairs heralded their descent.

Despite their rush down, Colter was impressed by their sudden slowing as they neared the bottom and reached their sister. Still, they didn't come to a complete halt until they were as close to her side as possible without bumping against her.

"You're okay?" Dane peered up at her, his expression anxious.

Before she could answer, Dillon reminded her, "Your forehead was cut."

"Yes, on a rock, I suspect. I've got a few stitches but I'm okay. And ready to sit down," she admitted.

"Sheriff Joe says he's gonna catch whoever shot Gabby." Dillon's lip quivered.

"He promised!" Dane's eyes flashed with fury.

"And he'll keep his word," Riley said as he stepped into the hall, adding, "although I suspect it was an accident and no one meant to hit Gabby. Now give your sister a little room." But Colter noted his voice wasn't harsh. "I know you've been anxious but you can see she's good, right?"

The boys shifted their gaze to Riley and nodded but didn't look inclined to move from her side.

"How about some brownies and milk in the kitchen," Lila stepped in smoothly with the suggestion.

Two sets of eyes lit up at the suggestion, followed by a quick silence as they trailed down the hall on the housekeeper's heels, but Colter didn't miss a glance or two back at Miranda. She was, he realized, the solid ground in their young lives. The only solid ground with Pederson gone. Riley offered his arm to Miranda who shook her head as she walked through the wide opening into the great room where McEnny stood waiting.

Colter noted the coffee carafe and a brandy decanter on a sideboard beneath a portrait of Miranda with the twins at a much younger age. He suspected it had been painted by a skilled artist from a photograph because they weren't posed. The three stood with saddled horses near a massive oak tree. One of the twins, and he couldn't be sure which at that age, leaned against the front shoulder of a stocky sorrel. The girl held the appaloosa she'd lost that afternoon, the ends of loosely held reins dangling from her hand. Her free hand rested on the other twin's shoulder. Wildflower-dotted hills rose in the background.

The girl in the painting had been pretty; the woman was more than that. Far more. Colter shifted his gaze to the sheriff who lifted a chin in acknowledgement of their arrival. He also lifted a glass which Colter suspected contained a bit of the contents of the decanter.

"Off duty conversation," McEnny said.

Colter nodded and crossed to pour small measures

into two glasses. He carried one to Miranda. She'd chosen to sit across the room in a straight-backed chair with minimal cushion. Having had a few sore ribs himself, he understood the wisdom of not sinking into the luxury of the leather sofa. He noted that Riley had helped himself to coffee before propping a shoulder against the wall near the entrance to the room, perhaps to intercept if either of the twins decided to rejoin them. A good move, Colter thought, if that were the reason. The conversation ahead wasn't anything the boys needed to hear.

Miranda met his gaze as she took the glass he offered. "Not my normal drink of choice," she murmured, "but I'll take it."

His glanced back at the sideboard, noted the cabernet and the label. He turned without comment toward McEnny and took a sip from the glass in his hand, before saying, "You got a plan?"

The sheriff shrugged. "Tomorrow, I'll head back out with a few more men, take the search further."

"Needle in a haystack," Riley inserted, "but me and some of the hands will scatter out as well. You say what direction and we'll go when you're ready."

Colter agreed. It would be as useful as searching the proverbial haystack but he also understood the lawman's need to do something. He suspected the ranch foreman needed that, as much, if not more.

"What about you, Bellamy?" McEnny glanced his way as he rose to add to his glass. "You going to join us in the hills?" He lifted the decanter with a questioning look and Colter shook his head. A negative to both the spoken and unspoken question.

"I'll be hiring bodyguards for Dane and Dillon."

"The hell you say." Riley stared at him but he looked

more perplexed than anything.

Miranda, on the other hand, shook her head at the suggestion. "I can take care of my brothers."

Colter let his gaze touch the bandage across her brow and the painful-looking bruise along her cheek.

Judging by her expression, she caught his hint. "I was caught off guard today. That won't happen again." Her glare darkened. "Or do you still suspect I may have murdered my father?"

The sheriff raised his brow and Riley muttered, "What the hell," but Colter kept his attention on the woman.

"You've dropped down to least likely on my list." As he said the words, Colter knew they were true. "But you can't be with them every minute and you're going to need some time to recuperate." He had no plans of conceding anything, but an outright fight wasn't going to do either of them any good.

A tilt of her chin indicated she was more ready for a battle of wills than he was "Wes—their tutor—has a concealed carry license. He hasn't been carrying while he's been here, but he's willing. We talked about it."

"He may have your trust but he doesn't have mine. Not just yet." Colter knew his tone was hard and abrupt. He didn't much care.

Looking furious, Miranda opened her mouth and Riley held up one hand. "Hang on, Randa."

She turned to include him in her glare. "This is crazy, Riley! You know J.D. and I had Wes thoroughly vetted."

"For teaching credentials and possible criminal activities, maybe." Riley held her gaze. "But for background? Connections of some kind?" He paused. "I think … hope … Wes is exactly what he seems to be, a good guy and a good teacher, but—he takes a day off—and someone takes shots at you and the boys. Maybe it wasn't his hand holding the gun but we at least have to look."

Somehow Colter hadn't expected assistance from Riley but he'd take what he could get. The stakes were too high not to take every advantage and a cessation in hostilities would make his work that little bit easier. "How long has Wes been here?"

"Going on two years," Riley answered. "No. More like eighteen months, I guess. Right after Christmas break when their last tutor took off without giving notice. Wasn't it, Miranda?"

She nodded slowly. "Early January."

"Any idea why she left?" Colter asked.

Miranda shrugged. "She didn't seem to care for the isolation. She told me a time or two that she'd assumed the ranch was closer to town, easier and quicker to get to."

Riley snorted. "More like the boyfriend she left behind who was stringing her along decided he wanted her after all."

"What?" Miranda tilted her head at him. "She never said anything to me about a boyfriend. How in the world do you know that?"

Riley rubbed his jaw and shifted his gaze to the side. "We had a … a friendship … going."

"Well, for Pete's sake! Why didn't you say so when I was trying to track her down to see what had gone wrong and at least make sure she was okay?"

Riley's color darkened along with his expression. "I didn't know until she sent me a 'good-bye, I'm sorry' letter when she got where she was going."

McEnny relaxed in his chair, seeming to enjoy the exchange. Colter decided this was as good a time as any to drop his second bombshell. "Where can I bunk?" he asked Riley.

The other man didn't so much as blink. "Cabins are all taken," he said, turning his gaze toward Miranda. "If his purpose is providing protection for the twins, he needs to be close to them, I'd think."

She looked from Riley to Colter without reaction. "I'll ask Lila to find you a room. I'm going up to tell the twins goodnight."

The ranchman said his goodnights and left by way of the back door soon after Miranda left the room. Colter turned to look at McEnny who stared down into his now-empty brandy snifter. "I hope you have a deputy waiting close-by."

"Too smart to have a drink if that wasn't the case," McEnny admitted, lifting his gaze. "Deputy Mayfield has a cousin works for Riley. They'll either be playing poker or playing guitars in one of the cabins." The sheriff stared into Colter's eyes. "I don't like that you might be right … that J.D. may have been murdered. And, if that proves to be a fact, I like even less that your team figured it out before mine did." He got to his feet. "But I'll be damned if I don't like you." With that he set his hat on his head and walked out of the room. Despite the two small measures of brandy Colter had seen him down in quick succession, the man looked steady enough.

Colter followed McEnny to the wide doorway, half expecting the man to tell him the shooting changed things, that he'd take over lead on the investigation. But when he paused and turned, he asked, "Did you pick up that two-way?"

Colter nodded. "Before I picked up our patient."

"Keep it on."

He watched as the sheriff settled his hat more firmly

on his head and let himself out the front door.

Lila came up beside him. "Miss Miranda says you're to have a room upstairs."

He glanced at her and nodded. "I'll get my bag from the truck." With his hand on the doorknob, he paused. "Can you send someone to the pharmacy? I have a suspicion Miranda doesn't plan to make that happen. They gave her something at the ER but tomorrow is when the pain will hit the hardest, and the pharmacy should have her prescription ready."

The housekeeper sighed. "That girl never has liked medicine of any kind. They're closed by now but I'll see to it first thing in the morning. Thanks."

The room was spacious, the furnishings classy but simple, the décor plain, the wide-planked floor bare. Colter found the design interesting with the king-sized bed backing a wall that was open on either side. Behind the wall, he found a bathroom with the largest shower he'd ever seen. Without a doubt, the tile and fixtures were expensive but they were as plain as the bedroom furnishings. He showered, tucked his pistol in the drawer of the nightstand and slept well for the first half of the night.

His first thought was that he'd been awakened by the full moon that washed the verandah with light. But, after another moment, he heard the slow, rhythmic creak of a porch swing or rocking chair. Slipping on his pants, he opened the sliding glass door enough to step out.

Miranda stilled the swing with the tip of one foot on a wide wooden plank. She turned her head slightly as he walked the length of the porch to reach her.

He thought of the prescription waiting to be picked

up. "Are you in pain?"

"Only my heart," she said at last.

"I'm sorry." There wasn't much else he could say. Just the two words. She wouldn't want sympathy from him but he understood loss.

He eyed the rocking chair that someone had left angled toward the swing, as if from a conversation. He didn't imagine she'd want conversation from him either. Regardless, he took the seat and leaned back but he didn't rock.

"I suppose I woke you." Her voice was quiet, not a whisper, but soft like the brush of the evening breeze against his arm. He wondered if she needed to talk after all.

"You and the moon, I guess."

"It's rare for anyone to be in this wing but me, so I'm used to coming or going without worrying about waking others."

He thought about that a moment. "Where are the twins?" He would have expected their rooms to be close to hers.

"Opposite wing. Wes' room is on one side of them. Lila's on the other."

"J.D.'s?"

"Middle wing, over the kitchen and opposite the front entrance. This was always the guest wing but, when J.D. decided to homeschool the boys, I gave Rachel my room and moved out here."

"Their first tutor…"

"Yes, Rachel Bailey."

A whippoorwill called and Colter paused to listen, enjoying the sound. There weren't many whippoorwills in downtown Albuquerque.

"Were the boys upset when she left?"

When she cut her eyes at him, Colter realized that wasn't what she expected him to ask or say. After a moment, her lips quirked in a half-smile. "They were upset they might get into trouble."

He hazarded a guess. "They didn't like her?"

"I think they liked her just fine. They liked playing tricks on her even more. She was … gullible."

He snorted. "Not a good match for a couple of lively boys."

"No," she acknowledged, "and I think they're somehow worse because they're twins. But her credentials were excellent and her professors gave her glowing recommendations. She was worth a try."

He gave her a look. "First job."

It wasn't a question but she nodded. "Fresh out of college."

"What about Wes? What's his story?"

When her sharp gaze met his, he knew she realized the path his mind had traveled and answered with more depth. "Again, excellent credentials but combined with a solid history and work references. He's older than he looks. The twins are his third position. He was with his first student for six years and the second for nine. Kids grow up and private tutors, the good ones, work themselves out of a job."

Despite the lengthy history in his profession, he'd have the tutor checked but all he said was, "Must be hard on them sometimes."

"It would be for me," she admitted.

And, almost as if on cue, one of the twins called from the darkened room behind the swing. "Randa?"

"I'm here, Dane. You can come on out."

He did, but reluctantly, giving Colter a sidelong glance as he passed. He eased onto the swing beside his sister. "Couldn't sleep, buddy?"

"I miss J.D."

Interesting, Colter thought. They all called him the same; whether father or boss or friend, he'd been J.D. to all of them. He listened as Miranda soothed the boy, watched as she left to walk back to his room with him, then got lost in his own thoughts as the moon shot sparkles of light through the leaves of the tree limbs sheltering the house.

She was gone so long he didn't expect her to return. She'd pulled her bedroom door closed behind them and could easily have slipped back into her room and never let him know. He turned his head when her door re-opened and she stepped out with a bottle of wine and two glasses. Her curves were outlined in moonlight and he felt an unexpected and unwelcome awareness of her as a woman. As young as she was to now be running her father's small empire, Miranda Pederson was no child. She was, however, off limits.

"I wasn't sure you'd still be here but you're welcome to join me," she said, lifting the bottle toward him.

When he saw an ornate stopper had already replaced the cork, he got to his feet and took the glasses, holding them while she poured the wine. She replaced the stopper and set the bottle on the wide porch plank before accepting a glass from him and sinking back onto the swing.

"I'm pretty sure alcohol doesn't mix well with pain meds," he commented.

"I suppose it's a good thing I don't plan on taking any."

Her response came as no great surprise. "Dane get settled?" he asked as he took the rocker once more.

"I let him climb in with Dillon. They're in the same

room but they each have full size beds. Dillon never noticed Dane was gone but woke when I tucked him in." She shook her head. "They were arguing with each other about who could spit the farthest."

"I can spit pretty far myself," Colter said. He smiled at the look she gave him, but his smile faded with his thoughts. It was the kind of argument young boys had, and they were too young for what life had dealt them. "I can't imagine losing my dad at that age." He couldn't even begin to think what it would have been like.

"Hard at any age," she murmured, staring down into the glass she held.

He nodded. There didn't seem anything he could say that wouldn't sound like a cliché. "You're young to be a mother to them." He knew he'd said the wrong thing as soon as the words left his mouth.

She lifted her chin. "I'm old enough and tough enough. The Bellamys aren't taking them from me."

He met her look with one just as firm. "That's not what we do."

"From what I hear, you do damn well what pleases you."

Because he heard more apprehension that antagonism, he kept his own response low-key. "Maybe you're hearing from the wrong people. I'm here to protect Dane and Dillon."

After a moment, she sighed and relaxed against the back of the swing. "And after that? What happens then? You go away and leave us in peace?"

He hesitated, then chose his words with care. "Every case is different. My primary goal is safety for Dane and Dillon," and for her but he suspected she wouldn't want to hear that so left it unsaid, "not only for the present but long-term, but also justice for J.D., for his loss as their father because, for all appearances, he was a good one." Colter wasn't ready to say J.D. had been a good man but he hoped that proved the case for Miranda as much as for her brothers.

"And after that?" she insisted.

"After that the company becomes a resource for the boys and for you as their guardian."

"The company. Welles Enterprises?"

He nodded. "The Slade Agency and the Bellamy Ranch are part of Welles Enterprises."

"Once you're done here, we won't need anything more from you."

"You may not. The twins may not. But we'll be there if you do. We take care of our own. If that means stepping on toes, we step."

"Even mine?"

It was a pointed question asked in a straightforward manner but he caught the slightest curve of her mouth in the moonlight.

"Even yours … but it's not part of the plan."

She took another sip of wine, leaned her head back and closed her eyes. "Duly noted," she said, her voice soft.

"You don't sound threatened by it."

"Not in the least."

The faint ripple of laughter that accompanied her response was both surprising and pleasant and he smiled in the dark.

Chapter Nine

Colter was in front of the bunk house well before daylight. He watched as Riley pulled his truck to a stop and killed the headlights without cutting the engine. The other man stepped out, brows drawing together at the sight of Colter. "Problem?"

"Nothing new. I wondered if you had a horse I could borrow for a couple of hours."

"Reckon. Where're you headed?"

"The hill above that lake. Miranda saw a flash, like glass or maybe a mirror, moments before she heard that shot fired."

Riley grunted. "Wait here." He took a moment to move the truck out of the way then headed into the barn. It didn't take him long to return, leading two saddled horses, one a bay and one a sorrel. "You know the deputies were sure to have crawled all over that place yesterday and they'll be back at it again today?"

"I'm sure they gave it a hard look along with a dozen other places and I know you plan to head out with some men and do the same," Colter acknowledged.

"But you need to see for yourself."

Colter nodded. "There are a lot of hills out there."

Riley studied him a moment, his expression disgruntled but not angry. He swung his leg over the bay and wheeled the horse around.

Colter fell in behind him, content to let the older man take the lead. He knew the ground and this was his ranch. It had to be eating at him that Miranda had been hurt under what he'd consider his watch. It damned sure ate at Colter and for much the same reason.

By first light, they were on the nearest hill, looking down at the lake. The surface glittered with varying shades of silver. Colter dismounted and studied the terrain, mostly grass and rock and scrub trees. Glimpses of water were visible from more than one angle through the branches of a stand of young pine.

Colter shifted from spot to spot with his binoculars until he identified the likeliest angle for the shot that killed Gabby to have been fired and not been hindered by rock formations. Once he was satisfied the position was viable, he slipped on a pair of thin leather gloves and began searching the ground.

Riley watched him for a moment before asking, "You really think you'll find that spent cartridge?"

Colter nodded. In his opinion it was worth the time and the effort.

"No professional would've left it here to be found."

Colter straightened and met his look. "If that shot had

been made by a professional, Miranda would be dead."

He wasn't surprised when Riley flinched and turned his gaze from Colter to the mountains in the distance. When the older man didn't comment, Colter returned to his search and, within moments, pulled a shell casing from a scattering of needles. He noted the markings on the end. They weren't pristine but close enough for a respectable guess. He held it up to Riley who studied it before giving a nod.

Riley set his jaw and turned toward his horse. "I need to get back."

Colter understood the anxiety that gripped the other man. A 6.5mm Creedmoor was accurate over a remarkable distance. Accurate and powerful. Meant to kill.

By midmorning, he was leaving the ranch for Albuquerque. He called the sheriff on his way out.

McEnny grunted at his find. "Creedmoor, huh? Pretty popular for deer and elk."

Or a horse, Colter thought, but didn't say.

"A hunting rifle, then. Could have been there awhile." Again, Colter held his peace and McEnny sighed. "Doubtful, I know."

"Not from the looks of it."

"Just the one cartridge?"

"Just the one. I have it with me if you want me to bring it by on my way out for fingerprint testing and to verify the markings as Creedmoor."

Colter waited through the silence that followed.

"I can't imagine any fingerprints would have survived the heat in the barrel," McEnny pointed out.

"It's a long shot," Colter agreed, "but possible." And

McEnny knew as well as he did that few states had unlimited resources, and even fewer would consider the death of a horse a high priority.

"What would you do with it? If my department wasn't involved, where would you take it?"

"To our lab in Albuquerque." Colter was careful to keep his voice neutral.

"Top of the line," McEnny speculated out loud.

"It is. And we still might not find anything."

"Maybe nothing to find," the sheriff concurred.

"Maybe." But maybe there was.

McEnny was smart but he had his pride and Colter was patient. He waited him out.

"I suppose it'd be best if you took it there." He cleared his throat. "I have the bullet from Miranda's horse in front of me. Picked it up this morning. Might be best if you took that with you as well."

"I'll swing by," Colter offered.

"I'd be obliged."

"You'll be the first to have the lab report," Colter said, and meant it, as he ended the call and made the turn for a quick stop in town.

Colter reached Albuquerque in good time in fast-moving traffic, stopping first at his apartment and then the laundry service he used more often than not. He met Jonah for lunch and a quick update on their cases. So far, neither of them had made much headway. Added to that, Jonah seemed distracted, almost edgy at the start, although he relaxed as they compared notes on progress, or the lack thereof.

Colter tucked the contact information for the twins'

bodyguards into his shirt pocket and glanced at the single sheet of information on Wesley Harper. "This is pretty thin."

"What can I say?" Jonah gave a shrug. "Those two have a very boring tutor. Smart, decent, dedicated … but boring. Excellent references from previous positions. Clean background check."

"And he's good on the concealed carry?"

"All legal and current on range time."

Nodding, he turned his attention to the first of two folders Jonah had prepared for him. He read it through, lingering over the summary of points on the last page. "So, Robert Bentley is financially solid—not rich but comfortable—but his health is deteriorating due to excess of pretty much everything he enjoys in life. Prime beef, cigars, beer. Beat one bout of stomach cancer, being monitored for the likelihood of another. If he's still bitter over his child bride leaving him for his not-too-much-younger neighbor, no one can tell. Hasn't mentioned her name in public in the decade since."

Jonah grunted. "Would she still be considered a child bride after five years of marriage?"

Colter gave him a look and shrugged. "Maybe not a bride but she didn't catch up to his age any. And there doesn't seem to have been any reconciliation between the two men, not that they were great friends in the first place, from anything I can see."

"Maybe not, but they were at least part of the same social scene until Bentley withdrew after his wife's exodus."

"Maybe she was part of the social scene and all he did was tag along to please her," Colter suggested. "I don't see much mention of him prior to their marriage but Pederson dabbled in local government from time to time."

Jonah gave a snort at that. "Dabbled? Some would call it sticking his nose in to stir a few pots."

"All for the good of the community." Colter would have done at least as much as Pederson under the same circumstances. Calling out politicians with broken promises, letters to the editor about city situations that needed correcting, putting pressure on local officials at town meetings.

"Didn't hurt his own business, either," Jonah pointed out.

Nor did Colter have a problem with that. "He was part of the community," he answered mildly.

Jonah leaned back in his chair and propped his feet on his desk. "Seems you've taken a liking to our victim."

"I think I would've liked the man," Colter admitted, picking up the second folder. "Haven't learned anything to make me dislike him other than him taking a hankering for his neighbor's wife. Hard to know what that situation was like from a distance."

He felt Jonah's watchful gaze and looked up again. "Don't," he said.

"Don't what?" Jonah pushed back. "Don't remind you that you're a good man and you were a good husband? Don't remind you that Dana's choices were never about you? Everything that was there started a long time before you ever knew her."

Colter waited for the familiar flash of irritation and was almost surprised by its absence. "I know," he said finally, quietly, "but I still feel bad for her."

Their eyes met and Jonah nodded. "Nothing wrong with that. Feel bad as you like. But not guilty."

The guilt, Colter realized after a moment, was absent as well. When had that happened? He shook his head slightly as he opened the folder.

The file on Arthur Newland didn't give much more information than what he'd already heard from McEnny but it did reveal some unknowns that drew a small hmm of curiosity from Colter.

"What do you think?"

Colter looked up and realized Jonah had been watching and waiting. "It's … interesting," he acknowledged. His tone spoke volumes.

"Old history. I know. Even so."

"Yeah, even so. How'd you get a copy of the original contract between them?"

"It was part of the lawsuit and I stumbled across mention of it in some of the news articles. Seems like the ranch, the lawsuit … it was all big news back then. All I had to do was pull in a favor to have the actual document tracked down and copied for me."

The biggest find was the deed to the original Newland ranch, a land grant as most of the Bellamy Ranch had been a century ago. The boundaries of that grant weren't any larger than what Pederson brought to the table but it was all Newland had. But then the same was true of J.D.'s original land purchase, which was his contribution to the partnership. For a moment, Colter wondered what had prompted the two men to create a partnership, whose idea it had been.

There might be something in the complete trial transcript which was obtainable, but he wasn't sure the why of the decision would be worth the tedious reading even if it was there to be found. When he said as much to Jonah, his cousin shrugged. "I'll put one of the juniors-in-training on it. It will make for good practice."

Colter nodded. "If there's anything there, let me know.

If any of his family look like a possibility for revenge, I'll get back with you."

He went back to his reading of what Jonah had provided. Though the physical center of the partnership holding, the two original parcels, Newland's as well as Pederson's, had become almost negligible through the years as they purchased surrounding lands together. The kicker for Colter was that the original contract remained unchanged and the spend for the additional acreage wasn't added to the recorded values. That was true for both partners but it was Newland who got burned.

When the contract was dissolved by court decree, Newland lost his original properties and much of his money. It was through his own fault, to be sure, but still bound to have been a crushing loss at the time, which led to more loss down the line.

"Why the hell would a man double-cross a partner who's helped him make a small fortune with no sign of that slowing down? Especially knowing what was at stake?"

He spoke the words aloud, more to himself than to Jonah, but Jonah chuckled and gave his own opinion. "There're as many answers to that question as there are leaves on a tree but it almost always comes down to one, maybe two probabilities."

Colter snorted agreement. "Greed or jealousy."

"Or some combination thereof."

Still thinking about the ramifications, wondering why Newland had made such a dumb move, taken such a risk, Colter straightened the papers and a half-page newspaper clipping slid from the pile. A glimpse of the headline had him taking a closer look. It was more of a human-interest piece than real news and emotionally but evenly done. An unexpected emotional cost to Arthur Newland was that his first wife and stillborn daughter were buried there on the land that he'd put at jeopardy and lost. Pederson had offered him a personal easement so that he and any relatives could access the cemetery. Newland turned it down vehemently and publicly, immediately following the outcome of the trial.

The article gave Colter a glimmer of an idea. He pushed it to a back burner, but he didn't plan to leave it there.

Colter drummed his fingers on the table lightly, and Jonah sighed and said, "I know. We still have more questions than answers. To be honest, I don't like how this is shaping up. It almost feels as if we're looking for two shooters. That tire shot was classic marksmanship. Missing Miranda and hitting her horse … amateurish."

"Unless the horse *was* the target. Two different guns, two different bullets, two different targets. An additional layer of skill there." And Colter didn't like how *that* was shaping up.

His cousin frowned. "But what would be the point?"

"When we know that," Colter said, "we'll know who killed Pederson."

Before he left, he and Jonah reviewed some cases and findings from a couple of their junior agents and made new assignments to a few others.

The energy that was Albuquerque hit him anew as he stepped out onto the sidewalk in front of their building. In another hour or so, rush hour would start winding down as the night life began heating up. The city held a rhythm that he enjoyed when he was in it but didn't miss when he wasn't.

From there, he had one last stop to make before heading back to the Pederson ranch.

Chapter Ten

In spite of their bitter ending, Colter would rather have buried Dana in the Bellamy private cemetery on the ranch. He'd wanted to … his father had begun the arrangements … but his mother had intervened as gently as was possible for her powerhouse nature. "Dana's heart was never here," she'd reminded. "We shouldn't hold her body hostage." The words had hurt as much as the manner of his wife's death but Colter had known the truth of them. Dana had once loved him as much as she was capable of loving but she'd loathed everything about the ranch. And its isolation most of all.

The first of the few times they'd visited the Bellamy ranch as a couple, she had flinched at the site of the gravestones, several of which were well over a hundred years old. "Don't ever put me here." Her vehemence had startled him.

And she'd been adamant, even hysterical, in the hours after the truck rollover that had broken her body in too many places and killed the man who'd been behind the wheel, that she never wanted to see the ranch again. When the hospital staff had convinced him those truly were her final hours, Colter had done his best to assure her that he'd do whatever she asked of him. Despite everything, she was still his wife. She'd looked at him with her eyes dulled by the drugs they'd given to ease her pain and said, "Don't put me in the ground."

He hadn't. His visits, rare and far between, were to a small cemetery inside this city she'd loved. He'd known for months that he was ready to move on but still he came, although less and less often.

He glanced around him, acknowledging the peace of the place, as peaceful as the valley that housed generations of Bellamys and Welles and Slades. Niches and urns of ashes filled the room. The ceiling of tinted glass panels sloped upward on support beams where they deflected sleet and snow of winter storms and reflected the brilliant sunlight of long summer afternoons in air-conditioned comfort.

Dana's urn was midway around the room and kept company by the gentle rushing of a water feature. Colter walked closer, then settled on one of the several benches. Usually he talked of the earlier, happier memories. Today, he was silent, letting the emptiness wash over him, an emptiness that was neither good nor bad. The frustration, the anger, the grief ... all were gone but nothing yet filled the space they'd taken.

When he got to his feet and walked away, he knew he wouldn't be back.

* * *

With Miranda's permission, Wes had taken the twins to visit a couple of the museums in Santa Fe. She and Wes had discussed the trip in depth the evening before. He and the boys were joining another homeschool tutor and his charges for breakfast just inside town and staying together until they left for home. Wes had retrieved his gun on his weekend visit home and she'd asked him to keep it at hand but not allow the twins to know. The thought of not having them underfoot made her tense but nor could she keep them prisoners. If someone wanted to hurt the boys, that could easily have happened when Gabby had been shot and she lay unconscious.

Missing their chatter, Miranda ate dinner on the patio then walked to the main barn to assuage her restlessness. Before college, she'd gone through a phase of wanting a show place, a barn with cobblestone or brick pavers for flooring and chandeliers hung from the center beams. Now she was glad for it to be unchanged from the durable, functional structure that J.D. had created long ago. Part of the foundation that had raised her.

She walked the hall in the shadows of early evening, rubbing a nose here and there, before she stopped at Gabby's empty stall. J.D. had called him Gabe in deference to his registered name of Zip's Gabriel. Miranda had changed that to Gabby after her first ride when he'd nickered at everything from an inquisitive prairie dog to a hawk that swooped too low. Her heart ached with missing him even as burgeoning fear nipped at her mind.

She'd had to fight the urge to keep the boys penned close to the ranch. Every moment she couldn't see them, was a moment that worry crowded the busy thoughts she tried to keep at bay.

Too late, now, to wish she hadn't agreed for them to eat in Santa Fe before starting home. They could have visited one museum in the morning and started home after lunch, leaving the second museum for another day. There were, after all, dozens of them in the area, all of them good and educational and a fun field day.

"Everything's fine," she murmured to herself as she switched the light off at the barn entrance and walked the path back to the house. "They're fine."

And then her cell phone buzzed in her pocket.

Wes' voice was terse but low. "We're being followed."

Her heart jumped. "Followed? You're sure?"

"Well, I'm not James Bond but, to check my gut, I left the interstate and made a loop around a truck stop. When I came out, the vehicle I'd noticed was waiting near the on-ramp and fell in behind me again. Shall I call 911?"

Her mind raced. "Where are you? You have your gun, right?"

"I'm about an hour out from the ranch and, yes, I have it. Even so…"

The unspoken implication hung between them. The gun was of little use while he was driving.

"Give me a minute," she said. "I'll call you right back."

She didn't need to ask specifics of where they were. She had an app on her phone and those of each twin that allowed her to pinpoint where they were at all times. After a quick check to confirm what she thought, she called Colter Bellamy. In a simpler world, McEnny would have been the logical person to call. She no longer lived in that world.

He answered her call after one ring. "What's wrong?"

"Wes and the twins are between here and Taos, headed home. He thinks he's being followed."

Colter fired a number of questions at her and she answered as calmly as her dread allowed, giving their location at the time of Wes' call and the make and model he was driving.

When she finished, all he said was "I'm not far from the ranch. I'll be there soon."

And then he was gone.

Hands shaking, she called Wes back long enough to let him know to expect Colter or some of his team to be within reach soon but to trust no one as long as the vehicle hung with him. Then she waited and paced, staring down the long drive as she watched for headlights. She started walking when she caught the first glimpse of them between hills.

The truck pulled to a stop and Colter stepped out, coming toward her with a long, relaxed stride. He was on his phone, still talking when he stopped, expression still, his eyes sweeping her face. It was only in those eyes that she could see the banked anger. He paced and gave orders and listened, his gaze sweeping her now and again, that anger leaping high with each glance.

After what seemed a lifetime, he ended the conversation and stopped in front of her. "Our helicopter has your tutor and the tail covered. He's about eighteen miles out from a small mom and pop restaurant right by the highway. Have him pull off there. If the tail stops near the highway again, have Wes pull to the rear. I have a car and backup waiting. He'll swap with the driver and he and the boys will wait until you say go."

"What happens if things don't go as planned? If whoever's following him doesn't stop ... just keeps trailing him around to back of the restaurant?"

"Wes and the boys go inside, use the restroom, get

drinks to go. If possible, our guy will block the tail. Then he'll get out of his vehicle, pop the hood, and curse all mechanics loud enough to be heard and long enough to make sure Harper and the twins get back on the road safely."

"And if he can't block him?" Miranda hated the quiver in her voice.

"He shoots the tires and holds a gun on the tail until help arrives. But, if things go as planned, they make the switch. Our guy leads the tail back out onto the road, then turns east at the next intersection. When it's clear, Harper and the boys can leave. They'll have a two-vehicle escort all the way."

When she got Wes back on the line, her first question was, "Can the boys hear us?"

"Not if we speak in a conversational tone. They're watching a movie, ear buds in."

"There's a small restaurant coming up soon. You're between eight and ten miles, by now, I'd think. You'll notice a helicopter overhead….?"

"I see him. Friendly skies, I take it."

"Yes." She breathed a sigh of relief at his easy tone. "Stop at the restaurant. Pull to the rear. There's a car waiting for you. You and the boys will change vehicles with the driver. If the person following you doesn't stop near the highway, take the boys inside and call me back."

"And what shall I tell the twins? They're too smart for much subterfuge and it would seem things are not going to settle anytime soon."

Miranda closed her eyes for a moment. That was her fear as well. "I don't disagree, but now is not the time. Tell them you reported the car sounded funny so I sent a rental." Wes was right. They were going to figure things out sooner rather than later so she'd have to get ahead of that. Just not at the moment. "Take a few minutes, make a deal of figuring out the lights, blinkers, and whatever. I'll call back when it's okay for you to leave. There will be two vehicles pulling out with you. Not sure if they're cars or trucks but, if you notice, just know they're okay."

"I got it." He hesitated. "Miranda?"

"Yes?"

"Don't worry. I won't let anything happen to the boys. You have my word."

It took a moment for her to speak past the sudden knot in her throat muscles. "I know you won't, Wes. Thank you." She hesitated, hating to break the connection. "I'll be back in touch soon, okay.

"I see lights ahead. I think this is my stop. Talk in a bit."

Miranda took a deep breath and met Colter's gaze. "I'm going to kill whoever is doing this."

He shrugged. "You're welcome to whatever is left of them."

When the next call came from the chopper, he put his phone on speaker. Miranda could hear the sound of the blades hitting air. Colter's gesture surprised her, but she was grateful.

"We're good on the bait and switch." The speaker sounded as if he were having fun. Miranda supposed more likely than not that he was. "The tail is following our decoy on their road to nowhere. Kids and escorts are good to go."

Colter nodded at Miranda and she made the call to Wes. When the call was done, she gave a sigh of relief and turned toward the house. Colter fell into step beside her as his phone rang again.

"Boss, did you want an intercept? The stretch ahead

is fairly empty and a full moon is making things easier. I could give our decoy a heads up to slow down and put the chopper down behind the tail."

Colter paused before responding. "No, *fairly* isn't empty enough. If we're dealing with an amateur, he may do something stupid and get someone hurt or killed. I doubt we'd get enough intel to make it worth the risk." Miranda thought he sounded disappointed. "Can you get a read on the tag?"

"Tried. It's been smeared with mud."

"Figures," Colter grunted. "Even a rookie knows that trick. Fall back enough where you're not noticeable and follow them until they get where they're going but have the decoy do an about face at some point and head back to town."

"What will happen then?" Miranda asked when he broke the connection. Behind her curiosity was real anxiety at what might be attempted next.

"The best scenario is that whoever was following Wes will realize they've been duped and head off."

She fought an urge to ask the worst scenario. She didn't want to know and she didn't think he'd tell her anyway. "If your guys don't intercept, how do we figure out who's paying that person?"

"If we're lucky, their final destination will give us a hint. I'm not all that hopeful, though. Nor am I sure the driver, whoever it is, was being paid. None of this has the feel of a professional. An expert wouldn't have been made by Harper. I'm glad your tutor had his wits about him, but still, the tail made a rookie mistake waiting in plain sight to pick him up again. The next one may be smarter."

Miranda fell silent and Colter could almost hear the thoughts rolling through her mind. "Gabby's death wasn't an accident. They weren't shooting at him, but the shots weren't accidental." She took a deep breath. "They weren't hunting out of season. They didn't miss at target practice."

He hesitated but there wasn't anything to gain with a lie and, even if he still had doubts about the intent of the shooter, it changed nothing. The animal would still be dead and she would still be grieving. Knowledge was power. Even painful knowledge. Still, he sighed before admitting, "Doubtful. All of that."

"I was in the way of someone getting to the boys." Her voice was quiet. "I still am."

"You'll be protected as will the twins."

They'd reached the front verandah and she cut him a look as she pulled one of the chairs away from the wall. "I don't care about protection. Dane and Dillon are all I care about now. Don't shut me out. I want to know what you know, when you know it."

He took another chair and shifted it to face her as much as the front of the house. "You may not care about your protection but those boys need you. Besides, you're a Bellamy by default."

"The hell I am. I'm a Pederson … as are they."

He smiled and shook his head. "It's possible to be both."

"Don't shut me out," she said again, and it was a warning.

The last thing he needed was for her to decide to take things into her own hands. "I won't shut you out but that road runs both ways." He let silence fall at her lack of response, giving them both time to think. They couldn't battle one another. It would put the twins at greater risk. He thought of the things he'd learned so far and the things he needed to know. "If you find something, remember something, that may be part of this, I need to know."

She lifted her chin, searching his face with her gaze. "Deal," was all she said.

They sat in silence until Wes pulled up with the twins. Colter watched her pretend that all was normal in their world and that no one was willing to kill her to get to her brothers.

The boys filled the air with excited chatter, all they'd seen and done. Their favorite, it seemed, remained the Rattlesnake Museum in Old Town and ice cream at lunch. The Maxwell Museum of Anthropology received no more than 'it was kinda cool'. Miranda seemed to be doing her best to comment and react normally but he saw Wes watching her and knew the effort fell flat with him as well.

When the housekeeper stepped out of the house, Miranda gave her a tired smile. "Lila, there you are. I think these guys are tired and then some."

Lila nodded. "It's late, for sure. Later than I thought they'd be." She shot the tutor a look.

Wes shrugged. "Had a bit of engine trouble." He high-fived his charges. "See you in the morning, boys. Pop quiz on what you saw and learned today." He gave a low shout of laughter at their quick protest. "I'm kidding. I promise."

After they allowed the housekeeper to hustle them inside, Wes turned to look at his boss and asked in a low voice, "What now?"

"I'd like to keep them under lock and key," Miranda admitted, "but they don't deserve being forced to live that way."

"No, but…" Wes sighed, "I felt rather inadequate today. Sure, I carry but that wasn't enough for the circumstances."

Colter held his peace until Miranda looked at him and said, "I'm out of my league."

The confession surprised him and impressed him even more. "Most people would be," he assured her, "but we're not out of mine. Get some rest and we'll figure it out as we go."

He wasn't being honest. His plan was mapped out with his team and ready to put into play once he shared it with Miranda. But he had no intention of taking that sharing beyond his team and Miranda, herself. Yeah, he'd done a background on every person on the ranch. All of them seemed no more and no less than what they appeared, but his trust level wasn't high enough to take a risk, not when two young lives were at stake. Maybe the plan hadn't been to kidnap and hold for ransom but that was the first thought that came to mind. And kidnap victims rarely fared well. There were other possibilities besides a demand for ransom. None of them good. Revenge, if that's what it proved to be, could be the ugliest of motivators.

Miranda gave him a look but followed Wesley inside. After a moment, Colter stepped inside as well. Lila stood at the end of the hall and watched as he locked the door. He turned to face her and she shrugged unapologetically.

"Sometimes they forget," she said. "I don't." He could feel her eyes on him as he mounted the stairs. Apparently, she didn't trust any more than she forgot.

Colter paused as he opened the door to his room, sensing her presence before he stepped through the opening. He shut the door behind him as Miranda flipped the switch across the room just inside the door that opened onto the upper verandah.

"You're unexpectedly trusting … considering your line of work."

He shrugged. "I didn't leave anything here that I don't want found."

She turned and walked out to the verandah and he followed, leaned against the railing and faced out over the lawn, as she'd done. Then he waited.

Her silence lasted longer than he anticipated but he had patience enough for longer than that.

"You don't figure things out as you go."

He lifted a brow, impressed yet again. "No?"

"No. You walk in with a plan and you execute it very precisely." She turned to face him, putting her back to the rail and crossing her arms in front of her. "So, what *is* it? What's your plan?"

He tried to ignore what his body was telling him about how she looked in the moonlight, her breasts framed by the arms she had crossed at her waist. Even worse was that his mind was urging him to defend and protect. He didn't mind when the urge was in regard to two nine-year-old boys. He didn't need to have that mindset regarding a woman. Even more so, not this woman. At the moment, she needed about as much protection as a mountain lion. But still, that was what he felt.

"I need to place one of my team with the working side of the ranch."

"In with the hands…"

He nodded.

"I'll let Riley know."

"It needs to be more … organic … than that."

Her look was dubious. "Organic?"

"As in not planned."

"Even though it's planned?" At his nod, a frown creased her forehead. "So, Riley needs to make up some story for the rest of the guys."

"Not exactly."

He saw when understanding dawned right along with fury. "You want me to lie to Riley? What the hell?" She pushed away from the railing and he watched without saying anything more as she walked the length of the verandah then spun to walk back, stopping in front of him. "I trust Riley, I don't care whether you do or not."

"I don't trust much of anyone, at this point, but I don't *distrust* Riley."

"Then why the deceit?"

"Look, it's hard for people who aren't used to keeping secrets to *remember* to keep them. I gather Riley is a straightforward kind of guy. Subterfuge is never going to be his strong point."

She took a deep breath and released it. "I agree with that."

"A slip of the tongue around the wrong person can mean the difference between life and death for Cheney," he added, pressing his point. "Honestly, I wouldn't be telling you if you didn't have a part to play in getting her on board."

She seemed to take less offense to that than to what she saw as an aspersion toward Riley but her brow lifted as she honed in on one aspect of his comment. "Her? This Cheney is female? And you want her mixing with a bunch of ranch hands?"

"You don't trust your men?"

"Oh, I trust them," she said tersely. "They'll be hands off and respectful. And they won't be distracted as long as she's old and plain."

He sighed. "Well ... not exactly, but Cheney is the best I know at what she does. All of which is a part of why I need your help."

"And the other part?"

"Simply that you don't have any empty positions to fill even if I were bringing in a man. If you did, you'd already have been looking and everyone here would know it, most with suggestions for who to hire. Hands don't quit the Pederson Ranch. They're rarely fired because your screening process is rigid." He'd done his homework. "They retire from here but they don't quit."

"I can agree the typical hand who applies with us isn't female. The bigger issue is that, you're right, we don't have an opening. That said, how do you propose I get her on board without notice?"

As she was talking, she crossed the verandah to the swing and sat. With no more than a brief moment of hesitation, he joined her.

"She'll be noticed," he said. "No way around that. The key is no suspicion. She's twenty-six and looks sixteen. She'll show up claiming to be eighteen and with just enough of what appears to be bruises covered with make-up to rouse Riley's suspicions. I think we'd be safe to believe he'd bring those suspicions to you."

"Interesting." She nodded. "But, yeah, Riley would beat a path to my office. He's a softy for kids and women, most of whom he thinks are helpless."

"But not you."

She snorted "Riley knows I'm as tough as I need to be. So, what then? When Riley asks me what to do...?"

"Suggest he have two of the men share a cabin for a little while and put her in the empty until you do some checking. You can both agree she's not as old as she says ... believe me she doesn't look it ... and that she may be an abused runaway."

"I still don't like the idea of lying to him," she said unhappily.

Colter didn't argue the point, just waited until she gave a sigh of acceptance.

"You said she was one of the family and the best at what she does ... which is?"

"Reading people and knowing when things are about to go south. More importantly than that, she's the best sharpshooter I know." He let the word hang between them but she didn't flinch.

"What does that gain us if she's with the ranch hands?"

"Nothing, which is why you'll make sure she's given things to do near the house and barn during the day. She'll have the opportunity to mix with the hands at breakfast and dinner, get a read on them when they're not working so they're not distracted by her. And she'll be close to Dillon and Dane during the day while you and I do a bit of detective work away from the ranch."

"Get a read on the hands?" She glared at him. "That's crazy! These men have been with us for years. All of them. I trust them with my life."

"You *are* trusting them with your life. You're also trusting the twins' lives. And every single one of them would maybe die to protect you. But one ... one may not ... one may be bought."

Miranda took a sharp breath, and he waited.

"I don't like it, any of it. But I'll do it. So, she'll be the bodyguard for the twins?"

"No. They'll be here tomorrow. They'll guard the perimeter of the house and barn area as long as the boys are home. If the boys leave the ranch, they follow, different vehicles."

She pressed her lips together. "The twins are too smart not to notice."

"I agree. That's why you should let them know what's

going on. I suspect they're already suspicious about their trip back from the museums."

"I'll think about it."

Colter studied her set expression and knew it wouldn't help to push her. He might have to, sooner or later but he'd wait and see for now.

Chapter Eleven

Miranda cleared her afternoon to take the boys riding after their lessons were done. Her ribs were still sore and her forehead throbbed when she went too long between aspirin but she put her game face on.

Beneath his wide-brimmed cowboy hat, Dane frowned when she winced as she swung up into the saddle. "Randa? You okay?"

"Maybe you shouldn't ride Sadie today," Dillon said. "She pulls on you."

That was true. The mare hadn't taken well to any of the light, training bits Miranda had tried so far. She was a quiet girl, not inclined to flighty fits and starts but, when she got irritated, she would push down into the bit, pulling at her rider's hands on the reins.

Miranda warmed at their concern for her and had to

make herself not smile with the pride she felt. "If she does anything that makes my side ache or if I get tired, we'll switch up, okay? Y'all can take turns riding her. But she needs to be ridden as much as possible." Unless she proved herself not trustworthy or willing, she would be Gabby's replacement around the ranch. She was a stout, well-bred mare with a head full of sense. She had to grow up a bit, but Miranda felt she'd get there with a little time.

She watched as the boys exchanged solemn looks. Like most twins, she supposed, they had a silent way of communicating that was just between them. Then both turned to look at her at the same time and nodded.

"As long as you promise," Dillon said.

"I promise," she answered, equally as solemn. "Besides, we aren't going far. I need to get out of the house for a while and wanted some company. We'll stick close to the house and barn, in case I get tired." That worked for an excuse while she figured if, what, and how much to share with them. She wondered what J.D. would have advised and the irony of that thought made the breath catch painfully in her lungs.

"Randa?" Dane peered at her from his saddle.

"I'm good," she lied swiftly. "Let's ride alongside the road first then circle around the back. Lila promised warm peach cobbler and real cream when we get back."

Some of the tension eased from Dillon's shoulders as she gave him a smile and said, "Lead the way."

It was the twins who made the conversation she needed to have easier. Who, in the end, gave her no choice. The ambling hour ride she'd planned turned into two. The air held the first hint of autumn dry but without any of the cool to come. She made sure to keep the roofline of the ranch house within her sightline but otherwise let the twins choose the route. There were several paths through the trees but eventually all of them circled around to the stream of water that began somewhere near the top of the mountains and ended in a small pond not too far from the back of the barn.

They were almost back at the barn when the drone of a plane made Dane look up. "Darn," he muttered. "I thought it might be the helicopter that followed us home last night. Who was that, anyway?"

She shot him a glance and was relieved to find the gaze fixed on her was curious rather than anxious. "Someone who works with Mr. Bellamy."

"He said we could call him Colter," Dillon told her.

"That's fine as long as he doesn't mind."

"But why would the helicopter follow us and not land if he wanted to see Mr. Colter?" Dane persisted. Dane, although as well-mannered as his twin, was always the one who would push for answers, even more so if things didn't add up to what he thought they should.

"Let's stop up here and let the horses drink and we can talk about that." She was relieved that her voice remained as steady as she wanted it to be. As steady as her brothers needed it to be.

After letting the horses have all the water they wanted, they slipped hobbles from their saddles so the horses could graze on what little grass there was on the rock-strewn hillside. Miranda sat on a small boulder a few feet from the water's edge. The boys pulled off their socks and boots and rolled up their jeans to wade, but after no more than a few minutes, both returned to her side.

"So?" Dane said. "What gives?"

They'd know something was up if she gave a non-answer. Anytime Miranda said 'we can talk about that' there really was something to talk about. Something real. Neither she nor J.D. had lied to them and Miranda wasn't going to start now. She could say a topic was off limits, as at times it was, and they'd back away. She couldn't do that. Not when lack of knowledge could put them at risk down the road. Or sooner.

And still she pondered what to say.

"Is Mr. Colter really a fake deputy?"

She sighed. They were connecting all the dots already. Dillon was watching her with that wise-beyond-his-years gaze. "Not fake," she said. "Temporary. There's a big difference. Sheriff McEnny gave him that badge, so it's real and has authority behind it."

"So, why's he here? Because somebody shot Gabby? Riley said he expected it was some hunter."

"Sheriff McEnny is concerned about that," she admitted. "He knows our hands would never be careless and no one else should be on our property, hunting or otherwise, if we don't know they're here. Mr. Bellamy is keeping an eye on things for a few days."

"And the helicopter pilot … he's watching out here, too?" Dillon looked thoughtful.

"Not exactly," she began, still wanting to choose her words carefully but Dane snatched that opportunity away with his next comment.

"The helicopter flew off right before we reached the ranch. He was watching *us*."

She gave a huff of laughter, mentally throwing her hands in the air as she acknowledged, "That's true. He was watching to be sure y'all were safe and we can expect him to be watching again when you leave the ranch."

"Because J.D.'s not here to watch out for us?" Dillon asked.

Miranda's brief amusement faded. "Partly."

"Is that why J.D. wrecked? Because he didn't have anyone watching out for him?"

Miranda's heart broke all over again at the look in Dane's eyes. She wanted to protect them. Always. From everything.

Swallowing hard against the lump in her throat, she finally answered, "We're not sure, yet, but … maybe."

"Who's watching out for you?" And that's when she saw the fear she'd hoped never to see in their eyes.

"We are," Dane answered his brother fiercely. "Me and you. We're watching out for her."

Miranda took a deep breath. "We're watching out for each other. All of us. Me and you and Lila and Riley and Wes … and everyone here, all of the hands who loved J.D., who love you."

"And Mr. Colter," Dillon added. "He's watching, too."

"He is." She might not like all of his methods or his bossiness but she was sure of that much and one thing more … at the very least, Colter Bellamy was one of the good guys. The problem, she suspected, would be to back him out of their business when any threat of danger was behind them. "And now it's time for us to get these horses to the barn and fed."

Dillon insisted on riding Sadie the remainder of the way to rest Miranda's arms. The boys were growing up too fast and she knew that J.D.'s death would hasten that process. It was one of those things she could do nothing about but, as some would say, pray. Miranda wasn't much for prayer. Or … maybe … prayer wasn't much for her.

Lila was waiting when they reached the house. True

to her word, there was peach cobbler still hot from the oven and the boys had their pick of heavy cream Lila had whipped that morning or ice cream from the freezer.

When Dane and Dillon were settled at the kitchen table, Lila gave her a look. "Mr. Bellamy is waiting for you in your office."

"Thank you, Lila."

"I don't know that I like him," Lila said with a sniff, "but I made him coffee."

Miranda chuckled. "Then you at least don't hate him."

Lila handed her two bowls of cobbler topped with her whipped cream. "No, I don't hate him. Should be plenty of coffee left in the carafe. Ring if there isn't."

Colter sat sprawled in one of the easy chairs, the ankle on one leg crossed against the knee of the other, his laptop cradled against the crossed leg. He looked up as Miranda walked into the room.

"Hi." Miranda noted that Lila had opened the drapes as she usually did by mid-morning but none of the lights were on. Apparently, the glow of the computer screen was enough for Colter to see whatever had the frown creasing his face.

The frown eased as she lifted the bowls with their warm scent of peach and cinnamon. "I'm about to spoil my dinner. You're welcome to join me."

He nodded and watched as she placed the bowls on the low table in front of the sofa. As he stood and crossed the room, he gave her a look as if to judge her mood at finding him making himself at home in her space. "Thanks."

"What has you looking unhappy ... more so than usual?"

He grimaced. "I guess I've not been the most pleasant person to be around."

"Not much reason for any of us to be," she admitted. "I have to try, though, for the boys. Their world is shattered and I need to patch at least some of the pieces back together for them. And add that to keeping them safe."

The words were her concession, her acceptance of the grim facts Colter had brought to the ranch. J.D. wasn't dead because of a wreck. He was dead because someone wanted him dead. Miranda had never deluded herself that J.D. hadn't made some people unhappy, even angry, but murder was out of the realm of her understanding and experience. But she was a swift learner and whoever thought her brothers were an easy target could think again.

"You can trust their safety to me." Colter was watching her and, she didn't doubt, reading her thoughts at the same time. He kept a steady gaze on her and at her silence he added, "It's what I do and I'm damned good at it."

She returned his look and nodded. "As long as you keep me in the loop, every minute, every step. The first time you fail to do that, the gates of this ranch will be closed to you and an army of tanks won't get you through."

His lips twitched. "We don't have an army of tanks so I'll make sure I don't need them."

She hesitated. "That frown you were wearing when I came in ... something new?"

"Nothing unexpected. Whoever was following Wes shook my team. They pulled into the parking garage at Albuquerque International. The frown was because I should have had a ground team take over when they got close to the city limits. Air cover has as many disadvantages as it does advantages."

Her shoulders slumped but she didn't say anything

about what he clearly considered a failure on his part. He'd accomplished far more than she would have known to do. More than what she suspected the sheriff would have been able to accomplish. Because of that, the twins had made it home safely.

She looked up to find him watching her.

"Let's talk about Bentley."

That surprised her and she said cautiously, "Jerica's husband."

"Ex," he reminded.

"One of them," she reminded wryly, adding, "Neither marriage lasted long enough to account for anything."

"You didn't like her."

She leaned back against the sofa. "I never knew her, not really. I met her, we exchanged comments about the weather, that's about all. We didn't have enough in common to maintain a conversation for any length of time. She wasn't interested in the ranch. I wasn't interested in her latest nail color. But … no … a woman who could walk away from her babies? That's not someone I could ever like. In spite of all that, Jerica and J.D., and whatever went on with her husband, that was all a long time ago."

"It was," he agreed. "And there may be nothing there, but it's a cage I'd like to rattle."

"Just to see if anything pops its head up?"

He nodded. "Just to see."

She shrugged. "Seems to me there's a lot of water under that bridge. Why now?"

"Because feelings fester. Because people are unpredictable."

"What would you suggest?"

"Maybe a visit. Both of us."

Miranda lifted a brow. "I suspect I'd be as welcome as

a rattlesnake. We'd need a good reason if we want him to so much as open the door to us."

"It would be neighborly to let him know we'd had a bit of trouble, could be trespassers he'd want to keep his eyes open for, maybe take some precautions with his own cattle."

She frowned, thinking. "He's mostly retired, I think."

"Mostly, yeah, but he's still running a few head."

"It might work," she smiled faintly, "but I doubt it will get us an invitation to sit and talk awhile."

"I don't disagree. Still, it might get us something." He paused at the clatter of boots on the stairs, a moment later Dane and Dillon were in the room.

"Miranda, the new Minions movie is out! Can we go?" Dane almost quivered with excitement.

"Tomorrow is Saturday. Wes could take us," Dillon suggested helpfully. "He likes Minions, too. He said so."

"Wes is going home for the weekend." It was his parents' fiftieth wedding anniversary. No small deal. And she wasn't sure Wes was up to another round of good guy-bad guy. Nor was she. Wes was too good of a good guy. "How about next weekend?" And maybe all of this would be resolved, please God.

Dane's face fell. "What if it's gone?"

"Minions?" She tried to keep her tone light. "No way, dude. They're way too popular. A new release is in theaters for weeks."

"Could you take us then?" Dillon asked. She could tell he was trying manfully not to beg.

Colter caught her eye. "Seth and Angel will be here tomorrow," he reminded. "As good a time as any to meet the boys."

The body guards. He hadn't told her their names yet

but she didn't have a doubt that was who he meant. And she still wasn't convinced it would be good for the boys to meet them. To even know they existed. That there was a reason for their presence at the ranch.

Colter didn't press further. He waited, watching the twins stare at their sister with pleading looks.

She said a silent prayer before nodding slowly. "There's a couple of guys who will be hanging out with y'all when you leave the ranch until … until things are easier." She didn't qualify *easier* but Dane nodded knowingly. The helicopter, she thought.

Colter cleared his throat. "A guy and a gal … Seth and Angel. They'll be here in the morning."

Miranda had assumed Angel to be a last name. Her mistake.

"Will they be with us all the time?" Dillon looked intrigued at the thought.

"No," Colter answered. "Most of the time you'll never see them but they'll be close if you need them. If you leave the ranch, they'll go, too, but not always in the same vehicle. We can make an exception for a movie. No reason for them to miss out on the Minions."

Somehow Miranda doubted the Minions were on this Seth and Angel's don't-miss list but she was equally sure they'd be well paid to sit through it. She watched the boys carefully but saw nothing but curiosity in their expressions. She didn't want them to live afraid. All she wanted was for them to be safe. If Colter trusted this duo, then so would she. "Maybe you and Riley could spend the day showing them around the house and barn tomorrow and hold the movie until Sunday afternoon." With any luck, that would give her time to get comfortable with them, with this whole idea. "Will that work?"

Dane nodded solemnly but Dillon grinned. "It's a deal."

Moments later they were scrambling back up the stairs to whatever they were watching when the Minions advertising crossed the screen. They weren't permitted a lot of television time and they treasured what they did have.

Colter was waiting when Miranda turned a questioning gaze his way.

"If we're going to have this Seth and Angel guarding the boys, why do we need an Annie Oakley to come, as well?"

"Seth and Angel will be focused on keeping Dane and Dillon safe. Cheney will be focused on everyone else." The ranch hands, Wes, Lila, Riley. Colter didn't completely trust any of them at this point. Except Miranda although, initially, he'd been as distrustful of her as he was everyone around her. He'd never seen her with J.D. and he knew from experience that an offspring was capable of killing a parent and a woman was capable of murder. But he'd seen her with her half-brothers. She'd kill for them as fast as she'd die for them. And no way in hell had Miranda caused the death of her appaloosa.

Chapter Twelve

Miranda had planned to tell Riley about the body guards first thing the next morning but Cheney arrived first. She knew something was wrong as soon as Riley came into the office and she caught sight of his expression.

She watched in silence as he filled a coffee cup from the carafe and turned to look at her. "We've got a problem," he growled. "She was sitting on the top rail of the corral when I come out this morning."

Miranda's heart sank. "She."

Riley nodded, taking it for a question. It wasn't. It … she … had to be Cheney. Damn it. Colter could at least have given her a day or two heads-up. Or maybe that's what he'd done and she hadn't recognized it for what it was. Now the girl was here for Miranda to deal with right on top of the bodyguards who would arrive at any time.

"She," Riley emphasized. "And says she's eighteen but she's nothing but a kid. Fifteen, sixteen at the most … maybe even thirteen or fourteen. Hell, I don't know."

"What does she want?"

"A job. Claims to be an experienced ranch hand." He snorted.

"We can't discriminate based on sex," Miranda said carefully, "but we don't really need anyone, do we?"

"We for certain don't need a kid."

"Did you ask for ID?"

"I did, and she's got some, but it's fake. Not even a good fake. Says her name's Cheney Smith. Someone's been hitting on her pretty good. She's wearing some heavy makeup but I can't say it's doing much to hide the bruises on her face."

"Maybe we should call McEnny," she suggested, feeling her way.

"She'll run and could wind up in a worse place from what she ran from."

Miranda knew she wasn't good at subterfuge, but it seemed she wouldn't need to be. Riley was caught up in the girl's plight.

"What do you suggest?"

Riley scratched his forehead. "Maybe Lila can find her something to do in here. Dusting or something. She can't bunk with the men even if she can ride a horse and rope a cow, which I got my doubts."

Miranda shook her head. Lila could keep her busy, no doubt, but tying her up with housework wouldn't accomplish Colter's goal. "I'm not unsympathetic, Riley, but we don't know her. Those bruises could have come from a pimp or from a drug dealer. I'd rather she not be near the boys until we know more about her."

He took a deep breath and straightened. "Damn, girl, you're right. She could be suckering me in. She had tattoos," he muttered the last, as if making a point to himself.

Miranda felt bad at the look of horror that had swept his face at her words. "Or she could be what she claims to be. And tattoos are like jewelry, a reflection of personality, not character." Somewhere down the road, when all of this was over and resolved, she'd have to tell him the truth. He was not going to be happy with her.

"That may be but she don't need to be around Dane and Dillon 'til we know for sure." He rubbed the back of his head, looking more stressed by the minute. "We can't send her packing."

"Maybe you could double up a couple of the hands and give her a cabin to herself? Assign her tasks like cleaning saddles and oiling bridles, helping Pete muck stalls. Real work, all of it, but things where she can't get hurt until we know what she can do and where you can keep an eye on her."

Riley gave a slow nod. "Yeah. I can do that. That's not a bad idea at all. Why don't you walk out with me and meet her? Maybe you can get a better read on her."

Miranda wasn't sure that was such a good idea. But then, again, neither was she sure it wasn't. Thinking again how very much she wanted to strangle Colter for *his* good idea, she followed Riley to the barn.

Whatever she'd expected, Cheney wasn't it. Miranda's first glimpse of her was just what her disguise projected, a young teen sitting on a bench at the opening of the barn, back slumped against the weathered wood. She jumped to her feet as they walked up, straightening her shoulders as if to impress in spite of ill-fitting clothes and a shapeless wide-brimmed hat that shielded her face, but not enough to hide unsightly bruises she'd attempted to cover with makeup. Then she swept the hat from her head in a quick movement, her gaze met Miranda's, and everything changed.

Miranda had a swift impression of flawless skin, wide-set green eyes, and red-gold curls cropped close. Cheney's eyes met Miranda's then she ducked her head as a young person might do. If Miranda had not known better, she—like Riley—would have judged the frightened girl to be no older than early teens. The steadiness in that quick glance eased Miranda's tension.

"Cheney," Riley said, "this is the boss lady. Ms. Pederson."

Miranda took the hand Cheney offered, felt the callouses in her firm grip. "Miranda," she corrected, giving Riley a quizzical look. No one here called her Ms. Pederson. Most of them had watched her grow from gangly pre-teen to the woman who helped them catch and deworm and vaccinate cattle every spring.

"Cheney, ma'am, and I'm grateful for a chance here." Her voice was low and quiet.

"Is that your first or last name?"

"Just Cheney, please," she said and looked down at her scuffed boots.

Riley exchanged a look with Miranda and she shrugged. "That will do for now, I guess." Riley knew they kept meticulous records of employees, even part time help, but she knew he'd expect her to be lax this once if only for a little while.

The weight in her chest grew heavier. She'd never lied to Riley. Ever. Not even by omission. She accepted the temporary necessity but she didn't like the feeling at all.

"Riley will get you started with some things that need doing. If you need anything or have questions, see him. You'll eat with the other hands but I expect you to keep your distance otherwise."

"Yes, ma'am. That won't be a problem."

Of that, at least, Miranda felt certain. She sighed as she turned away. She was going to have a lot to answer for later. But that's when she'd deal with the fallout. Later.

Colter knew something wasn't quite right when he caught a glimpse of Miranda striding toward the house and paused to wait on her. She hadn't seen him yet or the pair who stood beside him on the front walk. Her gaze was fixed on the ground ahead of her, her focus on the thoughts inside of her. He could almost see her wrestling with whatever worried her. And that, he knew, was why few civilians could provide adequate protection for themselves or the ones they loved. They couldn't detach from two of the most powerful emotions, love and fear for those they loved.

He called to her when her path would have taken her toward the side door. Looking up, she veered toward them.

"Good morning."

She echoed his greeting but turned her attention to the new arrivals. "I'm Miranda Pederson."

Angel Whittaker took the hand Miranda held out to her and gave her name. Seth Reynolds did the same. Colter tried to see them through her eyes and couldn't. He'd known them too long. Angel, older than him by a number of years, looked as soft as her name, feathery silver hair cut short, a sweet smile when she showed it, but that was rare, and odd-colored eyes the deep purple of a storm cloud on a summer afternoon. If he could have but one person at his back in a knife fight, it would be Angel. Seth was equally improbable-looking as a body guard, his face was round and unlined, his brown eyes placid. His reaction speed with a pistol was deadly. The unlikely duo had partnered for years and never let Colter down.

Although he watched as Miranda met each of their steady gazes, shook each of their hands, Colter hadn't a clue what impression they made on her or what she was thinking.

"They have a map of the ranch but they'll stay away from the ranch hands and close to the house, one on duty, one off, around the clock. If the twins leave the property, whoever is on goes with them."

"Riley needs to meet them." Miranda's tone was firm.

Colter nodded. He'd expected that and didn't have a problem with it. They weren't investigators and didn't need to be secretive about their movements. Being out in the open, as it were, did put them more at jeopardy. That was a risk they expected and accepted as part of this job and were being paid well to take. Colter needed time to figure out the who and the why of Pederson's death. In the meantime, the safety of J.D.'s sons remained paramount. The more people who knew two professionals were guarding the twins, the better.

He waited as she sent Riley a text message and it didn't take long for the foreman to make his way around to them. Colter watched and listened as she made the introductions, keenly aware of Riley's gaze on him the entire time.

And it was to Colter that Riley addressed his question,

and he didn't care that both were hearing every word. "These two are your family? Both of them? So, you trust them?"

Colter nodded. "One of them will have the boys in sight at all times but it's important the boys are together."

"They're not often apart," Miranda inserted, "but I'll make sure Wes understands."

"Where's the other going to be?" Riley asked gruffly.

"Sleeping. This is around-the-clock surveillance," Colter explained. "One will sleep. One will watch. After this weekend."

"What's happening this weekend."

"Wes will be away with his family," Miranda said. "It was planned some time back and I don't see any reason to change that plan. Seth and Angel will spend the afternoon with the boys and take them to a movie tomorrow."

Riley frowned. "I don't like them being away from the ranch."

"I don't either," Miranda agreed, "but I also don't want them to feel like prisoners. I have no earthly idea how long this will go on."

Colter met the gaze she turned toward him as she spoke. It wasn't a question but he answered anyway. "Not long." He intended it as a promise he meant to keep. He looked at Riley. "They'll need a place to hook up their camper, nothing fancy, a hose for water and an electrical connection will do."

Riley sighed but assented with a jerk of his chin. "We can manage. Got a couple of places that have been used in the past. They can take their pick."

"And could you spare them a couple hours of your time to explain your operations and show them the layout of the place?"

Riley looked from Angel to Seth, then back at Colter and nodded. He didn't look any happier but his stance had relaxed in acceptance of what was best for Dane and Dillon and, perhaps, at being included in the overall plan. As they walked away, Riley already talking with the other two, Colter turned back to Miranda.

"Busy morning?" Colter asked, remembering her tension when he'd first spotted her heading toward the house.

"No busier than usual. Just dealing with an unexpected arrival first thing."

He winced as her eyes narrowed at him. She'd known Seth and Angel would be here today. So, Cheney had arrived as well and earlier than he'd anticipated. At least they'd had that discussion up front. It wasn't as if she had been a complete surprise. Hopefully, she'd been on good behavior. With Cheney that wasn't a given.

"What did you think of her?"

"I never would've guessed she was anywhere near twenty-six, and I was ready to do battle over the bruises on her face. They look horridly real. But her eyes," she hesitated, "her eyes give her away."

Colter nodded. "The window to the soul… but" he added, "she's wise enough to make eye contact as little as possible and she'll stay in character at all times. With Riley. With you. Alone in her cabin."

"And she's more of the family? A Bellamy or Welles or Slade?"

He nodded but didn't elaborate. Until she decided otherwise, she was just Cheney. Her story was her own to tell—or not tell—as she chose.

Chapter Thirteen

Miranda kept her gaze on the landscape ahead but she felt Colter's frequent glances her way. "It would have been faster to drive," she said, as the trail twisted around another outcropping of rock.

"Harder to turn us away if we wander over the hills."

She couldn't argue the point. "Maybe, but it gives Bentley good cause to fire a shot or two at us for trespassing."

He cut her a look. "You think that likely?"

"To be honest? I don't know what I think, anymore." At least the twins weren't a worry for today. How much safer could they be than with two bodyguards? She'd talked with both Seth and Angel again that morning and been reassured in spite of herself. They were a bit of an odd couple but they had the same steady look in their eyes. J.D. always said you take a person's measure by what you read in their gaze.

She shifted restlessly in the saddle, then quieted herself when the young mare she was on sidestepped in a skittish move.

"You're not wearing the badge the sheriff gave you," she noted.

It wasn't a question, but he answered anyway. "No need. This isn't official sheriff's business. We're making a neighborly visit to let Bentley know we've had a problem with trespassers and to ask if he's had any. Like someone shooting at a woman and two young boys on a morning ride."

Her heart thudded at the reminder. The sound of gunshot. Gabby faltering, then falling. She forced a deep breath past the tightness in her chest. She felt Colter's eyes on her, appreciated his silence.

A bird winged low and she focused on the slow glide of wings as it lifted itself above the trees.

"And while we're on dress code," he said, keeping it casual, "you don't dress like a cowgirl."

He was trying to distract her. She was grateful and forced herself to a light tone. "For one, I'm not a cowgirl. For another, what antiquated notion do you have of how cowgirls look?"

"Multi-colored jeans, tops with sequins, and painted straw hats."

She snorted. "You've been to too many rodeos."

He slanted her a lazy look that was anything but. "You're saying those weren't real cowgirls?"

Ignoring the way her pulse responded to him, she countered, "Depends on your definition. They're horsewomen, some of the best. Most are barrel racers, some are breakaway ropers, some are both. Some come from a ranching background, some from farms, but as many from cities and towns. Not all of them have sorted steer for a sale, or branded a calf, or moved herds into valleys for the winter."

"How old were you?"

The memories made her smile. "The first time J.D. put me in a saddle in front of him I was all of two. It was spring and we counted babies born."

"Your first pony?"

"J.D. had a serious disliking for ponies. My first horse was a retired rope horse, slow but sweet and not an ornery bone in his body. Perfect for a little girl."

"Good memories," he said.

He was looking at her as if that were a feeling he understood. Maybe he did.

"Boosie was the horse that taught me to ride."

Colter chuckled. "Boosie?"

"Yeah, Lila wasn't amused because she knew which of the hands had ridden the horse before he was retired and why the cowboy was retired right along with the horse." She shrugged. "But that was his name and it stuck. He also taught me self-sufficiency and patience. If I wanted to ride, I had to figure out how to get a saddle on his back. Before I could saddle him, I had to brush him from forehead to fetlocks."

"More kids need to learn that kind of self-sufficiency and patience. We wouldn't have near the drug epidemic."

"Not every child has the access and the opportunity. Not every child is born a Bellamy," she smiled to take any sting out of her words, "or given the chance to be a Pederson."

"That's a fact and I never fail to count my blessings."

"Me, either," she agreed, remembering the things Lila

had told her about her real father. No, she stopped herself, some other man may have been a part of what created her in a physical sense, she couldn't pretend otherwise, but J.D. was her real father. Her only father. He was the example she lived by, the example she would choose by. If she ever chose again. She wasn't sure that would happen.

J.D. had given her a foundation and a better beginning than would have been possible without him. She wondered about Colter at Dane's and Dillon's age, about his birthright as a Bellamy.

"Were you actually raised on Bellamy Ranch?"

He met her look with a nod. "Rode, roped, sorted cattle, branded steers, all of it."

"It doesn't sound much different from life here. And you traded that for investigative work?"

"Not traded, just explored my options. Doesn't mean I won't go back to it someday."

Odd, she thought, that they'd never met when both their ranches were in the northern part of the state. But, considering she'd been homeschooled, as were the twins, and that J.D. had limited his low-key social life to Taos while the Bellamys frequented galas at the state capitol, perhaps not so odd after all.

She was about to say as much when they topped a hill. "There." Lifting her rein hand, she gestured toward the bottom of the hill. "Bentley's house lies beyond that cluster of aspens."

"We're on his property?"

"Have been for about half an hour."

"Are you ready?"

"As long as you're doing the talking." Her tone made it a statement, but she raised her brow in question.

Colter gave her a steady look and nodded, then he

nudged his horse forward down the slope.

Bentley's place gave an appearance of old-world charm. Both the main house and the huge barn next to it had been crafted with generous use of brick and weathered silver wood. Everything appeared in good shape. The landscaping wasn't lush but it, too, was well-maintained and the lumber on nearby corrals looked to be in good repair.

Colter reined his mount close to the barn and studied the layout.

"What are you looking for?" Miranda asked, her voice quiet.

"Nothing in particular. Hoping to get some insight into the man and his state of mind." Nothing here gave the appearance of a man drowning in thoughts of revenge. But the old cliché *looks can be deceiving* existed for a reason.

One of the hands stepped out of the barn as they rode past, then followed them as they moved closer to the house. Colter's back didn't itch at his presence but he didn't relax his guard, either. He dismounted at the wooden fence closest to the house and waited as Miranda stepped down. When she wrapped her reins around a fence post, he did the same.

She gave him a glance and he nodded toward the arched entry of the verandah. Taking a deep breath, she walked to the mahogany-stained door and knocked. He followed close behind, while watching her back and keeping an eye on the man who had followed them but stopped a respectful distance back from their dismount.

Colter wasn't surprised when Bentley himself opened the door. They were expected. He hadn't caught a glimpse of anyone following when they'd crossed over to Bentley land but suspected they'd been glimpsed on security cameras. He'd seen a few scattered around Pederson's place as well.

Bentley looked a lot like his photos but he had more physical presence than Colter expected. Not a tall man, maybe five feet, eight inches at most, but his shoulders were those of a working man, well-muscled and squared with pride, and his chin held high. He had pale gray eyes and a steady gaze.

"Good morning, Mr. Bentley," Miranda said. "I'm Miranda Pederson."

"I know who you are." He shifted his look toward Colter. "And you're the new deputy sheriff."

"Temporary." Colter held out his hand. "Colter Bellamy."

Bentley's handshake was reluctant and brief. "I know that, too. You may as well come inside." He stepped back from the opening

Miranda ducked her head, hiding her smile at his grudging tone. It wasn't much of a welcome but, then, Colter hadn't expected much.

Before stepping inside from the tile of the verandah, Colter glanced behind him. With their welcome, however lukewarm, made clear, the hand who'd trailed them from the barn faded away.

The inside of Bentley's home proved as well-kept as the outside. Rather than a wide hall at the front, as there was at the Pederson place, the entry opened right onto the great room with furniture as expensive but more elegant than Pederson's. The mosaic floor tile, bare of rugs, was spotless.

Bentley chose an armchair and gestured toward the

sofa which faced it. "Coffee?"

"No, thanks." Colter let Miranda's answer stand for both of them.

Bentley tilted his head and studied her for a moment. "Not a social visit, I suspect. Heard you had a little trouble across the way."

When she nodded and stayed quiet, he turned his attention to Colter who said, "More than a little. Shots were fired at Ms. Pederson and her brothers. You're the closest neighbor. We wondered if you'd seen any sign of trespassers on your property."

Bentley shook his head. "J.D. made lots of enemies."

His tone was neutral but his faint smirk less so. Because of that, Colter decided to be blunt. "Successful men often do. Are you still one?"

"Successful, or an enemy?" When Colter didn't respond, Bentley leaned back in his chair. "Successful enough. Hard to be enemies with a dead man."

Miranda didn't make a sound but Colter noted the sudden flexing of her fingers.

"It's my experience that grudges don't stop at the edge of a grave."

"Maybe not," Bentley returned, "but even if I carried one all these years, I wouldn't hold a woman and two kids accountable for a man's actions." He shot Miranda a look. "I may not feel any grief at your father's death but I am sorry for your loss and I don't bear you any ill will. And I'd fight a cougar bare-handed rather than see a young'un hurt."

Still, Colter thought, it was possible a grudge remained and even been recently fueled. "Losing the lease on those fields to J.D. must not have sat well with you, all things considered."

"I haven't lost it yet," Bentley said.

"But you can't renew it."

"No. I can't." Bentley lifted a shoulder. "But it doesn't matter, anyway. I'll be shipping those calves in the fall. They're already sold."

"You might want to keep an eye out, place an extra guard on your cattle," he suggested. "The Pederson Ranch will be doing the same." It was as much a warning as a suggestion.

"Not much left to guard. I've been selling my herd the last year or two. I've kept a few prized breeding bulls and several good producing cows, but they'll be hobby more than a living. I'm ready for retirement and no one to leave anything to."

Bentley was a cool one, but the last was said with at least a hint of the animosity that Colter had found missing up to this point. Pederson had robbed Bentley of his wife and the opportunity of children with her. The woman wasn't blameless but she wasn't around to hold accountable. Nor was Pederson. But his family was. Maybe he'd fight that cougar, Colter thought, or just maybe he'd willingly turn one loose on them.

Colter stood and placed a business card on the low table between them. "If you run into trouble, call."

"Why?" Once again, Bentley's gray eyes gave nothing away of his thoughts or feelings.

Colter shrugged. It was a legitimate question. "Being a decent neighbor and expecting one in return." He gave the words the faintest inflection. He wouldn't issue a threat but he wanted the other man to understand him.

Bentley understood. He grunted as he got to his feet.

"Thanks for the thought. I'll see you out."

"I suppose he has good reason for hard feelings," Miranda said as they walked back to their horses.

"Reason enough for resentment," Colter agreed as he freed his reins from the fence. "But not for violence."

"You still think he's a possible suspect?" It was hard for her to reconcile Bentley's calm demeanor with that of a murderer.

He studied her over his horse's back as she unwrapped her own reins. "You don't?"

"I'm not the expert," she admitted with a shrug. "You are. But he seemed so … so dispassionate and it was all so long ago. Why now?"

"You're trying to apply logic to murder." He looked the slightest bit amused as he swung up into the saddle.

"Not logic," she said, trying to sort through her thoughts as she followed suit. "I don't think taking a life is an act of logic. It's an act of passion."

"For you, that might be true—even for most people— but not everyone."

"Taking a life?" She shook her head and nudged her horse back the way they'd come.

"As many people murder for expediency as for any other reason." Colter lifted his own reins and his horse fell in step with hers.

"Expediency." She repeated the word.

"Sure. I want what you have. I want something and you're in my way. You witnessed something that could send me to jail. And don't forget kill for hire. I'm sure I could come up with a few more and none of them require strong emotion. Something as simple as I don't like the way you look. I don't like the way you're looking at me."

"But there's always a reason."

He lifted a brow. "A reason? Yes, but not always a good one."

When she stopped her horse and simply looked at him, he did the same.

"Who exactly are you?"

He looked pained. "I thought we'd established all of the fundamentals."

"No, I mean when you're not being a Bellamy, watching out for kith and kin."

"There's no such time. It's who I am and what I do."

"The Lone Ranger," she murmured, then cocked her head as a thought occurred to her. "Only for kith or kin."

"Not only but mostly," he admitted. "Somehow they seem to keep us busy enough without taking on outsiders."

"Ever?"

"It's rare … but if something piques our interest, we can be persuaded."

"Like money?"

She wasn't surprised when he shook his head. "Has to be more than that. Much more."

She felt his gaze on her back as she rode on. She'd never considered Jerica a very interesting person but she'd certainly come from an interesting family.

Chapter Fourteen

The remainder of their ride back was quiet and unrushed. They followed a different route, one that took them splashing through several streams of water. Again, he let Miranda lead although he'd spent enough time in the hills since his arrival to keep his bearings. She seemed lost in thought and Colter had a few of his own. It was true he still considered Bentley a contender for the guilty party, but he would look harder elsewhere. Even then, he wouldn't look away. Not entirely. The man might not be high on his list, but he'd stay for now.

At the moment, he needed to let Miranda know about the spent cartridge. He moved his horse closer and said her name.

After a glance at his face, she gave a small sigh and an even smaller shake of her head. "What now?"

She was silent until he finished talking, and there really wasn't much to say in the end.

"Two shooters?"

"Doubtful." More than, in his opinion. "I think one shooter, two guns."

"And not an accident or coincidence."

"Not an accident and I don't believe in coincidences." He recalled saying the same to the attorney. "Not when murder is involved."

Again, silence. He could almost hear Miranda's thoughts as she absorbed the implications.

"I can't think of anyone angry enough at both me and J.D. to want to kill us," she said at last. "Aggravated with one or the other of us, sure, but … angry enough to point a gun and pull the trigger?" She shook her head and the look she gave him was filled with bewilderment.

"Anger might not be the motivation."

"Greed?" She shook her head. "The only two who stand to benefit from my death would be the twins."

"Ever heard the saying, revenge is a dish best served cold? J.D. made a few enemies. Some you may know about and some you may never have heard their names."

She stared at him with a hint of horror in her eyes, then took a ragged breath. "Liz is right. I need to make a will, name a guardian I can trust to protect the twins, sooner rather than later."

He could almost feel her tension and, as much as he would've liked to reassure her, nothing was guaranteed. J.D. Pederson, for sure, hadn't expected to die moments before reaching home that day. The fact that Colter, as well as any of his team, would put himself between her and a bullet without hesitation might not be enough to save her. There were too many unknowns as yet.

As they neared the ranch house, Colter noticed her checking her phone several times. He had no doubt this revelation had increased her concern, added to her anxiety. Then she frowned, a faint frown, and one that didn't set off any alarms with him.

"Problem?"

"I have an app on my phone that lets me keep up with the twins' devices."

"Are they not where they're supposed to be?" Wherever they were, he was confident of their safety with Angel and Seth.

"They left the theater on time and had lunch at one of the local restaurants." She sighed, but then her mouth curved slightly upward. "Now they're at their favorite ice cream parlor."

He was glad to see the hint of a smile and gave her one in return. "If that doesn't sit well with them later, their current custodians can manage the consequences."

They parted ways after unsaddling and grooming the horses. Riley stood waiting at the front of the barn to talk with Miranda, and Colter headed in to make a few phone calls.

Riley pushed his hat back on his head and gave Miranda a searching look as she approached. "That old coot still as ornery as ever?"

"He didn't ooze with charm." She shrugged, trying to be fair. "I don't suppose he has any reason to feel the least welcoming toward any of us, but he didn't fire bullets over our heads."

"I doubt he's ever fired a gun in the direction of anyone," Riley said firmly. "Over their head or otherwise.

Going over there was a wild goose chase."

"As you told me it would be," she acknowledged, giving him a rueful glance sideways, "but it didn't hurt anything to talk with him."

Riley snorted. "I suppose not if you enjoy pissin' people off."

Miranda thought about that for a moment, looking down at the path ahead of her. "You know, I really don't think we did. To some degree, he seemed to enjoy the opportunity to let me know his disdain, even disgust, for J.D. If there was anger…" she shook her head, "I didn't see much sign of it."

"Boys had a good day," Riley said, changing the subject as easily as he'd started it.

"They're back?" A tautness she didn't know she had eased along her spine.

"Rolled in half hour or so ago, changed, and headed straight for the pool."

At his words, the tension threatened to return. The boys were excellent swimmers but they were still boys and not cautious enough for her liking. "Lila's with them?"

"Settled under the umbrella with a book and a glass of lemonade. Bodyguards are in the pool with the boys helping them work off popcorn covered in butter and soda and ice cream and whatever they let them have for lunch. God alone knows what that was," he finished with a grunt and a half-grin which belied a somewhat grouchy tone.

He fell into step with her as she turned toward the house and she took the opportunity to ask, "How did the girl … Cheney … manage today?"

"Kept her busy around the barn like you said. She sat on the bench and oiled leather for a full four hours without complaining. Just kept looking around her uneasy like."

The feeling of disloyalty, that stab of regret, returned. Riley deserved better. She couldn't give him better, not just yet, but she would, and as soon as possible. "She stayed close to the barn?"

"Until the hands returned for lunch." He frowned. "She didn't sit down with the rest. Took the sandwich cook handed her, then walked down the drive and back again."

"Do you think they make her uneasy?"

He seemed to think about that a moment before he shook his head. "Didn't seem anxious around 'em. When she reached the end of the drive, she stood watching the road both ways for a while. My guess is she's waiting for something bad to catch up with her. Like she's afraid whoever messed up her face might be following."

Miranda hated that she couldn't share the reason for Cheney's watchfulness. Even as she understood the need, she hated it. She heard shrieks and laughter as they rounded the hedge that separated house and yard from the working part of the property and her heart lifted. She hadn't heard either of the boys laugh since J.D.'s death.

Riley fell back and disappeared once she reached the pool. That was his way. He liked to keep an eye on things from a distance and he didn't mind their early morning meetings but he was most comfortable at the barn and with the ranch hands.

Miranda paused at the far end, enjoying the moment. Seth was in the deep end, Angel in the shallow, with the boys in the middle as they played a vigorous game of 'keep away.'

She made her way around the edge to the grouping of chairs. Lila got to her feet at her approach. Tilting her head slightly, she searched Miranda's face with her gaze, then gave a quick nod. "About what I expected. A waste of your time."

"Too soon to tell."

Lila rolled her eyes and Miranda gave her a rueful smile. Lila, like Riley, was not one to mince words or make them prettier than the truth required. Still, Miranda believed her own rebuttal. It *was* too soon to tell if their visit would stir things up or bring anything to light.

"Are you ready to take over here so I can get dinner started? They weren't hungry when they got home but another hour splashing about in the water like this and they'll be starving."

Miranda looked down at the heavy layer of dust coating the toes of her boots and the hem of her jeans. "Give me five minutes to change?"

With his phone held to his ear, Colter stepped out of his room onto the porch that looked down onto the pool where two of the Slade Agency's most lethal bodyguards played pool games with a murder victim's sons. He'd heard Miranda go into her room next to his a few minutes ago and he watched now as she walked back to the pool in a white one-piece swim suit. He knew he was staring; knew he should look away. Her legs were as long as he'd imagined and—considering he'd rarely seen her in anything but blue jeans—surprisingly tan.

Pulling his mind back from where it had drifted, he focused on the conference call until its conclusion, which wasn't long. None of them were. Ongoing investigations, like the Pederson case, were recapped, briefly and succinctly, ensuring key investigators for the Slade Agency stayed current on the status of everything in progress. The practice began years earlier when one of his uncles was murdered, leaving the family scrambling to pull the pieces of his investigation together sufficiently to save the client and send his uncle's killer to the chair.

Recalling the grief and the anger of those months, he reminded himself that whatever thoughts he might have for Miranda as a woman came a distant second to the safety of her, Dane, and Dillon. Listening to the young voices drifting up from the pool, he thought about his own summer days growing up and traded his jeans for shorts and a tee. He went down through the house rather than the outside stairway and stopped in the main room long enough to mix two drinks.

Miranda looked up from watching the boys as he approached, a smile lifting the corners of her mouth as she took in his cutoffs and flip-flops. "You look like a country boy."

He held one of the drinks out to her. "I *am* a country boy. This place is fancy compared to where I was raised."

Although fancy wasn't the atmosphere of the Pederson home. If pressed, he supposed he'd describe it as comfortable, in good repair but showing the soft patina of a little age.

She took the drink and sipped, watching as he kicked off his slides and settled at the edge of the pool beside her, feet in the water. "Fancy? Compared to the Bellamy Ranch?"

"Our house was large, most of them had to be for all the kin coming and going," he explained. "But nothing was custom made or top-of-the line."

Her thoughts weren't on interior design. They were on family dynamics. "Most of them?"

"A lot of family still live on the ranch ... Slades and Welles and Bellamys. A lot more have moved to other towns or cities or even states. After I moved to Albuquerque, Dad had it gutted and the interior rebuilt. Mama now has everything she did without all those years."

Angel moved to join them. Still in the center of the pool, Seth flipped first one boy then the other from his shoulders at the deep end. They came back again and again, begging for more.

"How'd the day go?"

"I had fun." Angel gave him a quick smile. "Not often I get to say that on a job this serious. They're young and they're funny, but they're wise."

She angled her position so that she faced Miranda as much as the pool. "They're as anxious for your safety as you are for theirs."

Miranda's forehead creased and she took a deep breath. "I know. I hate that for them. I don't know how to reassure them."

Angel shrugged. "I told them Colter had your back. That he wouldn't let anything happen to you."

Colter felt Miranda's gaze shift his way and she shook her head. "I'd rather they believed I can take care of myself."

Angel snorted. "They're men. One day they'll outgrow that and become real people."

Miranda grinned and, unoffended, Colter gave a short burst of laughter. He tended to agree, although there were a few in his family who wouldn't. Not all of them had experience with strong women, like Angel and Cheney and, to a lesser degree, like Miranda. He wasn't sure she could ever pull the trigger on a man staring her down, even one threatening her life with a gun in his hand, without hesitation as Angel could. But to protect Dane and Dillon, yeah, she could do that. Colter's plan was to make sure she never had to.

After a few more minutes of play, Seth and Angel eased out of the pool. Angel gave Colter a questioning look as she wrapped a towel around herself. "Usual morning meeting, Boss?"

He nodded.

Seth didn't speak, just returned Colter's nod as the pair matched strides in the direction of their camper. They'd chosen a place not so near the barn as to be conspicuous in their comings and goings but near enough to mingle when they saw a need.

Without missing a beat, Colter grabbed a ball from the net full of water toys fastened to edge of the pool and moved toward the deep end.

He called Dane's name a split second before tossing the ball his way. Dane caught it and sent it hurling toward Dillon. They formed a triangle edging further away from one another with each pass to keep things interesting. The boys' shrieks filled the air as they raced each other to catch every throw. Sunlight sparkled across the waves they made.

Dillon finally missed a toss his way. After retrieving with the exuberance of the young, he hesitated then moved closer to Colter. A faint questioning frown creased his forehead.

"Did somebody hurt J.D. because he was a mean old buzzard?"

Colter felt every muscle tauten as he took in the sudden look of misery on the boy's face. He had to force a calmness before asking, "Did you hear someone call him that?"

Dillon nodded. "He said it." His voice quavered. "He always said it."

'Who said it?" Colter persisted, still keeping his voice

quiet and even.

"J.D." Dillon took a deep breath but didn't look away. "Every time he got sick or hurt himself he'd say he was a mean old buzzard, too mean to die. Sometimes he smiled but sometimes he didn't."

Colter took a deep breath of relief. "No. That's not why. J.D. meant to reassure you that he was plenty tough and could handle things that needed handling."

But he hadn't been able to handle something and that something had gotten him killed.

"Someone hurt him," Dillon persisted. "That's why you're here and Angel and Seth."

Colter met Miranda's gaze, saw her anguish at Dillon's sorrow, her worry at his anxiety.

"Yes, someone hurt him. But they won't hurt you because we *are* here."

"And they won't hurt Randa."

"No," Colter said, "they won't." Not unless they made it past him first which would mean he was no longer breathing and he didn't intend to let that happen.

The air held a chill as Miranda gathered the boys to dry and change for dinner. She gave Colter a nod from across the pool. He nodded in return and climbed out on the other side. After a quick shower and change he went back out, taking the path to the farthest cabin where Cheney waited for him.

She had the old wooden chair under her tilted on two legs, the ladder back against the front wall of the cabin. She raised the cup in her hand as he got close. "Hey, boss. Coffee's fresh."

Colter lifted a brow. "Good way to bust your behind."

"Mine to bust." Her smile was more of a smirk but, then, it usually was.

Chuckling, he stepped inside to fill the mug she'd placed beside the coffeepot, then walked back out and leaned against a porch post to face her. "Anything?" he asked.

"Early days for that question." She sighed. "But I know time is critical. And, no, not so far. Everything and everybody seem to be just what they seem to be. Riley's suspicious as hell."

"He's supposed to be."

"I know."

Cheney was holding back. He'd known her too long not to know.

He waited, then asked, "What's up?"

"Nothing of consequence."

He waited and she scowled. "One of the ranch hands … he's not much more than a kid, I think … I've caught him a time or two standing at the edge of the path, staring at the cabin and he followed me half over that hill out back."

Colter stilled. "He know you caught him at it?"

She gave him a look.

"So that's a no. What are you going to do about it?"

"I just did, since you pushed," she said, tilting her head at him questioningly to add, "and since I suspect you don't want me to blow my cover."

His grunt held as much irritation as it did amusement. He didn't need the reminder she could handle whatever came her way, with or without his help. "You're right. I don't. What's he look like?"

"Five-eight or -nine, maybe one-fifty, pale hair that needs a wash and a trim. Scraggly beard that needs shaved.

Good shoulders, though, and a straight back."

"Looks like he stared long enough for you to get a good look. Consider it handled."

Cheney nodded and her next words told him she did, indeed, consider it handled. Her mind had already moved on. "I'm glad Seth and Angel are here. Those are two cute little boys." Then she lifted a very direct gaze to his. "We're missing something, Boss. It has to be here but we're missing it."

"Maybe. Or maybe it isn't. Pederson made some enemies. I'll keep looking there."

"And I'll keep looking here."

Riley sat on the long bench in front of the barn as he passed back by. He gave a nod as Colter looked his way. "Noticed you met the girl."

Amused, Colter didn't point out the fact that he would've had to do some standing and gazing down the path for that 'noticing'. All he said was, "Miranda told me she showed up out of nowhere … and what little she knows of her story. I'm not crazy about her being here."

Riley bristled. "Can't say as I'm crazy about you being here, either, but both decisions are Miranda's to make."

Colter gave a grunt of laughter at the other man's blunt honesty. "Fair enough. Even so, I plan to have someone in my team dig a little, see what teens have been reported missing in the surrounding counties."

"I imagine they'll be sorting through more than a few," Riley was quick to point out, so quick Colter wondered if he felt a little defensive about not having the resources to do the same.

"They get paid to do that sorting."

Riley rubbed the bristles along his jaw and stared off into the distance before returning his gaze to Colter's. "Truth be told, I kinda don't mind knowing you'll do that. Randa put some worries in my mind, thinking the girl might be mixed up in some kind of drug mess."

"Plenty of that going around," Colter acknowledged. "And always worth worrying about."

Colter turned as if to go and then hesitated, turning back. "Who's the kid with the scraggly mustache?"

"Got a couple match that."

"Both light haired?"

"Nope. Marley's hair is as brown as his skin. That'd be Grayson. Why?"

"Noticed him a time or two standing out near the girl's cabin. He wasn't doing anything wrong as far as I could see. Standing and staring. I wondered, is all."

Riley scowled. "Might be nothing wrong, but might not be doing what he's paid to do. I'll take care of that."

Colter nodded and turned to leave but Riley spoke again, turning him back. "You mind letting me know if you find something on the girl? Something that makes her not a good person to have a around Dane and Dillon?"

"You and Miranda both. I don't suspect I will, but it never hurts to check and double-check."

Riley's shoulders eased a little and he nodded.

Colter headed back toward the house. Subterfuge, necessity that it was, always left him feeling uncomfortable. Fortunately, he'd learned to live with that discomfort long ago. It came with the job.

Chapter Fifteen

An early evening storm rumbled and flashed in the distance as Colter combed through the latest round of files sent his way, some pending cases, some potential new clients. Most were not his and tagged with an info-only heading. The drapes were pulled wide and the occasional lightning streaks drew his gaze from his computer screen to the sliding glass doors.

He'd been at the small corner desk little more than an hour but hadn't yet heard Miranda come upstairs. But he wouldn't unless she crossed the upstairs balcony. It bothered him that he listened for her but not to any great degree. Interest was one thing, intentions were another. He had no intentions.

When she did step out of her room and past his door, she held a nice Cabernet by the neck of the bottle in one hand and two glasses in the other. She didn't so much as glance his way but lifted the two glasses slightly as she passed.

He smiled ruefully and followed her out. Instead of the swing, she sat in one of two chairs which looked out over the open hills in the distance. Between the chairs stood a small table, one he didn't recall seeing previously, where she'd placed the wine and the short-stemmed Bordeaux glasses. She'd poured wine into both, so he sat and picked up the one closest to him.

"What next?" Her question held neither weariness nor discouragement and not much patience, either, he decided.

"What do you know about a man named Newland? Arthur Newland."

"He broke faith with J.D. on their contract. J.D. took him to court and Newland lost."

Colter nodded and agreed, "He did. A pretty devastating loss."

She shot him a look. "You think he shouldn't have?"

"The court made the right decision. The only reasonable and fair decision."

After a sip of wine, Miranda nodded. "I was young—involved in the working aspect of the ranch but not at all in the business end of it—when all of that happened. After the jury decided and the judge ruled, J.D. gave the entire court transcript to me and had me read it line by line. It took days."

"Not very fascinating I would imagine."

"On the contrary." He could see her faint smile as she continued, "J.D. made at least half a dozen school lessons out of that court case ... on the worth of a man's word, on ethics in general, on trust-but-verify, on good business practices in general, on when to give grace, when to give up, and when to dig in, and on an iron-clad contract—even between friends."

"I'd say those were some pretty good lessons."

"J.D. was good at finding ways from real life to teach me the things he needed me to know."

"You miss him." Even as he said the words, he felt uneasy with himself. She was a client. He couldn't afford to see her as anything other than that.

"I do." Her voice was low, almost too quiet to hear. "Every day. Every time the twins look at me missing him, trusting me to keep them safe, depending on me." She took a deep breath. "Why did you ask about Newland?"

He pulled his thoughts back to the impersonal, back to the case that, after all, was his reason for being here at this ranch and at this moment in time. Justice for J.D., safety for the woman he'd loved as his daughter and safety for his sons.

"He committed suicide a little over a year ago."

"How horrible for his family," she murmured.

"Also eliminates him as a suspect..."

She tilted her head at his tone. "But?"

"He left a son ... not all that much older than you ... whose mother and baby sister are buried in the middle of Pederson land."

"J.D. offered Newland a permanent easement." Her answer was swift and her tone defensive.

"Which he turned down," Colter acknowledged. "But the son may feel otherwise."

"Enough to murder J.D.? After all these years?" The look she gave him was as dubious as her words.

"The suicide of a family member can trigger all kinds of long-buried thoughts and feelings ... trigger any number of actions."

"So, you want to meet him, get a feel for him, like you did Bentley." She shrugged. "I don't know ... seems a little far-fetched to me."

"Sometimes solving a murder is as much about eliminating suspects as it is identifying them."

She tipped the bottle, adding wine to the glass she hadn't yet emptied. "Fine. Where is the younger Mr. Newland."

"Santa Fe."

She stared into her glass thoughtfully. "I have an appointment in Santa Fe. We could combine."

"We could," he agreed. "And maybe have dinner with my folks. They've asked to meet you."

She looked up startled. "Me? Why?"

He shrugged. "Family."

"I'm not a Bellamy or a Slade or a Welles."

"You'd be wrong there. Dane and Dillon are blood relatives. The emotional as much as the legal tie between the three of you ... that makes you their family as well."

She set her glass on the table and stood. "I'll meet them. But that's all. No strings."

He smiled in the dark as she stepped back into her room. Those strings, more like threads, were already in place. Threads of protection, threads of loyalty. By the time she understood that, she would also understand they didn't bind or restrict or govern. She could walk away. Most didn't. Some, like Cheney's parents, did exactly that. As Jerica Pederson had done.

Which reminded him that he had yet to see a file or report on the twins' mother. He wasn't overly concerned for her well-being. She'd left Pederson and given up all rights to her sons long ago, by default, if not by intent. A judge had ruled in J.D.'s favor and granted full custody within weeks of her walking away. It seemed unlikely that

Jerica would be targeted by anyone but her first husband—and Bentley remained low on Colter's list of potentials for J.D.'s death. Even so, he'd see if Jonah had verification on her current whereabouts. Whether she and her most recent were still in Australia or if they had returned stateside.

The next couple of days were quiet but it was a brooding kind of quiet, weighted with afternoon storms and sluggish nights. No one, not Angel or Seth or Cheney, heard or saw anything worth reporting. That was a good thing as far as Seth and Angel were concerned. Their primary purpose was the safety of the twins. For Cheney it was a frustration Colter heard each time she reported in to him.

Newland's son lived in one of the nicer outskirts of the small city. His property was well-landscaped with a sweeping view of mountain peaks in the distance.

"That view must be stunning in the fall when the aspens turn to gold," Miranda murmured as Colter followed the winding paved drive through several acres.

They'd timed their arrival for mid-morning to accommodate her early afternoon appointment with Clark & Sons. Colter parked in front of a four-car garage and she turned to find his gaze fixed on her.

"That view is one of the many things which bring the hordes of tourists to Santa Fe summer, winter, spring, and fall."

"And the history and the food and the arts … the museums and opera," she defended with a smile. He lifted a brow and she chuckled. "And, yes, the ski resorts and the shopping. Still, Santa Fe was my favorite birthday trip destination. J.D. picked it the first time, a few months after my mama died, my first without her. I picked it two other birthdays."

"No Disney World?"

She laughed. "I can't even imagine J.D. in a theme park." Her laugh faded as she gazed at the sprawling designer's dream of a home in front of them. "He was a good man but I doubt the younger Mr. Newland will agree."

Colter nodded as he opened the truck door. "I suspect you're right but we'll know soon enough."

Miranda joined him at the hood of the truck.

Before they'd reached the end of the walk, the massive double doors were opened by a gentleman of indeterminate age in black silk pants and tunic. Not Newland, Colter knew, from the photographs that accompanied the files Jonah had forwarded. This face was unlined but the hair, brows, and mustache were a soft silver. The man nodded at their approach and stepped back in welcome, but Colter handed him a card before they entered. "We're not expected," he cautioned.

The pleasant expression did not falter. "As I'm aware, however, if you'll step into the foyer, I'll announce your arrival. Mr. Newland is not averse to unexpected company. My name is Evan, by the way."

Colter exchanged a glance with Miranda who shrugged before following Evan into the home. Just as the exterior did not follow the predominantly adobe architecture of Santa Fe, the interior reflected modern aesthetics. Colter found it boring but recognized the wealth reflected in the polished marble flooring.

Evan did not keep them waiting long—or rather his employer did not—and they were soon led into a long sunroom bathed in light despite the numerous shade trees that occupied a wide strip of property beyond the wall of glass. The younger Mr. Newland, Colter judged mid- to upper-thirties, was on his feet and waiting. He nodded at Evan who looked at Colter and Miranda. "Would you prefer coffee or tea? Lemonade? Or perhaps wine?"

When Miranda gave a small shake of her head, Colter opened his mouth to decline for them both but Newland said, "Bring it all, Evan. Or rather ask Ms. Hillburn to do so. You should join us."

Newland looked at Colter. "Welcome, Mr. Bellamy, and…" he looked at Miranda.

"Miranda Pederson."

"Ah." That was all. The one syllable that could mean anything, Colter thought. Or nothing. Then, "Please. Have a seat."

Newland waited until they chose a small sofa, then took one of two arm chairs opposite them. He sat forward, back erect, but otherwise seemed relaxed. Certainly, his expression was tranquil. Evan returned and settled in the second arm chair.

"So, Mr. Bellamy, I've heard of your family, of course. And," he nodded at Miranda, "I've heard of your father."

"Whom I recently lost," she said.

"My condolences." A slight rap at the edge of the room drew his attention. "Ah, Ms. Hillburn, thank you."

The woman carried nothing, but two young men behind her bore trays they placed with care upon the low table in front of the sofa. The young men walked away and the woman poured tea into thick mugs and handed one each to Evan and Newland before turning to Miranda.

"Water, please," Miranda said at her expectant look. Colter suspected it was more to be polite and show appreciation for her efforts than from thirst.

When the woman glanced at him, he shook his head. "Nothing, but thank you."

As she exited the room, Newland gave Colter a considering look. "How may I help you?"

"Actually, I'm simply accompanying Ms. Pederson at a difficult time."

Newland shifted his gaze. "The loss of a parent is … difficult."

"I'm aware you recently lost your own father as well," Miranda said, "and I'm terribly sorry for your loss. That, plus my father's accident are why I've come."

Although Newland's expression didn't change from polite concern, Colter was conscious of Evan tensing and shifting in his seat.

"Indeed?"

"In reading through some files, I came across some early documents and discovered that your mother and an infant sister are buried on Pederson land." She paused but Newland didn't comment. "My father gave yours permanent and legal rights to visit their graves."

Newland nodded and leaned back in his chair. "Which he never did."

Miranda nodded. "I know your father and mine parted on bad terms."

"Due to the unmitigated stupidity of mine," Newland returned bluntly. "But that's nothing to do with you or me."

"No, it isn't but I did want to extend the right to visit their graves to you."

Newland tilted his head and sighed. "I'm sure you're still grieving and emotional and this is a kindness but, to be honest, I scarcely recall my mother. My stepmother raised me and I'm grateful every day for the time I had her. As much as I appreciate your kindness and your empathy, I won't be visiting my mother's grave nor my father's, for that matter. Hers, because I can't remember her. His, because I wish I could forget him."

Evan made a soft sound which Colter thought could as easily have been sympathy as censure.

Colter found himself watching the other man more than Newland who shrugged and continued. "I realize that sounds harsh to someone grieving their own loss, and I apologize if that distresses you."

"No apology needed. I realize families aren't always nice and cozy," Miranda murmured. Colter suspected she was thinking of her blood father, now, rather than Pederson. She glanced at Colter and got to her feet. "We won't take any more of your time but please know you're welcome to visit your mother's gravesite should you change your mind."

Newland stood when Colter did, although Evan, his expression pensive, remained seated as they walked from the room. Not until he opened the door at the front entrance did Newland give Colter a direct look and comment, "I noted on your card that you are with the Slade Agency rather than the Bellamy Ranch. It occurs to me to wonder if you accompanied Ms. Pederson in a personal or professional role."

It wasn't a question. Even had it been, Colter wouldn't have answered. "It was a pleasure meeting you, Mr. Newland."

He glanced at Miranda who smiled at Newland. "Thank you for seeing us."

Newland tipped his head with a pleasant look and murmured, "My pleasure," then watched as they returned to the truck. Colter noted the door didn't close until he had the truck turned and facing the way they'd come.

Miranda looked at him as they drove away. "That was interesting."

Colter chuckled. "To say the least."

"And wasn't he the nosey one."

"A bit."

"Odd, too. Both of them. I thought Evan was a servant when he opened the door but then I thought maybe something different."

"I suspect maybe both."

Miranda looked at him with raised brows and an expression of dawning understanding. "Oh … maybe so. Evan seemed a good bit older than Newland, but perhaps that was due to the odd coloring of his hair and brows."

"Evan also seemed a little edgy when you mentioned your father's accident."

"I didn't notice that," she admitted. "Do you think it means something?"

"Everything means something," Colter said as he left the drive and pulled back onto the main road. "Whether or not it's relevant to us is something else again." And that, he thought, was too soon to know. One thing he thought certain, if Newland had anything to do with Pederson's death, it wasn't due to grief at his father's suicide.

Chapter Sixteen

At the outer edges of the city, Colter pulled into the paved parking lot of a large but unpretentious looking steak house and glanced at Miranda. "Will this work for lunch before your meeting with Clark & Sons?"

"I like steak."

At her shrug and mild response, he smiled. "They have other options."

She studied the windowless plank board front. "Mexican or Native American are also good options." He chuckled and held the door for her as she walked into the restaurant.

A wall of windows overlooking a mountain ridge, polished wide-plank flooring, and white linen table cloths, each graced by a low bowl of fresh flowers, hit the senses in almost the same instant as the enticing aromas. A host in sharply creased jeans and a sports jacket walked toward them with a smile and they followed him to a table next to the windows. He left them with an array of menus.

"Talk about a hidden gem," Miranda murmured as she picked up a menu of Thai cuisine.

Colter grinned. "We're lucky to be eating early. They don't do any advertising—word of mouth does it for them—and by noon, there won't be an empty seat in the place."

"You're not looking at a menu," she accused. "You're getting steak, aren't you?"

At that, he gave a short laugh. "No, but I do know what I want and, yes, I get the same thing every time I come here."

"Often?"

Watching as she looked around in delight, he was unexpectedly glad he and Dana had never been here. "Not often, no, but as often as I can."

He realized his tone must have reflected his thoughts when Miranda asked, "Did I say something wrong?"

"No. You didn't. See anything you like?"

"Only everything."

Despite that answer, she selected sushi from the Thai menu as confidently as he requested the cedar-plank salmon.

He lifted a brow when the waiter left with their orders. "Sushi?"

"You don't like?"

"I do. I didn't picture that for you."

"And I expected you to order a rib-eye or Porterhouse."

"Are you suggesting we stereotyped each other?"

She laughed at that and the green in her eyes sparkled as she looked back at him. "Didn't we?"

It was the first time he'd seen that kind of carefree look on her face and it took his breath. A reaction he didn't care for but couldn't seem to help.

Fortunately for his thoughts, which had scattered for the moment, a sommelier stopped beside their table. "I've viewed your menu selections. Shall I pair something for you or do you already have something in mind."

Colter glanced at Miranda who smiled at the sommelier. "I'm feeling adventurous. A pairing. But a single glass, please. I have a business meeting soon."

Colter nodded as well and the sommelier turned away, looking pleased.

"Are you?" he asked when they were alone again.

She tilted her head, forehead crinkling slightly. "Am I what?"

"Feeling adventurous?"

"Is that a dare of some kind?" She sounded dubious.

His ripple of laughter surprised him as much as he suspected it did her. "No, not at all. You seem ... different ... this morning." Not weighed down, was his thought, but he didn't want to say it so bluntly, didn't want to remind her of all that waited for her in Taos.

Still, it was inevitable, he supposed, that her thoughts would go there. She looked pensive as she picked up her water glass and gently swirled the slice of lemon that topped the ice.

"I don't think I've drawn an easy breath since J.D. was killed. The grief was the hardest thing I've ever experienced. Knowing ... believing now ... that someone intentionally hurt him, took his life, and took him away from us, has been crushing. I've felt almost suffocated by fear for Dane and Dillon," she admitted. She raised her eyes to his. "I needed to get away for a little while. I wouldn't have, couldn't have, if I didn't know that your team were there guarding them. Riley and Lila, both, would give their lives for them, but they aren't professionals."

He nodded. "I don't think we're dealing with professionals, but I don't think that makes this job any easier." And maybe harder in ways, he thought. Professionals, while skilled, were often predictable. Amateurs were like bottle rockets lit by a kid. It was hard to tell which way they would head and almost impossible to dodge with any degree of accuracy. "What you can count on, though, is that Seth and Angel know what they're doing and they do it well." And Cheney was his ace in the hole. As far as payroll records indicated, there were no real newcomers to the ranch hands. But if someone wanted justice for past wrongs, real or perceived, events could have been put in motion long ago.

But Colter left all of that unsaid and turned the conversation to the mountains displayed beyond the panoramic windows. He wanted Miranda to enjoy this lunch. Her problems weren't going anywhere, but they could be put to one side for few moments.

"Are you a mountain climber?"

Her gaze followed his to the mountain peaks and she shook her head. "Not me. Nor a skier. You?"

"I've tried both," he admitted. "Once each."

"Sometimes once is enough," she agreed with a smile.

"What was a 'once is enough' for you," he asked.

"Ferris Wheel."

"Seriously?"

"One of those ridiculous, over-sized ones at a theme park. I was eight and hated every moment. In fact, I hated the theme park. Poor J.D. thought it would be a great birthday treat." Her faint smile told him she appreciated the memory more than she had the experience. "He made sure birthdays after that were all about horses and the ranch. Boring by most standards, I suppose, but it was what I loved."

He leaned back in his chair. "You've been a partner with J.D. in the ranch since age seventeen. My guess is you can tell within a few hours when a cow is ready to calve and you can judge from an aerial when it's time to move a herd to the next pasture. The scent on the wind is enough to give warning that a winter storm is headed toward the ranch. A glance at a spreadsheet you've created gives you the break-even price on beef as well as the profit level." He held her gaze and shook his head. "Boring? No. Not remotely."

Lunch, Miranda decided afterward, had been interesting. And the most interesting aspect was that she had found herself relaxing into their conversation as he'd talked about his family and the day-to-day operations of a business that she, and everyone else in the state, had heard about for years. But he'd given her glimpses into the personal side of what she'd always imagined was an impersonal conglomeration.

She'd known their history. Most anyone in the state did to some extent. But seeing Colter now, hearing him speak of them, not as a business aggregate, but as individuals with a blood bond gave her a different perspective. Life in Texas hadn't been easy for the three young couples. They'd fought with Indians and loved with them, fought outlaws and been outlaws. Life in New Mexico was no easier, but they hadn't come looking for easy. They'd wanted a chance at better. They found a friend in Kit Carson when they arrived and sent their roots deep into the rocky, mountainous soil.

She thought of J.D and could picture him doing the same, packing up his young family and leaving a land that had lost its welcome in hopes of finding a future with more promise. He had that kind of courage. She saw that in Colter.

She was sorry when the meal ended, when it was time to go. It had been a welcome interlude, but it couldn't keep her problems at bay.

As they returned to the truck, she realized she was dreading the meeting with J.D.'s money manager. Not because she feared an unpleasant surprise but because it was yet another step in the distance between the comfort of her memories and the strangeness of what awaited her in the years ahead.

Colter elected to wait in the truck with his phone and tablet, but Miranda had not a doubt that he watched as the door opened to her and she stepped inside.

Somehow, she'd thought to find large and lush. She did find the lush—at least a masculine version of it—but the space was small. Comfortably so. There was a front desk, narrow and elegant. And empty. Double doors beyond framed a massive desk she suspected was made from honey locust. The grain was similar to the side tables in the main room at the ranch. They'd been custom made from one of the trees felled by lightning a few years back.

She stepped close enough to knock on the doorframe and a man dressed in what she considered business casual turned away from the filing cabinet with a quick smile.

"Miss Pederson! My apologies. I let myself get distracted." He held out his hand. "I'm pleased to meet you," then added as his smile faded, "but not under these circumstances."

"Thank you." She hesitated, judging his age to be early-to-mid-thirties. "Am I meeting with you or your father?"

His smile returned. "I'm Jameson Clark." He turned the photo on the wide desk so that she could see. "These are my sons. Andrew is fifteen and Mason is thirteen. They're my retirement plan in a couple of decades."

Their wide grins reminded her of Dane and Dillon. "They're handsome boys."

"Smart, too. Not that I'm prejudiced or anything. But, please, sit down," he said, gesturing her not toward the chairs in front of his desk but toward the two arm chairs in an alcove angled toward one another.

She felt some of the tension ease from her shoulders. She liked him, almost instinctively. She was comfortable with him. None of this had been easy but she couldn't imagine him making it any harder.

When they were seated, he leaned slightly forward. "You wanted to meet and I was glad for the opportunity but you didn't specify concerns." He gestured toward a folder lying on the small table between them. "I have your father's key documents here and will be glad to go over them with you."

Miranda shook her head. "I reviewed the copies Liz … J.D.'s attorney gave me. Everything seemed very straightforward."

He nodded. "I've done business with Elizabeth Langley. She's a good person to have on your side." The slightest frown creased his forehead as he leaned back in his chair. "Ms. Pederson, I'll be honored to serve you as I did J.D. and will make whatever changes you'd like to how your brothers' wealth is managed, but I'll also understand if you have your own person, a different company, you prefer to work with."

"I didn't mention concerns because I don't have any and I don't want or plan any changes to what J.D. has in place. I hope you'll continue to manage Dane and Dillon's money as well as mine, if you will." She took a deep breath. "It was J.D.'s habit to establish a face-to-face relationship with those who helped him keep his life on an even keel. That's a habit he engrained in me and one I intend to continue."

To her surprise, Jameson looked away and blinked. "J.D. was a good man. One of the best. I'll miss him." He turned his gaze back to her. "I'll take care of your interests and his sons as carefully as I did his."

She smiled and stood. "Thank you. I know this has been brief and I'm truly grateful for your time but I won't take more of it today. It's been a long couple of weeks and I'm more tired than I can say."

He stood as soon as she did. "I'll see you regularly then, as I did J.D.?"

"Monthly without fail but call between times if we need to meet." She started toward the door.

"I'll keep you apprised of market changes and concerns."

She paused at the door. "Preferably not every small thing. I trust you to continue to make the same type judgement calls you did with my dad."

He chuckled. "No, not every small thing. J.D. and I agreed not to overreact to volatile markets unless they looked to become out of hand. If that happens, I'll be in touch."

"And, otherwise, I'll see you once a month or so." She stopped and looked him in the eye. "Losing J.D ... moving forward without him ... is the hardest thing I've ever had to face. Thank you for making this part of it a little less hard."

He nodded. "Call, any time, for any reason."

Colter was leaning against the hood of his truck, phone to his ear, as he watched her come down the walk toward him. He ended the call as she came close. "Everything okay?"

"All good," she murmured.

They climbed inside and he started the engine.

"He seems like a good person. I think J.D. chose well."

"Yes, to both."

It took a moment for realization to sink in. "You had him investigated."

"Of course." He turned the truck smoothly onto the highway for Albuquerque, leaving the picturesque 'city different', as it called itself, behind them.

"And Liz Langley? J.D.'s attorney?"

"Again … of course." He glanced at her across the truck seat. "Troublesome?"

She thought about that. Not so long ago, she would have answered in the affirmative. But that was then. "No. Not troublesome."

During the miles between Santa Fe and Albuquerque, she called Wes and Riley and Lila. They would have called her if all were not well, but it eased her to have that contact, to hear the words 'everything fine here, boss'. And it made her smile all three times. They all, every one of them, knew she preferred being called by her name rather than boss. J.D. had been boss, always would be as far as she was concerned. But still she smiled because of the affection in their voices when they said it just the way they would have said it to J.D.

Lila teased her with the fact that she was making one of Miranda's favorite meals for dinner that evening, Wes bragged on Dane's latest science project, and Riley warned her twice about Albuquerque's crime rate.

"I'll be on my toes, Riley, I promise."

She sighed as she ended the conversation and settled into the leather seat of the truck until the Sandia Mountains came into view.

"He doesn't like you out of his sight," Colter said.

"No. He and J.D. tag-teamed me when I was growing up. I was with one or the other until I left for college and, even then, I had to check in once a day, every day, sometimes twice. Things were a little different when I was out of school and back at the ranch for good. But since J.D.'s wreck, Riley's been worse than he ever was."

"You can understand that."

"I do. To be honest, I worry as much about Riley as I do the twins. They're so young and unaware and he's getting on in age and maybe not as alert as he once was."

"Don't underestimate Riley." Colter said. "He's as smart and tough as they come. He won't let his guard down. He just needs to know you won't either. Besides, he's right about Albuquerque's crime rate. Things are getting better, but we have more than our share."

She looked at the buildings that rose around them as they entered the downtown area. "We don't seem to be headed into the ghettos."

Colter smiled as he turned into a private parking garage where she had a quick impression of a uniformed guard posted on either side. He stopped at a security station and was greeted by name and the attendant tipped his hat to Miranda as Colter introduced them.

"You own the building?" she asked as he pulled forward into a space right behind security.

"This and a few more. We occupy one floor on each of the others and rent the rest of the space. We're more spread out in this one. A guest suite on the top floor. A large conference room and several small ones on another. The corporate offices for the Slade Agency occupy the floor right above the conference rooms."

She let that information soak a minute and then shivered. "Different buildings. If you're targeted, you're separated."

"One reason," he acknowledged. "Not the only but … yeah … one of them."

Her first thought was that she couldn't fathom having to worry that an entire, extended family could be at risk. Her second was that—not so long ago—she couldn't have imagined J.D. murdered.

He stepped out of the truck and walked around to open her door, giving her a hand she didn't need, but took as she climbed down. "We're a few floors up but I thought you might want to stretch your legs before we hit the elevator. There's a place to walk right across the street."

She glanced at him. "I noticed what appeared to be a tiny park," she admitted. "It looked nice."

"It is. I'll show you." He put his hand on her back and guided her back toward a gated walk-through entrance.

"Also, the family's?" she hazarded.

"You make us sound like a gang of mobsters," he said wryly as he entered a code on a brick column and the iron gate slid to one side.

She laughed at the image. Despite his demurral, she didn't miss that one of the guards moved attentively out from his post as they stepped onto the sidewalk.

The next moments blurred as she heard a shout and the squeal of tires before hands gripped her arms, whirling her back from the street and toward the building. Over the guard's shoulder, she caught sight of Colter as he stepped off the sidewalk, pistol drawn. He fired several shots at a retreating SUV. One struck metal. The vehicle fishtailed but was quickly righted and didn't slow.

Chapter Seventeen

Cursing fluently, Colter came toward her, his gaze skimming her from face to toe before he took a long breath. "You're okay."

"I am." She went for a smile but failed as she said, "That was fun."

He drew her in against him for a moment and for a moment, she let him. Then she stepped back and Colter turned his attention to the guard. "You're Freeman."

"Yes, sir." His voice was steady but his face was pale. Miranda judged him in his late twenties. Maybe.

"Thank you." It was simply said but Miranda saw how firmly Colter gripped the man's hand as he shook it. "We're headed up now. Come with us."

"Yes, sir," he said again, his voice a little less steady at the request or the fact that he'd just spun a Bellamy guest on her heels, although for the best of reasons.

Colter slipped his arm around Miranda again and they walked into the building and an elevator immediately on their right. There were no less than four uniforms surrounding them by now, although she couldn't have said where they came from.

Her heart was still pounding as the elevator doors slid closed, and she took several deep breaths.

Colter frowned. "Are you okay?"

"I am." But she wasn't.

Colter's frown didn't fade, and she knew he knew she lied.

As the doors slid open again, Colter looked at Freeman. "This is Ms. Pederson. Miranda Pederson. She's family."

She wouldn't have thought the young man's face could hold less color. She was wrong.

Again, "Yes, sir," was all he said.

They stepped out into a space almost too large to qualify as a hallway. She had an impression of pale walls and dark wood floors but an impression was all she had time to absorb. There was a crowd waiting for them. Within moments, Miranda found herself surrounded and escorted into a conference room with comfortable seating. She recognized no one, but a young woman asked if she or Colter preferred coffee, tea, or wine. Miranda shook her head but did her best to smile in thanks. Colter asked for a shot of whiskey, "God knows I need it."

A man who looked a lot like Colter, and appeared about the same age, was barking orders into a phone. "I want the videos in five minutes and any eye witnesses you can track down in ten."

Another man, with eyes and nose like a hawk, leaned against a wall, phone pressed to his ear. "Mr. Bellamy, yes sir, they're fine. Yes, sir, someone will be waiting to take your car. No, sir, no medical needed."

A woman in dark jeans and a white vee neck stepped into the room and Colter said, "Thank God, Hamilton, take charge. Freeman?"

The young guard stepped forward. "Sir?"

"Go with Hamilton. Cassidy?"

"Yes, sir." Another woman, this one in a suit, with cropped gray hair and large, dark eyes. Asian, maybe, diminutive certainly, but somehow impressive.

"Freeman is reassigned to Hamilton. Salary commensurate with position."

"With Hamilton, sir? He's a new hire, just getting his feet on the ground."

"He heard that motor rev and acted before he saw anything. If he hadn't, Ms. Pederson would be on her way to the hospital." Or the morgue. That thought rattled him more than he was comfortable acknowledging.

"Yes sir, done."

Overwhelmed, Miranda didn't even try to follow the several conversations going on within her hearing. She simply let the words flow around her. The young woman who'd asked what she wanted returned with a tray carrying a small whiskey glass and a large water glass as well as a glass of dark wine. Colter took the whiskey and placed both the water and the wine in front of Miranda. "In case you change your mind."

She took a sip of the water and stared at the wall in front of her. A moment later, she heard his voice again, close to her ear. "Are you okay?"

"No."

"I'm here."

"I'm glad." And she was, but she still wasn't okay. She

wasn't worried for herself but for the twins. They were so far away. What was happening? Anything? Nothing? How would she know? A wave of nausea hit her and she took another shaky breath.

"What?" Colter asked.

"My brothers. I need to know."

He stepped away and her gaze tracked him as he made a call while pacing the room. When he came back to her, he said, "Dane and Dillon are safe. I've moved Angel and Seth into the house and told them no one goes in or out until we return. Cheney is on high alert. I can promise one thing if nothing else. All three will die before harm comes to your brothers."

She closed her eyes and leaned her head against the high seat back. "Thank you." She'd never meant anything more, never been more grateful, and still she wanted to be home. She wanted to see them for herself. But she knew Colter had things to finish here if she were ever going to draw another easy breath over the twins.

A whirring sound had her straightening and opening her eyes. A screen lowered on a side wall and she turned her chair enough to better see the images that slid into focus then shifted to make room for the next. For a moment it was dizzying, like watching a kaleidoscope, but she focused on the center and found she was also able to absorb the ones on the perimeter.

She was, she realized, looking down at the front of the building from several angles and heights. What she had thought were stills proved to be videos as a bird dropped into view and landed on the sidewalk. Distant street sounds made themselves heard. The short, impatient beep of a horn. A siren far away.

The moment she and Colter emerged from the shadows

of the parking garage, she held her breath as did—or so it seemed from the sudden silence—every other person in the room. The guard stepped smartly from his position at the wall. She focused on him, saw his head turn sharply an instant before she heard the sound of a motor, loud in the silence now, yet not so loud that her mind had registered it in the moment.

She felt Colter place a hand on her shoulder, a light touch at the curve of her neck. The warmth and weight of it reassured as she watched the guard move closer to her. When an SUV—gunmetal gray with a glitter beneath the dirt that covered it—came into sight, the guard moved to intercept the step that would have taken her into the street, Colter right behind her.

It was clear the moment the driver stomped the gas. The engine roared and settled smoothly into a high-rate of speed.

Miranda felt again that dizzying moment when the guard had spun her away from the street and the fast-moving vehicle.

Someone must have given a command because the video froze at the moment the SUV was at its nearest position on the screen. Someone in the room spoke quietly but clearly into the silence. "An older model with a body-on-frame design. The driver's height appears between five-six and -nine. The mock turtleneck was worn to disguise the line of the driver's neck and jaw but, from the chin, this person does not appear bulky. The ballcap could cover a bald pate or a headful of curls pulled up and wrapped tight. The sunshades make it difficult to say anything about the shape of the eyes."

"Are you leaning toward a male or female?"

Everyone in the room turned to look at the man who'd

stopped in the doorway to study the screen.

"No, sir, I'm not leaning in either direction at the moment. The seat could be set at its lowest point or its highest."

"Making the vehicle difficult to maneuver when you factor in length of legs and knees…"

"…as well as arm reach. I concur. Now, if you'll let me continue with my assessment…"

Miranda caught her breath before it became an audible gasp but the rest of the room was swept by a faint ripple of laughter.

Even the man in the doorway chuckled. "Damn, Jade. Carry on."

"Thanks, Uncle Reggie. As I was saying … or trying to…" more laughter "we aren't looking at a master of disguise but someone who made a good attempt at hiding key factors. We'll use a facial recognition program to attempt an identification, just in case the person is in our database."

As the young woman continued speaking, the man's gaze swept the room and he started walking toward Miranda and Colter, circling the room to avoid passing in front of the projected images.

He reached them as Jade finished and asked if there were any questions. He nodded at Miranda and murmured, "Reginald Bellamy. I'm happy to meet you, Miss Pederson, but hoped for better circumstances over dinner this evening," then looked at Colter and nodded. "Son."

Miranda looked from one to the other and knew exactly how Colter would look in thirty years. Their bone structure was the same—the high bridge of their noses, their strong chins, the slight arch to their brows which, on a woman, would be elegant but gave the two of them slightly sardonic expressions.

"Dad."

Miranda could see the affection that passed between the two with that simple greeting and the look they exchanged.

"When we're done here, Jonah will be waiting in my office with the city police who need to take your statements. They're with Freeman now. We'll complete that business and talk after. Your mother has arrived. She's on her way up and she's not happy."

And that, Colter thought as Adrianne Bellamy stalked into the room, was another typical understatement. His mother could be graceful when the occasion called for it. Now was not that occasion. And, no, Colter thought as he stifled a wry smile, she was not happy and she'd be a hell of a lot less so if reminded that her family, more often than not, found her entertaining.

Her auburn hair, still long and silky, was coiled tightly at the back of her head. She hadn't bothered with makeup. She almost never did. Nor did she need it.

"Hello, Mama," Colter said as she stopped in front of him.

Her gaze—assessing, slightly anxious, and a great deal pissed—searched his face. "Reggie said you weren't hurt."

"No. I'm not."

Relief brought a return of her famous, or infamous, tart tongue. "So, why didn't you hit your target?"

Colter smiled. He knew where this was going. Bloodthirsty woman, his mama. "I hit exactly where I was aiming."

"Then you weren't aiming at the right thing. That driver should be on his way to the morgue."

With that, she turned from him and crossed to Miranda who stood as she approached.

"You're not harmed?"

"I'm fine, Mrs. Bellamy, but thank you."

"Addie, please." She glanced at the table. "You didn't have your wine and that water looks untouched as well." Without waiting for a response, she walked to the sideboard and flipped two glasses before pouring a shot of brandy in each. Returning, she handed one to Miranda and said, "Drink," then proceeded to down her own.

To Colter's surprise, Miranda did the same.

Addie looked toward her husband and nodded.

"Team," Reggie said, with a rueful look around the room, "we may now resume."

Jade concluded with the comment that one of Colter's bullets appeared to have hit the tire, flattening it, as he'd intended, another hit the hubcap, the third hit near the base of the bumper as the driver struggled to control the swerving vehicle. Despite the fact that the vehicle would have been limping along within moments after the tire was hit, it had not yet been located.

Miranda's nerves had settled, whether from the shot of brandy or simply from being surrounded by a team that exuded competence as well as confidence. As she walked into Reggie Bellamy's office beside Colter, Miranda took a quick look around before her gaze settled on the man and woman in suits that screamed plainclothes cop before moving to the man in more casual slacks and knit pullover seated at the small conference table with them.

All three of them stood, but one stepped forward.

"Jonah Slade," Colter said, by way of introduction,

"Miranda Pederson."

She took the hand he offered but instead of a shake, he placed his other hand palm down over hers. "I'm sorry for the poor welcome, Miranda. We'll do better next time."

They exchanged smiles before she turned with Colter to the officers, one seasoned with weathered features, the other younger with more than a hint of eagerness in her eyes. As soon as Miranda took the seat Colter pulled out for her, the officers returned to their seats. Colter sat on one side of her, Jonah on the other.

The officers introduced themselves and dove into the matter foremost on all of their minds. The older one, Gerard, took the lead. "We watched the video." Miranda's gaze followed his gesture toward a wall. The screen there was smaller and more discreet than the one downstairs but still larger than a monitor screen. "Do either of you recall anything beyond what can be seen and heard on the video? Take a moment and close your eyes if you need to." He looked at her first. "Ms. Pederson?"

"No. I've tried. I tried downstairs and as we were coming up from the conference room. When we arrived, I'd noticed the garden across the street. We were going there for a moment." She swallowed and took a breath. "The guard ... Freeman ... grabbed me before I saw or heard anything that didn't seem ... right."

He shifted his focus to Colter who shook his head. "I heard the SUV before I saw it, primarily because the engine sounded like a V8."

"That's a lot of power for downtown traffic," the younger officer, Williams, murmured.

"A lot of power under any conditions," Colter affirmed, "but even with that, I didn't associate it with any immediate threat. Not until it rounded the corner, and by then Freeman had reacted and pulled Ms. Pederson back so I pulled my gun."

"And discharged a firearm multiple times into a city street," Williams said.

Gerard shot his partner a quelling look as Colter answered without a hint of irritation, "With a clear line to my target, added to the fact that the driver was using their vehicle as a lethal weapon and a danger to anyone in their path." He looked at Gerard. "I'm sure you've checked my license and registration."

"I'm sure they're all still in order," Gerard returned, giving his companion another sharp glance.

Williams ignored the warning, "It's a good thing you own this building, given how close you were."

At that, Gerard stood. "Officer Williams, please wait for me at the elevator. Mr. Bellamy, your stint with the department isn't forgotten. The captain would welcome you back with open arms."

"Not a chance." Colter smiled, softened his words. "It was good training and good experience but not a career goal for me."

Gerard watched as Williams cleared the room then shook his head. "I'm her third and final opportunity as a trainee. The first two requested her transfer before a month was out. I'm doing my best but I don't think she's going to make it."

"Some don't," Colter said.

Miranda tried to feel at least a touch of sympathy for the young woman but couldn't muster it. If she was too hardheaded to learn from her mistakes, she was too hardheaded to succeed.

"Some don't," Gerard agreed. "We'll run a close-up of the driver through a facial recognition program."

Miranda noticed that no one mentioned that the Slade Agency planned to do the same.

"But you don't expect to find anything," Jonah said.

"Always possible," Gerard agreed, "but unlikely. This was an amateur attempt."

Miranda frowned. "And what would mark it as professional?"

Gerard gave her a quick smile. "Good question. An unremarkable vehicle in an unremarkable color. A less busy time of day. A less obvious place than the front entrance of the Slade Agency."

"But if they were already on our trail, perhaps this wasn't the intended time or place, but an opportunity seized?"

"Even more amateur," Gerard answered. "Pros plan to the nth degree. Few would jump on an opportunity for no other reason than it presented itself."

"And pros don't drive gunmetal metallic gray utility vehicles on a hit," Jonah inserted.

Miranda gave a slow nod. That was a standout color. Dirty but standout.

"So, we have an amateur," Colter agreed. "And probably desperate."

"Unfortunately, yes. Or getting there."

Chapter Eighteen

The officers left moments before Colter's parents walked into the office. Addie's gaze went straight to Miranda and she nodded as if reassured by what she saw.

"We'd planned dinner out but it's getting late. You'll want to be home tonight, I'm sure. Our chef is already upstairs and we'll dine there so you can be on your way home soon."

Reggie frowned. "Whoa. I thought they could stay in the suite here tonight and rest before heading back tomorrow."

"Miranda will want to get home to the twins."

Miranda looked at her with touch of surprise and more than a touch of gratitude. Beyond the sharp and maybe acerbic businesswoman exterior, Addie Bellamy had a mother's heart.

Addie looked at Jonah. "You'll join us for dinner, Jonah. We've more to discuss."

It wasn't worded as a request, but he nodded and smiled. "Of course. Thank you."

Miranda took a deep breath and nerved herself for more discussion, but Addie surprised her again by saying, "Let's go upstairs where we can relax for a bit before dinner. I want to hear all about those boys."

Upstairs, Miranda thought, was nice. Not sumptuous or decadent as she'd almost expected, just comfortably nice. One end of the room held a large dining table, which was being laid for dinner. The other end was a sitting area, a spacious one, where a coffee service was being arranged beside a bowl of flowers. The staff moving with quiet efficiency about the room were drawn in by greetings and introductions and amusing stories, while the family arranged themselves on eclectic furnishings that looked to have been chosen more for comfort than cohesion.

True to her word, Addie wanted to talk about Dane and Dillon, asking dozens of questions about their interests and lessons, and listening with concentration to Miranda's responses.

"And they have a tutor who homeschools them?"

"Yes. I did as well. We live so far out. J.D. always said sitting on a bus was a waste of daylight hours." She shrugged. "I think it was more because he liked having us around. I stayed far ahead of the school curriculum and the boys are as well."

Reggie nodded. "Leaves more time for them to learn what they'll need to know to run their own ranch someday."

For a moment Miranda wondered why he hadn't

assumed that J.D.'s ranch would come to them when they were of age then recalled the will had been probated and was now public. Even more probable was that they'd had access through Colter's role as deputy. The realization didn't bother her as much as it once would have.

"Do they want to be ranchers?" Addie asked.

"On what day of the week?" Miranda asked with a rueful smile.

Addie chuckled. "And which month of the year?"

"Exactly, but they're learning ranch life as well as academics and local history and culture."

"That's right." Reggie snapped his fingers. "They were leaving a museum when that tutor realized he was being tailed." He looked at Colter. "Did you ever ask him if he was interested in the formal training I suggested?"

Miranda raised her brow but Colter gave a quick shake of his head. "I told you I wasn't going to do that. He's far too valuable to the boys as he is. We can provide all the guards the boys will ever need, now and after this business is finished, if Miranda wants."

"I suppose. And Angel and Seth are guarding them now, right?" Reggie's brows were drawn together.

"They're in the house with them until Miranda and I get back, then they'll return to the perimeter."

"And Cheney's there as well?"

Colter did no more than nod but Jonah leaned forward at the name. "Cheney. How's she doing?"

"Seems solid," Colter answered him. "Has been for a while, Jonah, otherwise I wouldn't have brought her in."

Jonah frowned. "I've been trying to keep that girl alive since I found her."

And that, Miranda thought, was the least reassuring thing she'd heard all day.

* * *

Colter watched Miranda navigate the evening the way she had navigated the day. On some level, he understood how difficult all of this was, the caring questions from his parents, the easy conversation about everything but the vehicle rocketing toward her at deadly speed, being away from home, away from the boys when she was so desperately worried about their safety. He also knew nothing would be easier until J.D.'s murderer was found and punished.

But for now, he knew she wanted to be home, and he needed to get her there. As coffee and dessert were passed after dinner, he gave a subtle 'wrap it up' signal to his mother who gave him a nod and smile that were just as discreet.

His dad, however, missed their signal and had one last question as he walked them to the door. "Miranda, who stands to gain if you were out of the way?"

For a moment, she looked startled, then shook her head. "No one. I don't know. I haven't even made a will, yet. I sent Liz … my attorney … my thoughts. I'm supposed to meet with her this week to finalize." She took a deep breath. "I suppose the twins would … by default. And they are my primary concern. If something happens to me, they would become wards of the state."

Her stricken expression made Colter's insides clench. "I have no intention of letting anything happen to you." But it almost had today. The realization pricked. Hard.

"In any case, we'd never let them go to strangers," Reggie said. "They're family. Our family. And, as their guardian, you belong to us every bit as much as they do. Anyone who knows us, knows that."

Miranda almost managed a smile. "I suppose it's possible there's someone in Albuquerque who isn't familiar with Welles Enterprises."

Reggie smiled back. "Possible but not probable, but there may be someone too ignorant to understand what that means where family is concerned." He gave her a hug. "We have your back, honey. Yours and those boys."

Miranda thought she knew what that meant until they walked out of the elevator in the parking garage and two men greeted, then fell into step beside them, one before, one behind. They stepped into trucks parked on either side of Colter's and he waited until the first pulled out. Glancing in her sideview mirror, Miranda saw the other fall in behind as they turned onto the street.

"You think we'll be followed?"

"Actually, I don't."

"Your dad did?"

"Not him, either. He agrees we're dealing with an amateur, someone who took a dumb chance. This was Mama's idea, and stopping her when her mind is made isn't always an option."

She thought about that for a minute. Thought about something else. "If you weren't a Bellamy, how much trouble would you be in for firing shots into the street at that car?"

"It could have gotten … uncomfortable … but it wasn't the name that avoided a problem as much as my time on the city force. That and the fact that I donate hours every year, helping train new recruits."

"Do you enjoy doing that or do you have another motive?" She thought it a fair question, all things considered.

"Both. I do enjoy it but I also think it helps to cement relations, not with the Slade Agency alone, but with all private investigators."

She glanced back at the headlights following them at a steady pace, not too close, not too distant. The same with the tail lights in front of them. "Is your dad part of the Slade Agency?"

He hesitated and she thought he preferred not to answer but then he said, "In a sense. How much do you know about Welles Enterprises?"

"I know all of you own about half the state," she retorted.

He chuckled. "Not even close. In fact, some of the original lands, the three combined properties, were donated as a wild horse preserve a couple decades back."

"A drop in the bucket?" she countered.

"We still have enough," he admitted, "but there are a lot of us, near and far, those resources have to support."

"I also know what pretty much everyone knows," she said. "Welles Enterprises includes the Bellamy Ranch which is famous for its beef cattle and working horses, and it includes the Slade Agency … which is a private detective agency."

"That's the simplest answer. We provide security monitoring and protection for immediate and extended family and, occasionally, business associates."

He took his attention from the road barely long enough to shoot her a glance. "At this point, you're part of that 'extended' and pretty much stuck with it."

Her lips twitched in a smile she knew he couldn't see in the dark cab of the truck. She ignored the comment and the point behind it. "What function, exactly, does Welles Enterprises play?"

"Legal and financial oversight for every aspect of everything any of us do. Training programs. Educational foundations. Charities."

"None of which would appeal to you."

He gave a grunt and acknowledged, "Not in the least, but I'm smart enough to know it's all critical. As important, maybe more so, than the rest."

"So, back to my question. Is your father a part of the Slade Agency?" 'An employee of' didn't seem an appropriate description for Reggie Bellamy.

"He's one of the three current executive partners of Welles Enterprises."

So, she'd been in the presence of New Mexico royalty, she thought wryly, but all she said was, "A Bellamy, a Slade, and a Welles, I would guess."

"Most of the time but not always. When Welles Enterprises was established, there was one of each. Subsequent partners are named by a retiring one or in the will of a deceased. A few times a spouse has shown more of the strength, or more of the willingness, it takes to help run this company than a blood relative."

"And the other two partners ... the two who are family ... don't argue the point?"

"They can't. Succession was established in the original charter of the company."

She tried to wrap her mind around any family, or combination of families, having such a strong legacy, one that had survived through generations. "So, all of the descendants of the three original partners work for the company."

"Not all, by any means. Most elect to work for one of the branches, yeah. Some enter professions which lead them away but their welcome stands, if and when they decide to return. And anyone who stays but chooses not to be productive is choosing to leave."

She thought a moment. "And Jerica walked away from all that."

"Some do," he said. "More than you might think. The expectations on those who stay are high. And we have as many enemies as we have friends."

Miranda thought about Reggie. Despite his smile, something in his eyes had given her a hint of what his enemies would find waiting for them. She saw that same something every time she looked in Colter's eyes. She'd always thought 'like father, like son' a trite expression. It seemed she'd been wrong.

When Miranda fell silent, Colter could almost hear her thinking. The family was a lot. He'd always known that. What he hadn't known was that, for some, they could be *too much*. That had been true for Dana.

She didn't speak again until they were turning onto the highway toward the ranch. When she did, her question surprised him although he supposed it shouldn't have.

"What did Jonah mean about keeping Cheney alive?"

"Cheney's father was one of those who walked away. Her mama was dead and she was just a young teen, barely more than a kid. He left and took her with him before any of the family could intervene."

"Would they have? Intervened, I mean. He was her father."

"Not forcibly, no, but maybe he would have accepted help. Jonah was on a job when he stumbled across word of Cheney, her dad had gotten himself killed and she was in a bad place with some bad people. Jonah got her out but they both nearly died in the process."

"How old was she?"

"Sixteen."

"So … the tattoos…?"

"Yeah."

He parked in front of the sprawling ranch house and watched as she walked to the side entrance. She paused at the door and glanced back at him before going inside. He couldn't see her expression and didn't even hazard a guess at her thoughts.

He walked to where their escorts had stopped. They stood together at the hood of their trucks waiting for him and he wasn't the least surprised to hear that Reggie had ordered them to stand guard for the rest of the night so Colter could rest. It wouldn't have done any good to argue, so he thanked them and went up the outer stairs.

The upper verandah was empty, as he'd expected it to be, and he let himself into his room.

Chapter Nineteen

McEnny called not long after daylight. "We need to talk. I'll be at the café on Paseo at 8:00."

Colter didn't ask which café. There was more than one but not as far as the sheriff was concerned.

Colter was there ten minutes before McEnny arrived. Tired and irritable, but there. He was downing his first cup of coffee when the sheriff walked through the front entrance and came straight to his table.

The waitress was at McEnny's elbow with a cup and fresh pot before he'd even pulled his chair away from the table. He grunted his thanks and gave her a half-hearted smile. "Much obliged, Stella," he told her.

She wiped a spill from the table. "You get any rest after I left last night?"

Colter kept his gaze fixed on the liquid in his cup.

"Enough," McEnny answered and she walked away. "Ain't what you think," McEnny said into the silence.

Colter met his gaze. "Not thinking about much of anything," he said honestly, "except what you called me here for."

"My wife, Beth, has end-stage cancer. Stella's her best friend. When the pain gets too hard Stella comes and sits with her. They talk for hours until the pain meds take her under again."

"I'm sorry," Colter said, and he meant it far more than the words could convey.

"Me, too," McEnny said. "I wish it were me. I'd trade with her if I could but there ain't a damned thing I can do except be there."

"Then be there," Colter said. "Give me what you've got and go home and be there."

McEnny sighed. "All she does is sleep now."

"Then go lay down beside her and hold her while she sleeps." He had a feeling McEnny needed that as much as his wife.

The sheriff nodded. "I may do that. Later. But … what I'm going to tell you is going to upset Miranda some kinda' bad."

Colter eyed him. "Worse than hearing that the man who raised her was murdered, worse than knowing her brothers were targeted for possible kidnapping, worse than having her horse shot out from under her?"

McEnny sighed. "Not worse, no, but it's bad enough."

"I'm listening."

"J.D. wasn't where he said he'd be the morning he was killed. Deputy Gardner talked with over two dozen people who were at the auction, most of them friends or business acquaintances. No one saw him."

"At the auction? I thought you said he could've been and still not been noticed?" Colter still found that unlikely, with what he knew of the man, but very little could be ruled out at this point.

The waitress returned to fill their cups. She picked up the menus they'd laid aside and took their orders. When she was out of hearing, McEnny nodded. "That's true. It could've happened but I had a visitor late yesterday. Sherry Marks." He paused and sighed.

Colter stayed silent. He didn't recall hearing the name or seeing it in any of his digging through J.D.'s life. McEnny looked increasingly uncomfortable which Colter found interesting in itself.

"According to Sherry, J.D. was with her that morning."

"With her." Colter repeated.

The sheriff gave him a look and nodded.

"Huh." Colter leaned back in his seat. He could see why McEnny dreaded telling Miranda. Hearing it would cut deep. And that, he thought, was what happened when you placed people on a pedestal.

McEnny didn't seem to expect more of answer. "Her husband was on the list of people Deputy Gardner talked with. Gardner was with Oliver in the front room. Sherry stood in the hall eavesdropping and overheard Gardner's questions and Oliver's responses. She seems to think Oliver wanted her to hear it. Said he isn't normally a loud talker and I'd have to agree, always been softspoken. Anyway, Oliver told Gardner he wasn't at the auction that day so didn't know if J.D. had been or not. Sherry said that's where Oliver was supposed to be, where he told her he was going when he left the house that morning."

McEnny fell silent, and Colter frowned as he thought that through. "So, we have J.D. with another man's wife while the man was supposed to be gone and the man admitting he wasn't where he was supposed to be."

The sheriff nodded. "And maybe he was home all along. Home to see J.D. come calling on his wife."

"Did Ms. Marks ask her husband where he went when he left?"

"No. She's afraid to say anything."

"Pretending a marriage isn't falling apart won't hold it together."

"She's not afraid for her marriage," McEnny said grimly.

Colter caught sight of the waitress walking their way with her arms loaded and held his answer. He leaned back in his chair as she slid a plate in front of him and another in front of McEnny. They both picked up forks and started eating. Breakfast was a meal to be enjoyed hot.

Even then, the conversation couldn't be put aside. "So, if we mix that fear with a few possibilities, Marks could have suspected something between J.D. and his wife and put himself in J.D.'s path."

"That's what she's afraid of."

"It wouldn't be the first time that scenario played out," Colter agreed, "but why in the hell would he have taken away his own alibi when he talked with your deputy?"

The sheriff snorted. "People are stupid. Haven't you figured that out yet?"

Despite the gravity of their exchange, Colter chuckled. "I won't argue the point. So, his wife ... what? Suspects her husband killed J.D. and now fears he'll kill her?"

"Something like that."

"What's your plan?"

"I don't have any choice but to talk with Marks again. I'll do it myself this time. Thought you might want to be there."

"I do and I appreciate it. Are you going to bring him in for the questioning?"

"No, it's Wednesday. I plan to head out to the auction and catch up with him there, maybe have a casual-like conversation over a cup of coffee."

Colter nodded and turned his attention to the biscuits and red chili gravy on his plate.

The auction was packed with people and goods. Most of the space was devoted to farm animals in paddocks surrounded by potential bidders and to equipment laid out in rows, but there were also well-built booths with displays of local wares, anything from jarred pickles and jams to quilts and birdhouses. Although the event appeared well-organized, it was far-flung—spread over several acres, at least—and it wouldn't be difficult to overlook a person in that kind of mix.

McEnny seemed to know what interested Marks and they caught up with him making his way along a row of used engines that had been pulled and cleaned and laid on tarps.

Marks glanced up as they came close and stopped when they did. "Sheriff," he said by way of greeting before offering his hand to Colter, "Marks ... Oliver Marks."

Colter introduced himself.

"Got time for coffee?" McEnny asked, his tone easy as if it were fine if the answer was no.

But Marks seemed to know it wouldn't be fine. He sighed. "Sure." He turned and led the way to the small café which proved more of a screened porch attached to a room at the back with a window for orders to be taken and items passed through to waiting customers. The menu was scant … coffee, tea, and pastry of the day.

They took their coffee, in white ceramic mugs, and sat at one of the small, wooden tables.

"You know Gardner already asked me if I saw J.D. here the day he died. I didn't."

"Because you weren't here," McEnny paused, "but that's rare for you, isn't it? Not much kept you or J.D. away."

"It's one of the few things I enjoy these days. Farming has turned into a chore for some of us. The cost of everything we need to grow a crop or raise a pig or a cow is up, but the take-home pay of the people who buy from us is down."

McEnny stared into his coffee cup then lifted his gaze back to Marks. "What made you decide not to come that day?"

Marks didn't flinch. "The sight of J.D.'s truck turning into my drive. He wouldn't have seen my truck was still there. I'd pulled behind the barn, planned to throw a few things in the bed, and see what I could get for them."

"Are things that bad?"

"Things? No. Seeing J.D. follow my wife into the house, his hand on her hip? Yeah, that was bad. I sat in the barn, just sat, and waited until he left." He fell silent for a moment. "It was my fault she turned to him … my drinking … but I'm getting myself together now. Trying to, anyway. I didn't try to hurt him and I won't hurt her."

"So … what *are* you going to do?"

"Go home. Talk with Sherry and see if we have anything left to save after all these years together. Maybe see if she'll go talk to Father Elliott with me." He looked down. "Maybe she won't."

McEnny got to his feet and placed his hand on Marks' shoulder. "Sounds like a plan."

Neither Colter nor McEnny spoke until they were pulling back on the highway and then all McEnny said was, "Damn," and Colter knew he was thinking about his own wife, dying of cancer.

When they reached town, the sheriff stopped in front of Colter's truck, and kept the engine running as he asked, "What do you think?"

"Unlikely, but possible." Everything was always possible.

"Yeah, the crime doesn't fit the man." He shook his head and met Colter's gaze. "But he stays on the list."

"Do you believe his wife might be in danger?"

"I don't, but unless she asks for protection or he makes a wrong move, there'd be nothing I could do, anyway. Not officially. Unofficially, I plan to stay in touch with her, let her know there's help if she needs it. Or if she even thinks she needs it."

Colter nodded and stepped out, closing the door with a nod to McEnny. He wasn't looking forward to sharing what he'd learned with Miranda. She and Wes were with the boys on the lower verandah playing some kind of board game when he got back to the ranch. He gave them a nod and continued to the barn.

He passed Riley along the path and both stopped. Riley tilted his head. "Anything new?"

Colter skirted the issue with a shrug. "Nothing relevant. J.D. made a few people unhappy over the years but nothing I can see that would drive someone to murder."

"He wasn't a saint," Riley agreed, "but he helped more people than he hurt and he didn't hurt anyone out of meanness or ever on purpose. And that's the gospel."

Colter nodded agreement but, still, Riley looked unhappy. "What's on your mind?"

"I met with J.D.'s lawyer ... Ms. Langley." He shifted his feet. "J.D. was an old fool and a hard-headed one. He left me more than the little piece of property I agreed to take. I tried to give it back ... for Dane and Dillon ... Ms. Langley said the boys were fine and her job was to carry out J.D.'s wishes. Then she laughed and said there must be something in the water up here."

Colter waited. Riley was going someplace with this but he wasn't a man who knew how to hurry.

"Ms. Langley mentioned the will had been probated ... it's out there for everybody and their kin to see. Now I know you have that Seth and Angel team here guarding things. Wes carries when he's with the boys and he's handy with it. We had some target practice and he matched my score which ain't too bad. But whoever is out there knows Miranda owns the ranch. What if J.D. was killed because someone thought the ranch would go up for sale if he was out of the way? Miranda's *in* the way of that now."

"It's a possibility," Colter admitted. One of many.

"I'm thinking she needs a bodyguard."

Colter decided to ease into this one. "What are her thoughts on that?"

Riley kicked dirt. "She's hard-headed. Thinks I worry too much," he muttered. "Maybe I do, but she and them boys are all I have left."

"I can make the offer of one, Riley, but if she won't listen to you, I doubt she'll listen to anyone else."

"Could be she doesn't need to know he's there."

Colter snorted. "That only works in the movies, but I'll talk with her."

"Thanks. If not the ranch, she could get kidnapped for ransom or something and her mouth alone would get her killed."

"That pretty much only happens in movies, too. I'll try. I promise."

Colter watched as Riley moved on down the path. As much as he sympathized with the older man, he understood Miranda's need not to be cushioned. Or smothered. Even so, Riley had a point. Colter wasn't sure he would get far with it if Miranda had already refused.

Cheney met him at the barn as he'd asked. She led a horse from the stall for him, played at oiling a bridle while he saddled.

"Anything?" he asked quietly.

"Nothing."

"Nothing is good. I guess."

She ducked her head at his tone and he knew she was hiding a quick grin. Cheney didn't smile often.

"Yeah, I'm spoiling for a fight," he admitted. "Something or someone to hurt. Mostly, I'm just ready for this to be over." But that was only half of what he felt. The other half never wanted it to end. The stress of knowing Miranda and Dane and Dillon were in constant danger was wearing on him. The knowledge that he'd have no real place in their lives when the danger had been removed was unsettling. The thought stilled his hands.

Cheney's brow furrowed slightly as she watched him. "It will be, boss. Whoever killed J.D. Pederson will show their hand and you'll nail them."

He took a deep breath and smiled his thanks as he swung into the saddle. "I'll be back before dark. I've got some thinking to do."

His path wasn't aimless. He circled the house, looking for hidden weaknesses, looking for places to maximize strength. The more distant but much higher ridges provided the greatest risk from a high-powered rifle. If he were looking for an assassin, a professional hit, he'd focus there. Much of what had happened so far, especially the attempt to run them down in Albuquerque, told him to stay focused on an amateur, an amateur's knowledge and thought processes. That didn't make him rest easier. An amateur was more erratic, as this one was proving, and could get lucky, as this one already had. And whatever the purpose, whatever the quest, the dogged determination was clear.

But while one part of his mind focused on providing protection for Miranda and the twins, another part focused on the woman, on what he had to tell her about J.D.'s last actions the day he was murdered. He suspected she was too practical to consider him a saint but the man had taken her and raised her as his own. The revelation would shake her, fracture her memories of the man she loved as a father, and Colter hated being the one to do that.

Which admission brought him face to face with his feelings for her, which were as unexpected as they'd—initially—been unwelcome. When this was over, he didn't plan to walk away. That required him moving on from the last vestiges of guilt that had plagued him since Dana's death. It was time, he knew, to put those demons behind him.

He entered the barn from the rear as the sun settled on the distant peaks. After unsaddling and brushing his mount, he led him into a stall then went in search of Miranda. He didn't have far to go. She and Cheney were seated upon the bench out front. They weren't talking. He would have heard the murmur of conversation as he came down the aisle between stalls.

Cheney got to her feet, as Colter stepped out. "Night,

folks," was all she said as she walked away.

Miranda stood as well. "Lila will have dinner ready. How was your ride?"

"Quiet."

"See anything of concern?"

"No." He sighed as they walked away from the barn. "I almost wish I had." He paused and gave a casual glance around. "Did you and Cheney have a good talk?"

"Cheney? I don't think she's much for conversation, but being with her was … peaceful."

Colter snorted. "I don't think I've ever heard her and that adjective in the same conversation before. Intense, yes. Peaceful, no."

"I guess she has more sides than you've experienced, then."

"Miranda…"

She turned to face him, brows raised at his tone.

"We need to talk."

All she did was nod but he saw the apprehension in her eyes. "After dinner and the twins are settled." Her tone held as much resignation as anything. "I'll see you upstairs, on the verandah. Judging by your tone, I suspect I'd better bring the wine."

Chapter Twenty

Miranda sat in the swing and waited, trying to breathe evenly, trying to keep anxiety at bay. Whatever Colter had to say wouldn't be good news and she wasn't sure how much more of the bad kind she could take.

She'd looked in on the twins. Dillon sprawled on his bed, was reading an adventure novel, so engrossed he didn't even sense her presence. Dane sat at his desk, drawing another action figure. She'd have to arrange art lessons soon. He looked to have talent above average and she'd nurture that if she could. The sight of them steadied her but not enough to bring peace of mind.

When Colter joined her, she lifted her glass toward the table where a second glass waited beside an open bottle of Malbec and managed to wait until he'd poured his wine and taken one of the chairs near the rail.

"What did you see out there?"

"Nothing new."

His even tone didn't fool her. Something was troubling him. "Then what is new?"

"J.D. wasn't at the farmers' auction the morning of the wreck."

The stem of the wineglass trembled in her grasp and she was glad for the dark to hide it. "And…"

"He was with Sherry Marks."

It took a moment for her to absorb the implications of his words. "*With* her?" She took a deep breath, then another. "J.D. was with Oliver Marks' wife. Alone?"

"In the Marks home."

"That's hard to … fathom. He never so much as mentioned her name."

"He wouldn't have, would he?"

"Where was her husband, where was Oliver?"

"He was supposed to be at the auction. Same as J.D. But, before he left, he'd pulled behind his barn to put some things in the back of the truck to take with him. He saw J.D. drive up and watched as J.D. and his wife went into the house."

By now her hand was trembling so much she had to set the glass aside. "So, Oliver Marks saw them together and … what … killed J.D. out of jealousy?"

She recalled seeing Marks on the hillside where she'd scattered J.D.'s ashes. Had he been there to gloat? She couldn't remember if he'd come to the house after, but there had been so many…

"It could have happened that way," Colter's voice was quiet. "But I don't think it did. Neither does McEnny. We talked with Marks this morning. He has no more and no less reason than Bentley or Newland. They're all still on the list of possibilities. None of them higher on that list than the others." And none were really very high in his mind. That fact, more than any, kept him awake at night.

"With any of the three, we'd be dealing with some level of insanity, wouldn't we, some crazy craving for vengeance? It would benefit Marks nothing to attempt kidnapping the boys, even if he had the means—and I can't imagine he has the kind of money or connections to hire thugs to do that—or to kill me, supposing I was the target rather than Gabby. The same for Bentley and Newland, although they *do* have that kind of money." She looked at the shadow of him in the dark. "I'm right, aren't I?"

"About the insanity … clinically, yes … but of the most common type."

"Common?"

"Anger. Each of them has cause to feel angry. The level of antagonism combined with the level of violence in the reaction is what shifts that anger from justifiable emotion to provisional insanity."

"Well," she gave an unsteady laugh. "That all sounds logical enough."

For the first time since they'd been meeting and talking outside her room and his, he shifted from the chair to the swing beside her. And for the first time, she yielded to the temptation to rest her head on his shoulder.

"So, there's someone else out there. Someone we don't know about."

"Yet," he said softly.

What, she wondered, had J.D. done, who had he angered so much that they had taken his life, so angry that they would threaten his family? And how many others like Bentley and Marks, maybe even Newland to some degree, had he wronged?

"Miranda, I think it might be time to put someone close, to guard your back."

"No." The refusal was instinctive. The thought of someone watching her every more, even for her own safety, made her shudder. The twins had Seth and Angel. Then there was Cheney. That was enough. "Riley's here. Close."

"It was Riley's idea. He's worried."

"Then you'll just have to reassure him." Not until that moment, did she realize how completely she trusted Colter Bellamy. As shaky as her world felt, and it did, the shoulder beneath her cheek felt stable and solid.

As she'd done so many times as a young girl, Miranda went in search of Lila early the next morning. Miranda sat at the counter while Lila spread dough for the twins' favorite cinnamon rolls. Lila worked, listening in silence, while everything Miranda thought and felt spilled out in a rush of words ending with the most heartfelt of all. "I don't understand. That isn't the J.D. I knew."

"Isn't it?" Lila asked, gazing at her.

"You mean Jerica? That was different. She threw herself at him. You said so yourself."

Lila laid her rolling pin aside and wiped her hands. "Hand me your cup, that coffee's cold by now." She took her time emptying and filling the mug. She handed it back to Miranda before refilling her own. Miranda could almost feel her gathering her thoughts.

"Don't judge him too harshly for Sherry, for sure no more so than for Jerica. J.D. and Sherry were college sweethearts, the talk of the town and the favorite couple their senior year." She smiled at the memories then sighed. "Everybody thought they'd get married straight after graduation. For whatever reason, that didn't happen, and I don't think he ever got over her. Jerica was a substitute and a poor one."

"Jerica was a long time after college."

"She was and J.D. had women here and there in between but none he took serious or gave reason to take him seriously."

"So why Jerica and not the ones in between?"

Lila made a face. "Because Jerica had made up her mind and it wasn't long before she'd made up his, too." Lila set her coffee aside and picked up a saucer of softened butter. For a moment, she seemed completely focused on the spreading the butter evenly and carefully across the dough, then she asked, "So, Joe doesn't seem to be looking too hard at Oliver Marks for what happened to J.D.?"

"No, but I don't know that I could blame Mr. Marks," her voice cracked just a bit, and she hated that it did.

Lila looked up sharply. "Now you stop that, Randa. It's fine to take J.D. off that pedestal for a moment but never, ever forget that he adored you and you adored him. Whatever his sins—and God knows we all have them—he was a good and decent man."

Miranda nodded slowly knowing, despite everything, that what Lila said was true. J.D. had given Newland—the man who'd broken their contract, broken faith with him, tried to cheat him—a permanent easement to his wife's grave when not even a court order thought the other man deserved it. Yes, Bentley's wife had walked away from her husband into J.D.'s arms. Maybe J.D. was wrong but so was she, even more so because she'd broken her vows to her husband. If it hadn't been with J.D., it would have been with some other man. That the woman had walked away from her own sons was proof enough of that. She was a shallow person with a disloyal heart and would never be satisfied anywhere with anyone.

"But Oliver Marks was a friend."

Lila nodded. "To a degree. J.D. was friendly with a lot of people but not really close to anyone but you and Riley."

"And you," Miranda reminded.

"And me," Lila agreed. "Beyond that, Sherry was his first love. Neither a man, nor a woman, forgets that first." She stopped and let that silence hang before she went on. "No matter what mistakes he made, he's the same man who would sit for hours with a calf and bottle when a cow died giving life. The same man who drove to the next county because the shelter had a kitten that looked a lot like the one you loved, that little calico that some careless hand let his horse step on."

Miranda smiled even as she felt a slow tear slide down her cheek. "He thought I wouldn't notice they weren't just alike. I did."

"But you didn't tell him. Somehow, even that young, you knew it would hurt his heart. You have an old soul, Miranda. You always did. J.D. did, too. Y'all were so alike in that. Just remember, nothing J.D. did changes who he was or what he was to you. Don't let what you learn change him in your mind."

Getting to her feet, Miranda gave Lila a hug, the ache inside her easing as the woman rocked her into a familiar-since-childhood embrace.

"It's still hard to imagine J.D. sneaking around with a woman. He'd never shown interest in anyone, and," she hesitated, "he was almost as old as Riley."

Lila lifted one brow, and Miranda felt a twinge of horror. "No, do not say another word."

"Like what? That Riley's human and a male one, at

that." Lila laughed.

"I can't think about him like that." But, she reminded herself, there had been the twins previous tutor, Rachel Bailey. Miranda, for sure, hadn't known about that *friendship* but not knowing hadn't made it not true.

"Then don't. Don't think about it, but you probably do need to be aware that Riley slips away from time to time to see a friend down in Albuquerque."

"No," Miranda insisted, "I don't need to know that. Any of it." She turned to pour herself another coffee. "Why doesn't he just marry her and be done with it?"

Lila snorted. "Because he's married to this ranch. Just like J.D. was."

Miranda stared at her a moment then sighed and walked out, taking her coffee to the office. A part of her understood that this really changed nothing about how she was raised. Another part of her accepted that it did change how she *thought* about it.

Regardless, boring as it was, she was glad she had work to do. Reviewing the ranch accounts was preferable to any more revelations. She focused on numbers, pushing everything else aside for the next few hours.

Colter stared at the barrage of email on his laptop, most of it marked as information only. He scrolled past those, leaving them unopened. He stopped scrolling when he saw one from Jonah with Pederson in the subject line.

Jonah had forwarded a report from their forensics lab on the debris Colter had picked up at the site of J.D.'s wreck. Their examination checked a box that needed to be checked. He didn't actually expect the report to provide anything relevant to the investigation. He was wrong. A second bullet had been found embedded in the mangled sideview mirror which had been missing from the driver's side. The distance between tire and mirror would be vast for a sharpshooter. It appeared someone had gotten very, very lucky with that shot through the tire sidewall. Another solid nudge away from professional and toward amateur.

The email just below that was another report. This one had Colter leaning forward. Their facial recognition software confirmed the driver of the SUV was a woman but not much more than that. She wasn't in the agency's database and Jonah had added a quick note that the same had been true of the one used by the city, available to Colter if he wanted it forwarded. He didn't.

He sat back with a faint sense of disappointment. He stood for a moment and paced, trying to clear his head of the feeling that he'd missed something vital. The lower verandah was empty of all but him and the birds and squirrels who were fighting over what was left in the squirrel feeder. The birds had finished theirs and wanted more. Greed, he thought, frustrated. Always greed.

After a moment, he returned to the table and his laptop. Pacing didn't accomplish anything. He opened and stared at an enlarged photograph of the driver Jonah had sent with the report. It didn't matter that the color of eyes was hidden by sunglasses. Contact lenses changed that in an instant. The glasses effectively hide the shape of the eyes. Same with the hair, or lack thereof, which was hidden by the cap. Cut and color easily changed. Plastic surgery could add or remove ten years from a person's features, give the appearance of higher cheekbones, lower ears, a firmer or softer chin. But usually, only professionals went to that level. To a lesser degree, heavy makeup, carefully and expertly applied, could fool facial recognition software.

Heavy shadows here and there, contours created from varying shades. It could be done, but most amateurs didn't realize how easily and effectively.

He picked up the coffee cup Lila had filled for him earlier. Empty. He grunted and set it aside just as the housekeeper stepped out with full pot.

He gave her a smile and she returned it. "I wasn't going to speak if you were deep into something. Just thought I'd check to see if you need a refill."

"I do and I'm grateful."

She filled his cup, checked the cream and sugar containers, then turned to go.

"Lila?"

She glanced back. "Need something else? I'm pulling a cake out shortly. I could bring you some."

"I'm not hungry but I'm sure I wouldn't turn it down." He hesitated, going with his instinct. "Could you look at something for me?"

"Sure."

She stepped back as he turned his laptop to face her. After studying the photograph, she shrugged and looked back at him.

"No one you know?"

"Well, there's the cap pulled low and the turtleneck up high and with the sunglasses, but no, nothing I can see looks familiar but I can't see *enough* to say I don't know the person."

"Thanks," he said ruefully. "I was hoping you would see something I was missing."

She took a deep breath. "You know I'd like more than anything to be able to help. I take it this is what's called a person of interest?"

"The driver of the SUV that nearly ran Miranda down."

"Then I wish more than ever, that I could help." She shook her head. "That girl's more precious than gold to me." An edge of fear joined the grief still resident in her eyes. "This is all hard."

He watched as she walked back into the house and closed the door behind her but his mind wasn't on her. It was on the feeling in his gut. The one that wouldn't go away now that it had crept in.

Reaching for his phone, he pulled up Jonah's number.

"You found something?"

He heard the energy in his cousin's voice and hated to cut that short. "No, sorry."

"Damn, I'd hoped the photograph might trigger some kind of recognition."

"It triggered something but not that, no sense of familiarity. I want you to find Jerica."

"Jerica Pederson? As far as our records go, she's still in Australia."

"Look again. I want everything. Confirm where she is, who she's with, now. And everywhere she's been since she walked out on Pederson and their sons. All of that and any contacts that stand out."

"Based on…"

"Nothing but a gut feeling."

There was a long silence then, "That's good enough reason. I'll send an agent to Wyoming and one to Australia and I'll pull Darby for research, he's the best we've got at grabbing information from all sources and building a picture."

"I agree. He can make things fit that no one else sees."

"When do you need it?"

Colter's silence said everything.

"Got it. I'll put someone with Darby. They can pull the

information that's scattered across hard files and databases so he can focus on stitching things together."

"Thanks, Jonah. I know we have a lot going on." Pulling resources from job to job wasn't something any of them did lightly.

"Those two kids and your woman are top priority, right now. Reggie and Addie have made that clear."

Before Colter could argue the 'your woman' aspect, Jonah added, "I'll be on the road to you within the hour."

"You're coming here? Why?"

"Because I have gut feelings, the same as you. Mine says I'm needed there. *You* need me there."

Jonah broke the connection before Colter could argue. But he wouldn't have, he realized. He'd be glad for the backup.

The cake finished baking but it was Miranda who brought it out, a slice for him and a slice for her. Lila was close behind with a glass of iced water for each of them.

"Anything else?" Lila asked, glancing from Colter to Miranda. Satisfied with their nods, she disappeared back into the house.

"The boys are going to be jealous."

"Not true," Miranda settled into her chair with a sigh. "I served them and Wes before us. We're in the clear on any guilt trip."

"I'm glad you're here."

She had a forkful of cake halfway to her mouth and laid it down again. "Uh-oh."

"I'm sorry," Colter said, feeling like a clod. "Let's enjoy Lila's cake, then we can talk."

"Too late. I know there's something there now,

something you need to say and don't like doing it, but it's fine. Honest." As if to prove her words, she lifted the fork again and took that first bite.

Colter did the same, wishing he'd waited to broach the subject.

She took a sip of water and said, "What have you learned?"

"Not all that much. Not really. The driver of the SUV was female but we couldn't get enough of a visual to match to anything in our files."

"The bad guy files, you mean?"

He couldn't help the smile at her phrasing. "Not necessarily bad guys. Anyone of record which might be a bad guy. We also have photo ID for all of our employees and some from other agencies who cooperate with us."

"In case an agent goes rogue?" she said, sounding tongue-in-cheek.

He frowned. "You really have been watching too many movies."

"Not movies. Books."

"Regardless. Too much fiction."

She took another bite and he could see that she didn't feel rattled as quickly as he thought she might. "So, I have a theory."

"Which is?"

"What if I weren't the intended victim? I mean you were right there with me."

He gave her a look and nodded. "That's possible. I'm sure I've made an enemy or two, along the way."

"You sure didn't make a good first impression on me," she reminded him.

"I didn't intend to." He finished his cake and pushed the plate aside. "For now, though, we're going to go with my theory."

She took the last bite of her cake and swallowed before nodding. "That whoever killed J.D. is out to kill me."

"Or, at the least, to get you out of the way long enough to get their hands on the twins."

"For ransom or for full control of their future, because there's just not a strong enough motive with Bentley or Newland or Marks. At least not that would drive them to violence beyond J.D.'s death." She nodded. "I get that, so…"

"Yeah … so." Because of the future impact on Dane and Dillon, he didn't like where his deductions had led him, but he couldn't argue with them.

Miranda took a deep breath. "Jerica is that someone else. Has to be. She's the only person who could hope to benefit if I'm dead."

Colter nodded.

"And we don't know where she is."

"Yet," Colter said firmly.

He wasn't surprised that she'd come to the same inevitable conclusion. He was surprised at her calm. Surprised and relieved and unexpectedly proud.

Chapter Twenty-One

Jonah was in Taos by dinnertime and asked Colter to meet him at the diner in town. He glanced up and nodded as Colter walked in but he didn't smile.

Colter thought of Miranda as he'd seen her last, sprawled on the floor in the great room. Dane with his sketch pad, drawing what appeared to be alien creatures. Dillon with a graphic novel of some comic-strip hero. Miranda just soaking up the normalcy of the moment. But her eyes held a certain gravity as he left. She knew he was meeting Jonah.

Colter pulled out a chair and sat. "Tell me."

"It isn't good," Jonah said.

Colter snorted. "I knew that before I got here."

"That tattle publication got it wrong. Jerica Pederson is not in Australia. The woman with her husband on the yacht is about to be Jerica's replacement. The women look a lot alike. I guess the guy's got 'a type.' The not-yet-happy couple are just waiting for the divorce to come through."

Colter waited for the other shoe to fall.

Jonah sighed. "No one appears to be in residence at their Wyoming home."

"So, we don't know where the hell she is."

"No. We don't."

Colter eyed him, silently. Jonah wasn't done.

"That SUV … the one that tried to run you down…"

"Not me," Colter said, angry but not at Jonah. "Miranda."

Jonah nodded. "It was stolen from a car lot near Interstate 25 not far over the state line in Colorado. They never even knew it was missing. It was located early this morning by a couple of fishermen at a small lake just south of Santa Fe."

Colter took a deep breath. I-25 was the most direct route between Albuquerque and Wyoming. "That damn well seals it then." He'd like to think Jerica had stayed on I-25, heading to her Wyoming home. He knew it more likely that she had turned toward Taos—and the Pederson Ranch.

"It does." Jonah studied his face. "I'm sorry, Colt. This shouldn't have happened. We should have had a handle on this."

"That's on both of us, but we'll worry about that later. Figure out what's broke and what to fix. For now, how do I keep Miranda and those boys safe?"

"All I can tell you is what you already know … that you have the best of the best on the ranch. Seth and Angel. And Cheney."

Colter knew what it cost Jonah to so much as say her

name. Had always known. "And us."

Jonah nodded. "And us. Get some sleep Colt. I'll do the same. Nice room you gave me, by the way."

"No reason to let it go to waste, and I've never been sure whether to give it up or not."

Jonah stood and reached for his hat. "I think you made the right choice. Keep her close the next few days and, between the two of us and the team you have in place, we'll keep her safe."

Colter returned to the ranch and sat in his truck a moment staring at the house, then walked up the outer staircase and into his room. He stopped short of turning on the light, simply stood beside his neatly made bed and fought the need to see for himself that she was safe. That compulsion won and he followed his gut to the room next to his.

Her door to the verandah stood slightly ajar which made his blood chill but they'd have that talk tomorrow. For tonight, he stepped inside and pulled the door closed behind him and waited.

Miranda rolled over and murmured his name. He knew when she came fully awake. She flipped the covers aside, and Colter locked the door and shed his clothes in unhurried movements. Tonight, nothing was about being in a hurry.

Miranda woke to an empty bed and stretched in the predawn light. The faint creak of the swing on the verandah drew her as she slipped on a robe and followed the sound.

Her hair was a mess and her face bare of what little makeup she ever bothered to apply. She didn't care. Colter had seen her at her worst and at her best. He could take her or leave her as she was and *this* was who she was.

He was watching as she stepped out and tilted his head toward the small table. She picked up the carafe and began pouring coffee into the mug beside it. When he said, "Compliments of Lila," her gaze went to his.

"Did you get an earful?"

"Only about the boys and our lack of discretion."

"There is that," she said wryly. "Poor Lila, she just admitted to knowing about Riley slipping away to see *a friend* in Albuquerque. She's probably had enough *friends with benefits* revelations."

Colter lifted a brow. "Hardly that. I told her not to worry because I plan to make an honest woman of you."

She sank to the chair opposite the swing, holding the mug in both hands. She glanced down, surprised to see them so steady. "That almost sounds like a proposal."

"It is. When you're ready."

"We've known each other what … fourteen days?"

"When you're ready," he said again.

And she smiled, realizing it didn't sound like such a terrible idea, after all.

They parted at the base of the steps, but when Miranda started toward the kitchen, Colter reached for her hand and tugged her close again. "Stay close to the house today, and keep your pistol with you."

She frowned at his tone. "Something's up? Worse than usual?"

For a moment she thought he wouldn't answer, then he gave a nod. "Worse than usual. If you see Jerica, shoot to kill."

A cold chill slithered along her spine. "Jerica?"

He nodded.

"Where will you be?"

"I won't be far. Jonah's on his way from town. We plan to meet with Seth and Angel and we may ride out, see if we can find signs of anyone camping in the foothills."

"Camping?" She gave a short laugh and, recognizing near hysteria, followed it with a deep breath. "That wouldn't be Jerica, I can promise you." Fear nipped at her as she said, "You think she's here?"

"I think she's close. I think she has been the whole time."

"Watching and waiting," Miranda said flatly. When Colter nodded, she shuddered. "Be safe. Promise me."

He kissed her hard then stepped away. "I'll be back."

Whirling, she all but ran back up the stairs to her room, found her gun and loaded it. Then she went to Wes' room and made herself knock rather than pound on his door.

He opened it almost at once. Early as it was, his hair was wet from the shower and he was fully dressed. He frowned when he saw her. "Miranda? Are the boys okay?"

"I'm going to need you to make sure of that, Wes." She kept her voice as steady as she could. "Where's your gun?"

"In the nightstand, drawer locked, even though the gun isn't loaded."

"Get it and load it. Keep it and the boys upstairs in whichever room seems most defensible to you."

He didn't ask questions, just nodded. "Theirs, then. Mine has the verandah."

"I'll have Lila bring their breakfast and yours."

She knew he saw her fear for them in her face, when he touched her hand. "I've got this, Miranda. Whatever is going on, I've got them. I swear on everything dear to me, on my own family, they'll be safe."

Because she knew she would frighten them, she didn't go to the boys but left Wes to do what he needed to do. From there, she went to the kitchen, to Lila.

"Where's your gun, Lila?"

Startled, Lila put down the knife she was using to peel potatoes. "In my room."

"Get it, load it. Wes will keep the boys upstairs. Lock every door downstairs behind me."

"Wait! Miranda, where are you going?"

All she said was, "I'll be back." If she told Lila the truth, that she planned to use herself as bait, the woman who'd more than half-raised her would never let her go.

Colter and Jonah sat with Seth and Angel at a picnic style table just outside their camper. Jonah had pulled security tapes from hotels between Santa Fe and Taos covering the past few days. They spotted a woman with similar build and jawline in two different locations but in each the woman wore oversized sunglasses and a large sunhat.

Colter studied them with a sinking feeling. He wanted, desperately wanted, to be wrong. Miranda would be devastated if he were right.

Jonah elected to talk through everything they knew. Colter knew it was a good strategy but would rather have jumped into a plan. Jerica could show up any time, and in any vehicle, now that she'd ditched the SUV. And she would have the same goal in mind. Killing Miranda.

Miranda found Riley in the barn, grooming a horse tied

inside his stall.

"Riley, something's going on. Colter's worried."

He turned to drop the curry comb into the bucket at his feet and shook his head. "The man's been worried since he got here. Best I can tell it's part of his job."

"Jerica may have caused J.D.'s death."

The hall of the barn was gloomy in the early morning light but not so much she couldn't see his brows pull together at her words. "Jerica? That woman's been gone from here a long while."

"I know, but, think about it. It makes sense in a sick kind of way. With J.D. dead, I inherit the ranch. With me dead, the boys inherit. If the boys inherit, and Jerica decides to be a mother again, she has access to the ranch and control of the boys. If she lets them live."

Riley shook his head. "Whoa, now, girl, slow down. That's a lot to take in."

He looked tired, she thought. Older than she was accustomed to thinking of him, and worn out. The realization hurt her heart. "I'm sorry, Riley. Truly I am, but I'm frightened out of my mind." She took a deep breath. Colter had asked her to stay close to the house for safety but Riley had been protecting her since she was a little girl. He was older now than then, but his hand was no less steady. "I need you to ride shotgun with me."

"Shotgun." He shook his head. "What the hell, Randa?"

"If she's watching, she'll follow me. I'm sure of it."

"What then?" he asked with a slight shake of his head. "You planning a gunfight?"

"Not between the two of you. This is for me to do. You might be a better shot than me but I'm a better shot than Jerica."

A sound from behind sent a chill along her neck. Riley's

gaze shifted, over her shoulder, and he flinched.

"Well, that may be true, sugar," Jerica drawled. Not close. Not yet. "But the gun in my hand is better than the gun in your pocket."

Miranda kept her eyes on Riley, saw the horror on his face.

"Get her gun, Riley."

He shook his head slowly. "Jerica, don't."

"You knew where this was headed, Riley. You've known all along."

Miranda slowly turned to look at her. This Jerica was not the beautiful, shallow woman Miranda remembered. The rich life she'd lived hadn't done her any favors. Dissatisfaction had edged itself into the lines around her mouth and eyes. And those eyes, once lively with laughter even though at the expense of someone else, were almost dull, sparked only by the anger that pinched her lips

"I didn't," he protested harshly.

"Damn you, Riley, I knew you were spineless. What did you think I was going to do? Why would I want to know J.D.'s comings and goings? Why would you tell me?"

Nausea had Miranda taking short, shallow breaths. Not Riley, she thought as anguish shredded her heart, not Riley.

Even so, when he shouted, "Drop, Randa. Now!" she did, instinctively, and immediately wished she hadn't. Jerica fired a heartbeat after, and she heard the sharp intake of Riley's breath and the slow slide of his body against the front of the stall.

Things fell into place too slowly for Colter, terrifyingly slowly, beginning with the day Gabby had been killed.

Miranda had failed to let Riley know when she and the boys had moved on to the lake. Yet, as Colter repeated events and conversations, he heard Riley's voice saying, "I was on the other end of the ranch. Took me two lifetimes to get here." Had Dane known to tell Riley they'd moved on to the lake or had Riley already known just where to find them?

The sound of gunfire jerked him to his feet. His gaze went to Jonah's as he flung his chair aside and turned to run. The corrals and paddocks were empty of men, but horses wheeled in panic. Colter was still too far from the barn when the second sounded. Too far. And his heart dropped in his chest.

He and Jonah reached the front of the barn at the same moment. Colter positioned himself in a crouch on one side of the opening. Jonah did the same opposite him.

His first glimpse was of Miranda, sitting on the floor cradling a body, another body several feet away, and Cheney standing nearby, her back against a stall front.

Gesturing to Jonah, Colter stepped inside. His gaze went first to Miranda, at the tears streaming down her face, then to Cheney who looked at him and shrugged. "It's done, boss. Catch up with you later." Then she turned and walked out the other end of the barn but not before giving Jonah a long, expressionless look.

Colter knew she'd go straight to a place of solitude and heave her breakfast onto the ground. He'd done it too many times, himself, not to know.

He walked to Miranda and helped her lower Riley's head and shoulders to the ground and gathered her in his arms.

Chapter Twenty-Two

There was no ceremony, no gathering of mourners, no words spoken. Together, Miranda and Lila walked up the hill, carrying Riley's urn between them, sometimes stopping to rest or to wipe at the tears that flowed as memories swept them. Together, they scattered his ashes not so very far from those of the man who'd been his best friend, the man he'd ultimately betrayed.

Colter was waiting when they returned. Lila gave him a sad and weary smile as she stepped inside. Miranda walked into his arms.

After a moment, he stepped back and looked down at her. His expression made her heart squeeze. "Is something wrong?"

He nodded. "Beth McEnny died just after midnight. Joe called and asked me to meet with his team this morning, make sure things keep on track for a few days." He hesitated. "I don't want to leave you."

"I'm fine." And she was. Still grieving, still bewildered by the turn of events that taken J.D. and then Riley so swiftly, but, even so, she would get through this and anything else.

"I'll probably need to stay close to town for a few days." He looked more unhappy by the minute.

"I'm not going anywhere," she whispered.

"I'll be back," he told her.

But, even as he kissed her, she wasn't sure that he would. He was a Bellamy. He had another life, in another place, heavy responsibilities that didn't include this ranch. She and Dane and Dillon were safe. His charge was complete.

In the end, Colter stayed away longer than he'd planned. Joe McEnny returned to his office and Colter slipped from town to return to Bellamy Ranch. His father was surprised to see him. His mother was not.

Dinner was somber as he gave them the details that had not made it into a formal report. As far as the world was concerned, as far as anything that would be seen later, Riley had died a hero, unblemished.

The next morning, his father was out and about, early as usual. He found his mother downstairs.

"I know you can't stay, but I'm glad you came home, Colter. We've been waiting for you since we heard what had happened."

He smiled and hugged her. "I'm glad I came, too." But, no, he couldn't stay.

"Walk with me," she suggested as she opened a door and they stepped out into the wildflower garden that flourished just beyond the glass walls of the dining room. Beyond that space, the hills were nearly as raw and wild as the day the first Bellamys had laid eyes on them.

"How is Miranda?" Addie asked.

Colter looked out at the skyline. "We've talked. She sounds … at peace. More than she did, anyway."

"You haven't seen her."

He looked at her then. Her tone wasn't judgmental. Neither was her expression.

"No," he said at last. "I wanted to give her time and space."

Addie kept walking, unrushed but unhesitating, and Colter walked with her. "Time and space?" she repeated his words.

"To know what she wants. To be sure."

"You're thinking of Dana." She gestured toward a wrought-iron bench and they sat.

"It's hard not to."

Addie turned to face him. "Dana was weak. You can't blame yourself for that."

"I don't. I did, yes, but it's easier to see reality from a distance."

His mother nodded at that. "It always is." She paused. "You wanted Miranda to be sure … are you?"

There was no hesitation when he nodded. "I am."

"But?"

Colter stretched his legs in front of him and fixed his gaze on the horizon. "I've always thought I'd eventually come back here, live here. I know Dad expects it."

"And so you may … you and Miranda … eventually. As to what Reggie expects," she chuckled, "I've never let him get too comfortable with predictability." Her amusement faded and her gaze softened as she gestured around her. "All either of us wants is for our children to have the fullness and richness of life that we have." She turned to face him. "Let's go upstairs for a moment. I have something to give you."

He followed her back inside and up the stairs to the room she shared with his father. She opened a wall safe and withdrew a gold velvet jeweler's box.

Handing it to Colter, she said, "I retrieved this from the bank vault the day after you brought Miranda to Albuquerque. It once belonged to your grandmother and to her grandmother before that. No one knows for certain, but it's thought to have been a gift from Slade to Katherine Bellamy on the birth of their first child."

Colter opened the lid and gazed at the emerald clasped in gold.

"It will match her eyes," Addie said softly

Colter smiled, swept with love and gratitude for this woman who knew him so well. She was right. Between the green and the gold and the sparkle, it would match the color and the life in Miranda's eyes.

"Let me know what kind of wedding she wants. I'll make it happen. Small or large, it will be perfectly Miranda, just as she wants it to be."

"That's a big leap of faith," he said, smiling.

She smiled back. "Faith in my son has never required much of a leap." She touched his face. "Go now. Go home to Miranda. It's time."

It was dusk when Miranda walked from the barn after unsaddling Sadie. With the help of a lot of saddle-time, the mare was turning into a decent cow horse. Miranda, like Riley, had always believed she would, if given the chance.

Miranda missed Riley, every moment, every day. The grief was less sharp now and her memories bittersweet. She wondered, couldn't help but wonder, what role he'd played in all that had happened. Had he been in love with Jerica? Fooled by her? Or had he, like Jerica, been jealous and swayed by greed. She wondered, yes, but she suspected she didn't really want to know. She wanted to keep her good memories, wanted Dane and Dillon to keep theirs.

There were days when she felt at peace and days when she didn't. She'd have to hire a manager for the ranch. She wasn't ready to face the prospect of replacing Riley, but knew she'd have to think about that soon. She couldn't do all that the ranch needed to survive. She didn't even want to try.

More than Riley, she missed Colter, but she didn't call. He'd come back to her or he wouldn't. It was as simple as that. And as hard.

As she neared the house, her eyes lifted to the light streaming from the windows. Her thoughts went to the twins who were still grieving for J.D. and for Riley, but— like her—they were moving forward and healing as best they could. They would thrive. She'd see to that.

She stopped in her tracks when a movement on the upper verandah drew her gaze. Her breath caught in her throat as a man stepped toward the handrail, looking out at her. Colter.

Joy, unexpected and unbidden, swept through her, and Miranda lengthened her stride as she went to meet her future.

Thank you for taking the time to read *A Dangerous Inheritance*. If you enjoyed it, please consider telling your friends or posting a short review. Word of mouth is an author's best friend and is much appreciated.
Thank you,
Susan

***

Up Next:
The Bellamy Legacy continues!
Cheney is on enforced thirty day leave, under a psychiatrist's care after the shooting of their suspect. This is protocol for the Slade Agency. Although on official leave, she begs for work and is given a task by her team lead, to review and provide feedback on several files. One of those files, however, involves human trafficking, which triggers memories of her own past. Filled with a need for vengeance, Cheney sets out on her own to save several young victims. Jonah discovers what she has done, and big trouble follows.
Watch for this new Bellamy book in 2024

Also by Susan Yawn Tanner
The Bellamys of Texas historical series:
Winds Across Texas
Fire Across Texas
Storm Out of Texas

The Bellamy Legacy contemporary series:
A Dangerous Inheritance

New editions from Secret Staircase Books
The Scottish Highlands Romances
Highland Captive
Captive to a Dream
Exiled Heart

Coming soon ...
The brand new Cat Callahan mystery series!

A Warm Southern Christmas
(a historical romance novella)

Visit Susan's website to discover more about the author and her books. Sign up for her newsletter where she announces new books and exciting giveaways.

susanytanner.com

Susan Yawn Tanner is a bestselling author in the romance and mystery genres. When she isn't writing, she's either tending her horses or barrel racing. Although she lives less than an hour from the Gulf of Mexico, the white sandy beaches of Mississippi can't compete with the lure of arena dirt.